Emily,

Thank you so much... my patron!, Because of you, I get to share my dream with the world.

THE MIRROR'S GAZE

Rae P Muzzdrm (signature)

Other Books by Rae D. Magdon

Death Wears Yellow Garters

Amendyr Series
The Second Sister - Book 1
Wolf's Eyes - Book 2
The Witch's Daughter – Book 3

And with Michelle Magly

Dark Horizons Series
Dark Horizons – Book 1
Starless Nights – Book 2

THE MIRROR'S GAZE

BY
RAE D. MAGDON

Desert Palm Press

The Mirror's Gaze
Amendyr Series - Book 4

By Rae D. Magdon

©2016 Rae D. Magdon

ISBN: 9781942976189
ISBN (epub): 9781942976196
ISBN (pdf): 9781942976202

All rights reserved. No part of this book may be reproduced in any form other than that which it was purchased and without the express permission of the author or publisher. Please note that piracy of copyrighted materials violates the author's right and is illegal.

This e-book is licensed for your personal enjoyment only. This e-book may not be re-sold or given away to other people. If you would like to share this book with another person, please purchase an additional copy for each recipient. If you're reading this book and did not purchase it, or it was not purchased for your use only, purchase your own copy. Thank you for respecting the hard work of this author.

This is a work of fiction. Names, characters, places, and incidents are the product of the author's imagination or used fictitiously and any resemblance to actual persons, living or dead, businesses, companies, events, or locales is entirely coincidental.

For permission requests, write to the publisher, addressed "Attention: Permissions Coordinator," at the address below.

Desert Palm Press
1961 Main Street, Suite 220
Watsonville, California 95076
www.desertpalmpress.com

Editor: Kellie Doherty (http://editreviseperfect.weebly.com/)
Cover Design: Rachel George (http://www.rachelgeorgeillustration.com/)

Printed in the United States of America
First Edition — August 2016

Acknowledgement

Thanks go to my wonderful publisher, Lee, without whom this series never would have found a home. Thanks also to Kellie, my smart and supportive editor. Thanks also to Sy and Cal, for reading over sections of the manuscript and offering their valuable insights.

Dedication

To all the fans who have supported my dream of becoming a full-time writer. This one's for you.

Foreword

Dearest Reader,

    Before I present to you the astounding events that took place in the Kingdom of Amendyr during the Great War, I must explain how this account was shaped. The words themselves are taken mostly from the second diary of Lady Eleanor Kingsclere, née Sandleford. Without her precise (although undeniably embellished) record keeping, placing everything into a well-ordered timeline would have been impossible.

    However, Lady Eleanor's diary was not the only source used. Enclosed within its pages were letters exchanged between her and Cathelin Raybrook during the war. In addition to the diary and the letters, Lady Eleanor kept several sketches and poems, all signed "*Raisa.*" From these, and from a short written account authored by one Ailynn Gothel and edited by Lady Eleanor, I have drawn several of the descriptions used throughout this tale.

    And what a tale it is! Though I have devoted several years of study to the Great War, part of me still finds the story fantastical. In order to tell it properly, I have chosen to divide this manuscript into three distinct voices. During the course of my work, I found each to be equally important and could not justify elevating one narrative at the expense of the others.

    I pray you will not find this confusing. It really was the only thing to be done.

Your servant,

Rowena
Princess of Seria, Keeper of the Royal Library

THE MIRROR'S GAZE

Part One

Taken from the accounts of Lady Eleanor Sandleford, Cathelin Raybrook, and Ailynn Gothel. Edited and summarized by Princess Rowena, Keeper of the Royal Library.

Chapter One

Taken from the diary of Lady Eleanor Kingsclere

A FOUL WIND FOLLOWED the team of white horses as they galloped up the drive. They stood tall, proud heads lifted in defiance as the sky shook with thunder, but I could not make out the carriage behind them. Its shape was only a grey smear, blurred by heavy sheets of rain. I pressed my face closer to the kitchen window, but it was no use. I could not see anything.

"Well? Who is it?"

I sighed and turned away from the window. "I don't know, Jessith," I said to the tortoiseshell cat beside the fire. She was stretched out on her back, all four paws in the air, soaking in every bit of warmth she could. Her eyes were closed, but I could tell she was listening intently.

"Whoever they are, they picked an awful day to visit."

Jessith yawned, but made no move to get up. "And you picked an equally awful outfit to greet them in."

I stared down at the tan and white working dress and apron I had put on that morning. Although I was no longer a servant at Baxstresse, some habits were harder to let go of than others. "It's practical," I insisted, fighting a blush. I refused to let myself be embarrassed by a cat's opinion. "No one at the manor cares what I wear. Besides, Belle likes these dresses."

One of Jessith's yellow eyes cracked open. "She likes them because they're easier to take off, but that hardly matters now. You should prepare for company."

I ignored the comment, knowing a reaction would only encourage her, and stole another glance through the window. The carriage had drawn closer, and I could just make out the coat of arms on its side— two plumed quills crossed in an X, with a sword pointing down between them. "It's someone from the palace, but who? We aren't expecting anyone from Prince Brendan's court." Over the past three years, since Belle and I had helped him escape Luciana's magic spell, the dashing prince had become my fast friend. He was a frequent guest at Baxstresse, although I suspected his recent visits had more to do with my friend Sarah than me.

Jessith abandoned her spot and climbed to her feet. Her mouth opened in a wide yawn, showing off her fangs and the pink ridges of her throat. "There's only one way to answer that question. Go out and see what they want."

I wiped my hands on my apron and bent to tuck the edges of my skirt into my boots, grateful that I had chosen practicality over petticoats. Despite Jessith's complaints, it would hold up well against the rain and mud. Once I was finished, I scooped her into my arms and headed for the kitchen door, ignoring her noisy huff of protest. "I doubt it's Brendan. He always announces his visits. Of course, he has been stopping by more than usual lately."

"It's Sarah's fault," Jessith said flatly. Her expression remained sour, nose wrinkled and whiskers twitching, but she relaxed against my chest, only hooking her claws enough to find a grip on the front of my dress. "That fool of a prince can't stay away from her."

I gave her a chastising look as we entered the front hall. "That's unkind of you, Jessith. You didn't call me a fool when I fell in love with Belle. How is this any different?"

"Brendan isn't a fool for falling in love with a servant. It's being around Sarah that turns him into one. The two of them are insufferable. You weren't nearly so idiotic when you chose your wife."

I smiled. Coming from Jessith that was almost a compliment, although I was certain I had acted every bit of the fool she had accused Brendan of being. I began to say so, but someone else caught my eye. Matthew the stablemaster was standing by the front door. His wide-brimmed hat covered his face, and his work clothes were soaked through. He nodded in greeting, and I did the same. "Hello, Matthew. I take it you saw the carriage, too?"

"Aye, when I was out seeing to the horses. Brahms ain't afraid of thunder, but it makes Sir Thom jumpy." He gave me a once-over. "Are you wanting ta go out and greet our guests? That was a royal team coming up the drive."

"If you are, then put me down," Jessith said. "I'm not going out in that filth."

"Of course. We can't have you getting mud on your precious paws." I set her on the floor, and she sprinted over to Matthew, weaving between his legs without actually touching his stained pants. I pretended not to notice when he reached into his pocket for a lump of sugar and tossed it to the floor. Jessith was fond of any food she wasn't supposed to have, whether it was part of a cat's diet or not.

While she was distracted, I turned toward the large double doors. Matthew pulled them open, and I peered out into the rain. The carriage had come to a stop at the end of the drive and one of its doors was ajar. I waited for someone to emerge, perhaps one of Prince Brendan's courtiers, but the person who appeared instead surprised me.

A girl stepped out, perhaps ten years old. The rain had plastered her damp black curls to her face, and the edge of her white dress was stained with mud. Her skin was brown, much darker than most Serians or even the people of Amendyr, but her eyes were bright and wild. They fixed on me, and I knew instantly the girl was *Ariada*. The magic in her blood called to mine, and my skin tingled with warmth despite the cold blasts of air that whipped about my face.

I hurried out into the storm, untying my apron. Once I met the carriage, I wrapped it around the girl's thin shoulders to try and stop her shivering. Her dripping fingers clasped the edges of the fabric, and she swayed beside me.

"Are you all right?" I asked, hurrying to steady her.

The girl did not answer. She simply stared up at me in silence.

When I noticed Matthew running out to meet us, I wrapped my arm around the girl and turned toward the team of horses. Their sides heaved, and their coats were frothy with sweat and rain.

"Where is your driver?" I asked them, staring at the empty box. "Has something happened?"

"We don't have one," one of them said, not at all surprised that I could speak their language.

"Cassandra sent us," said the other. "She told us to bring the girl here as fast as we could. We've been running for hours."

My eyes widened in surprise, and I clutched the child tighter. Cassandra was one of Prince Brendan's magical advisors, along with her husband Cieran. If she had been desperate enough to send a little girl racing off through a storm without even a driver to look after her, something had to be wrong.

"Head for the stables," I told the horses, pointing to the other side of the manor. "Matthew will make sure you're warm and dry in there."

They whickered their thanks and allowed Matthew to lead them away. As soon as they were gone, I turned my attention back to the girl. She still seemed unsteady, and her skin was growing clammier by the moment. I rushed her into the manor, shielding her from the rain as best I could. The wind buffeted us until we stepped inside, and it took most of my strength to close the heavy doors against the gale. At last, they slammed shut, and the noise faded. "Are you all right?" I asked again in a softer voice.

The girl did not seem afraid of me. Instead, she looked curious as she studied my face. "I heard you. You spoke to the horses, and they understood."

I nodded. "I've always been able to speak with animals. I'm *Ariada*, like you."

Her eyes darted away from mine, and she hung her head. "No," she whispered. "I'm *Kira'baas*. You aren't like me."

The word *Kira'baas* sounded Amendyrri, tasting of magic, but I had never heard it before. I looked at her, eyes narrowed. "*Kira'baas?* What does that mean?"

Before the girl could answer, several voices called out at once. I gazed past her to see a small crowd of people gathered on the stairwell, all looking at us with concern. Mam, Sarah, and several of the servants were there, but one figure stood out from the others, and I smiled. Seeing my wife swiftly banished the last of the cold clinging to my skin. "Belle? I thought you had fallen asleep in the library again."

Belle lifted the skirts of her tan and white tea gown and hurried down the stairs to meet us. Instead of returning my smile, her face read disapproval. "What on earth were you doing outside? You look half frozen." She stopped abruptly at the foot of the stairs, finally noticing I was not alone. "And who is this?"

"I'm not sure. She arrived a few moments ago in a carriage with the royal crest. I just brought her in."

"Well, I s'pose the next step is to clean her up and get her warm," said Mam. She had always acted motherly toward me, and she seemed equally concerned for our unexpected guest. "You kept a fire going in the kitchen, didn't you, Ellie?"

"Of course she did." Sarah offered an arm to Mam along the way. "Good thing, too. Both of you look like drowned rats."

Jessith snickered from somewhere near my ankles, and the girl's face immediately brightened upon noticing her. She reached down to pet the top of Jessith's head, and to my surprise, Jessith allowed her touch despite the dripping water. She tilted her chin up so the girl could scratch under it, and a raspy purr started in her throat.

"Her name is Jessith," Belle said, stepping cautiously toward the girl. "How would you like to take her to the kitchen with you? We can get you some warm clothes."

The girl looked up at Belle, and then turned toward me, waiting to see what I thought. She had not appeared to be afraid of me or Jessith, but she seemed slightly mistrustful of the others as they drew closer. "That sounds like a good idea," I told her. "The kitchen's just down the hall."

After a moment of thought, the girl nodded. When Jessith started off toward the kitchen, she followed, with Mam and Sarah trailing behind. As I moved to join them, Belle fell into step beside me. She folded a protective arm around my waist and pulled me close, pressing a kiss on top of my head. "She's *Ariada,* isn't she, dear heart?"

"Yes," I whispered back. "I can sense it. But when I mentioned it, she used a different word: *Kira'baas.* Do you know what it means? Do you think she could be from Shezad?"

Belle froze half way down the hall. The others continued walking in front of us, not noticing we had stopped. She let go of my waist and turned to face me, and the corners of her lips tugged down in a worried frown. "I don't know about her, but the word isn't from Shezad. It's Amendyrri. I came across it a few times in the library when I was researching Luciana's..." Her voice trailed off, and she shook herself, banishing old memories. "Never mind. *Kira'baas* means 'Voice of the Dead'."

The footsteps ahead of us stopped, and I noticed the girl peering over her shoulder at me. She abandoned Jessith and began making her way back down the hall. "Are you coming?" She still clutched the apron I had given her. "I don't want to go alone."

I gave Belle a look to let her know we would finish this conversation later and went to meet the girl. She smiled when I reached her, holding out her hand. I laced my fingers through hers, casting one last glance at Belle to make sure she would follow us. She did, but a shadow remained over her face. Clearly, the word *Kira'baas* had frightened her.

Once we arrived at the kitchen, Mam wasted no time making our strange guest comfortable. She took away my soaked apron and replaced it with a warm blanket, guiding the girl into a wooden chair by the fire while Sara began heating up some of the leftover soup from lunch. Belle remained by the doorway, arms folded over her chest. Her gaze never lingered in one place for too long, but it always returned to our strange visitor.

The girl tolerated Belle's suspicious glances, and even Mam's motherly fussing, but her eyes found mine every few moments, seeking reassurance, and I tried to offer some comfort. I nodded Mam in Sarah's direction and drew a second chair in front of the fire and sat down. Once they were on the other side of the kitchen, I turned to face the girl. "Can you tell me your name, and maybe where you're from?"

Without so many strangers hovering over her, the girl seemed to relax. She gave me a weak smile. "Neva. I'm from Amendyr."

"Not Shezad?"

"No, but my mother was." The word "was" did not escape me. I had lost my own mother, and I recognized the slight hesitation as Neva explained. However, she didn't linger on the subject. "What's your name?"

"I'm Ellie," I told her, trying my best to sound reassuring. "It's nice to meet you."

"Ellie?" the girl repeated, staring even more intently at my face. "Then you're the one." Before I could ask what she meant, she wriggled free from the blanket. Reaching into a fold of her skirt, she withdrew a water-stained letter. "Cieran told me to give you this," Neva whispered.

I frowned, not understanding. "Wait, you were at Prince Brendan's palace? Well, I suppose that explains the carriage. If you're from Amendyr, what were you doing there?"

A shadow fell over Neva's face. "Cieran was taking care of me, helping me learn to use my powers. Then they came for me, and Cassandra put me in the carriage so they wouldn't find me. I wanted to stay and help, but she said I had to go."

I started to ask who "they" were, but Belle pushed away from the door and came to stand behind my chair. The fire cast flickering shadows over her face, hollowing out her cheeks. "Go on, Ellie." She reached out to squeeze my shoulder, but even the warmth of her hand could not guard against my chilling sense of dread. "Open it. The message might make things clearer."

I broke the seal, bracing myself for bad news.

Ellie,

You must forgive my brevity. There is little time. The girl I have entrusted into your care is Neva Velias, Crown Princess of Amendyr and rightful heir to the white throne. She escaped Kalmarin and her stepmother, with my assistance. I have kept her safe at Prince Brendan's palace for the past several months.

Somehow, we were discovered. We woke to find an army of monsters at our door. A powerful Ariada controls them, and she seems to be proficient in more than one type of magic. Her creatures took the dungeons, and all the prisoners there have been turned.

Cassandra and I must protect Prince Brendan and his knights, but Neva cannot stay here. The safest place for her is with the Amendyrri rebellion. Please, take her across the border. Some of my friends will find you there. You must also use the journal I gave you to warn Cathelin Raybrook of what has happened at the palace.

Above all, be cautious. The Queen's eyes are everywhere in both kingdoms.
Cieran

I stared at the message for several moments, jumping from line to line. *An army of monsters...all of the prisoners have been turned...all of the prisoners.* My fear became blind panic. The letter fell from my hands, and I clutched tight to the arms of my chair. If this *Ariada*'s monsters had taken the dungeons, it meant she was no longer locked away. Even though Cieran had not written it, I knew what he was trying to tell me. After three long years, Luciana was free.

"Ellie, she isn't here." Belle's hand squeezed tighter, but I barely felt it. "She can't hurt us." I shrugged away from her touch, nearly knocking over the chair as I leapt to my feet. I wanted to run. To hide somewhere she would never think to look. But if Luciana had escaped the dungeons, nowhere was safe. She would find me, and this time, she would kill me.

I lunged for the kitchen door, but Belle caught my wrist. She pulled me back, and I collapsed against her chest, burying my face into the dark, safe space where her throat ran into her shoulder. I trembled in her arms, but no tears fell. I was too terrified to cry.

"It's all right," Belle murmured, stroking my hair. "Everything is all right. I promise."

But I knew it was an empty reassurance. If Luciana truly was free, she would not hesitate to come after us. That was why Cieran had mentioned Cate. That was why he wanted us to flee for Amendyr. Not just to return this strange girl to her kingdom, but to escape from the woman who wanted Cate, Belle, and I dead. Something tugged at my skirt, and I tore my face away from Belle's shoulder to see Neva standing beside me.

"You're afraid of it, too, aren't you?" she whispered. "The thing that's watching us through her?"

It hadn't crossed my mind, but old memories came welling up, images of a burning eye set in silver and gold rings. I gritted my teeth, struggling to shut them out. Luciana was terrifying enough on her own. I did not want to remember the tainted magic I had felt through her sorcerer's chain. "What are you talking about?" I asked. "Who are you talking about?"

"You've seen it," Neva insisted. "I know you have. The thing that watches me through my stepmother has been watching you, too. I know how its magic feels when it's touched someone."

Slowly, I pulled out of Belle's arms and nodded. "Yes. I think so."

To my surprise, Neva took my hand. Her fingers were still cold, but I clutched them tight anyway. "It's already dead. It can't hurt you unless the person it's using hurts you. That's why Cieran had to hide me."

"How do you know all this?" Belle stared at Neva incredulously, but I knew she remembered the sorcerer's chain. Its power had almost killed her. She believed every word this girl was saying, just as I did.

Neva shrugged. "I am *Kira'baas,* Daughter of the Sixth Son. When the dead speak, they speak through me."

Chapter Two

Taken from the letters of Cathelin Raybrook, edited by Lady Eleanor Kingsclere

THE DARKNESS SEEPS INTO everything. It stretches through cracks between the stones, rises to the high, empty ceiling, reaches out over the floor in grasping fingers of shadow. Shadows need light to survive, but there is no light here. Only thick, choking darkness that clogs the air.

"Take the girl out into the woods." A voice, low and soft, but resonant enough to fill the room. "Kill her, and as proof that she is dead, cut out her heart and bring it back to me."

A cold beam of light pierces the blackness. It stabs through the dark like a lance of ice, falling on a man's terrified face. His skin is sallow, sweat is smeared across his brow, and his eyes are wells of fear. "But, my lady."

Another figure steps out of the shadows: a woman, tall, skin pale as snow. Her hair is equally fair, spilling past her shoulders in a shimmering waterfall. A crown of white gold rests upon her head, shining like a beacon in the black room. Her lips are a perfect cut of red in the landscape of her face, and they part, almost as if expecting a kiss. Instead, she speaks, whispering words that tremble like notes of music. "The girl cannot live. As long as she does, Amendyr will remain divided."

The man's eyes glaze over. The irises swell, but his breathing remains shallow, and his heartbeat batters his chest. He is terrified. "Yes, my lady."

"See that it is done." The woman moves away from the cold light, shifting aside to reveal its source: a mid-sized, oval-shaped mirror hanging against a stone wall. Its glass swirls with grey fog, and dark, fuzzy shapes shift behind its surface. She turns, running her hand over its smooth surface, and one of the shapes steps forward. A body? No, a face.

The face in the mirror was beautiful once, a lovely heart shape and a proud jaw. But her chestnut hair is rough and matted, and her eyelids *are scarred shut, twisted over empty sockets. The lady's hand comes up to rest on the mirror's glass, stroking along the eyeless woman's cheek. "If you fail to kill her, I will find someone else who can. My shaper will make someone else who can."*

The mirror flashes, and the face transforms. Her skin cracks, peeling around the edges like an old painting, and the color of her lips dulls to a putrid black. Her teeth sharpen, grazing the surface of a purple-grey tongue. The sickly sweet smell of rotting flesh clouds the room, cutting off the air to my lungs.

I woke with a start, jerking upright and clutching the covers to my chest. My heartbeat pounded heavily in my throat and my chest burned with each breath as I tried to spit the foul, lingering taste of rotted meat from my mouth. Although my eyes were open, it took me several moments to see where I was—still in bed, naked and shivering except for the wolfskin belt around my waist. Sweat rolled down the middle of my back, but my skin felt ice cold.

Fragments of the vision lingered at the edges of my mind, always present, but just out of reach. The longer I remained awake, the more disjointed the sounds and pictures seemed. I groped blindly, trying to recapture them, but they slipped away before I could fit the pieces together. Only one image remained—the face in the mirror. It swallowed my thoughts and seared behind my eyes. Her name had not been spoken, but I already knew who she was. The woman with no eyes, the same face that had destroyed my days and visited my nightmares.

The mattress dipped beneath me, and I looked down, regaining a little of myself as I stared into a pair of soft, familiar brown eyes. Larna. My *Tuathe*. Her angular face replaced the one in the mirror, and I sighed with relief. My pulse stopped racing as I let the covers fall around my hips. "I'm sorry. Did I wake you?"

Larna sat up beside me, stretching her arms over her head. "Aye, Cate, but it doesna matter. Morning's already come." She pulled apart the curtains behind the headboard and sunlight filtered in through the window, banishing the shadows to the far corners of the room. She turned to me, forehead furrowed with concern. "What were you seeing?"

I shifted closer, curling beneath one of her arms and tucking my head against her shoulder. My fear had retreated to a dark corner of my heart, but I still needed to be close to her. "I'm not sure. I saw..." My tongue tripped, and I swallowed before trying again. I needed to convince myself that I could speak her name. "I saw Luciana's face. But it wasn't her face. She was something else. Dead, but not." The sweet, rotting smell from my vision filled my nose and mouth again, and I had to grit my teeth to keep from gagging.

Larna stiffened against me. My mate held a special hatred in her heart for the woman who had raped and abused me. Still, her first instinct was to offer comfort. She kissed my forehead, brushing away the damp strands of hair that clung to my cheeks. "Someone canna be dead and alive together, *Tuathe*. Maybe that part of your vision was only a nightmare."

I was not so certain. Luciana had seemed frighteningly real to me, and I knew Larna would not understand. She always believed my visions, but she had not seen them, heard them, tasted them. She was not *Ariada*. "Luciana wasn't the only person in the vision. There were two others, a pale blonde woman with a crown on her head and a man attending her. The woman told the man to bring back her heart."

Larna looked at me in confusion. "Whose heart?"

"She didn't say, but I know she wanted it badly. No, wanted isn't the right word. She needed it. Needed it like breathing." The fact that the blonde woman wanted the heart was terrifying, but not surprising. It was a common ingredient in shaping and necromancy, a fact I knew through personal, gruesome experience. But the need...the hunger she had felt...that was something I did not understand.

"I am thinking I prefer your old visions. At least we could be understanding them."

I let out a snort, trying to ignore the tight coil of fear in my chest. "You mean the ones where I watched you die over and over again? No, thank you. These visions are terrifying, but losing you every night was even worse."

"These?" Larna eyes narrowed, and she gave me a searching look. "You mean this isna the first?"

"This was the first, but I'm certain I'll have more." I untangled myself from her arms. "The important ones usually come several times." Once I was free, I headed for the wardrobe against the far wall, regretting my decision to sleep naked. The cold no longer bothered me since becoming a wyr, but I felt exposed anyway. At Baxstresse, I never would have dared to walk around without my clothes.

Larna sighed, abandoning the bed and following me to the wardrobe. She had stubbornly refused to remove her own clothes from our travelling packs, but mine were hung and folded neatly inside. She folded her arms around my waist from behind, preventing me from reaching for my leggings. "Is there anything you might be doing to change what you saw?"

I shook my head. "No. I could tell the vision happened long ago. I can't prevent it."

"Then what will you be doing? Waiting?"

"Yes, I don't have much choice."

Larna caught the waver in my voice, felt the tension in my body. She had always been able to read me. Her hands trailed along my sides, cupping the swell of my hips, but she paused before going lower, waiting for me to tell her what kind of comfort I wanted. Normally, Larna had an open invitation to touch me however she liked, but with Luciana's memory still hanging over us, I was grateful for her caution.

My head fell back against her chest, and I laced my fingers with hers. The vision had left me shaken, but the longer I spent in Larna's arms, the more relaxed I felt. Being close to her helped ease my fears. "I can't decide whether I want you to take me back to bed or not," I murmured.

Larna dipped her head, and I gasped as the warmth of her mouth found my throat. My pulse raced, but I did not push her away. She was the only one my inner wolf trusted near such a vulnerable place. "Whatever you need," she whispered into my shoulder. "If you want to forget her touch with mine, I will be helping you. If you want to cry, I will hold you until the tears dry up. If you are needing anything…"

Tears of relief burned in my eyes. I turned in Larna's arms, but as I tilted my face up to kiss her, someone started banging on the door. I drew back in surprise and scurried to find my clothes instead. "Who is it?" I called out, balancing on one foot as I shoved the other into a fresh pair of leggings. Larna did not bother looking for her own clothes. She simply sighed at me, shaking her head in disappointment as her view disappeared.

"Ailynn. May I come in?"

The door swung open before I could give an answer. I whirled around, clutching my tunic to my chest to preserve some of my modesty. Just as I had feared, Ailynn stood in the doorway, gaping at us in surprise. Even worse, she was not alone. Her lover Raisa stood beside her, but thankfully, she was too busy glaring to see us. "Ailynn! What's the point of asking if you're going to barge in anyway?"

Ailynn seemed to come to her senses. She clapped a hand over her eyes as a vivid pink blush spread across her face. "I'm sorry," she stammered. "I'm not used to sharing space with other people."

"That's no excuse," Raisa insisted. She kept her eyes fixed on the floor, but I caught a hint of a smile on her face. "I'm so sorry, Cate. Sometimes I think she was raised in a barn instead of the same cottage as me."

"It's all right." I shrugged into my tunic, stealing a glance at Larna as I did up the belt. She had wandered over to our travelling bags, completely unaffected by our embarrassment. At last, she selected a shirt but seemed in no hurry to find a matching set of pants. "Just pick something," I begged. "I know the pack doesn't care if you're naked, but Ailynn and Raisa aren't wyr. You're embarrassing them."

That got through to her, and she hurried to finish dressing. "Sorry," she said, grinning slightly.

I sighed, reaching up to smooth her messy black hair. Larna always found a way to ruin it, short as it was. "There. You're mostly presentable now."

Ailynn uncovered her eyes, and I noticed her blush had crept all the way to her collarbone. "I really am sorry. I thought the two of you would be awake. Most of the liarre are already gathered in the grand theater, and I didn't want us to be late."

I glanced out the window in surprise. Sure enough, the sun was already high in the sky. "It's nearly midday. How did that happen?"

"The same way it is happening every day," Larna teased. "The birds call the sun up, and..."

I bumped my shoulder playfully against hers and took her hand. "Come on. I don't want to be late for the meeting."

"I admire your enthusiasm," Raisa said as we joined her by the door. "This is the sixth day, and the council still hasn't decided anything. I can't believe they don't realize the danger."

The mention of danger called up my vision again, and my smile vanished. "They're frightened. The Queen's forces are already slaughtering their way through Amendyr, and the liarre don't want to bring the war to their doorstep."

"That's exactly why they should fight," Ailynn protested. Her embarrassment shifted to anger, and the heat in her cheeks rushed to light her eyes. "If the Queen takes over Amendyr, what's left? Liarre territory. Joining the rebels is in their own best interest."

"We know that, but they haven't seen what Mogra's army is capable of."

Guilt tugged at Ailynn's face. "I should have made sure she was dead instead of running away. She's probably still out there, shaping the Queen's army. If...no, not if...when they come here, it will be my fault."

My heart ached for her, but before I could offer comfort, Raisa ran a soothing hand along the stiff line of Ailynn's arm. "It's not your fault, *Tuathe*. There wasn't time. We nearly died."

Ailynn let out a deep sigh. All of the anger drained out of her, and she turned to face Raisa, resting their foreheads together. It was a surprisingly intimate gesture, and I almost felt like an intruder in their world as she rested her hands on top of Raisa's swollen stomach. "I know," she murmured. "But she was my mother. I had a thousand chances to stop this, and I didn't take them."

I shared a glance with Larna, and she cleared her throat. "There will be other chances, Ailynn. If Mogra lives, we will be finding her, and you will be having an army at your back. And if the Queen's demons are coming here..." She smiled, and even without her fangs, I could see the predator underneath. "They burn as easy as anything else."

A little of Ailynn's confidence returned. She removed her hands from Raisa's belly and folded an arm around her shoulder instead. "I suppose you're right. Now, let's hurry. I've already made us late for the meeting." She and Raisa turned for the door together, and I followed, still holding Larna's hand in mine.

The four of us stepped out of our building and into the sunlight. The council had given us shelter right in the middle of Ardu, nestled among the flat, stacked-stone buildings, but the main street was empty and all the shops were closed. Everyone had already made their way to the grand theater to watch the debate.

"You'd think they would get tired of sitting after nearly a week," Ailynn said. "The council doesn't seem any closer to deciding than when we started."

"I can't blame them," I said. "War means lives lost. They have a right to be concerned."

"Don't look so worried, Cate." Raisa offered me a smile. "I'm sure the council will listen to you and Larna today. They can't put off their decision forever."

I sighed. Even though Raisa had misinterpreted the source of my fear, I did not mention my vision. Now was not the time. "I don't know what else we can say to convince them. We told them about the villages burning, about the Queen's army, about Mogra's *kerak* and shadowkin."

"We just have to keep trying," Ailynn said. "If we can force the issue to a vote, I think we have a fair chance."

I was not convinced. Waiting for a decision from the council was frustrating, but I wasn't sure we had the votes we needed. The arachniarre and feliarre representatives were firmly on our side, but Councilor Maresth and the equiarre representative were far more cautious, and the caniarre representative's behavior was almost hostile. "Not unless we can get at least one more councilmember to agree with us."

"We will," Larna said, folding a strong arm around my shoulder. "I know we will."

I remained silent as we stepped onto the street, praying she was right even as the face in the mirror flashed through my head.

Chapter Three

Taken from the verbal accounts of Ailynn Gothel, edited by Lady Eleanor Kingsclere

I SLUMPED IN MY seat, crossing my arms and gazing across the giant rings of the grand theater. It was the largest building I had ever seen, and almost all the benches were filled with liarre. Even after several weeks in Ardu, I had not grown used to the sight of so many faces. It didn't help that none of the faces were human. The tapered, twitching noses of the feliarre, the long, delicate muzzles of the equiarre, and the tattooed arachniarre with their needle-thin teeth still seemed strange to me.

Warmth brushed my wrist, and I looked into my lap to see Raisa's fingers lacing with mine. I gave her hand a squeeze and sighed. The liarre had treated us well for the most part, but I was still a stranger here and watching them debate day after day made me feel helpless.

"They should be starting soon," Raisa whispered beside my ear. "I can see Councilor Maresth just beyond the door."

I looked back up to meet her eyes, and a few threads of her golden hair brushed along my cheek. I tucked them fondly behind her ear, stroking the soft line of her jaw with the backs of my fingers. "Remind me to cut your hair later. If I hadn't braided it this morning, it would be down to your ankles."

Raisa shook her head and pushed my hand away, reaching up to check that her braid was still there. A few strands had escaped, but that wasn't unusual. With so much hair, some of it was almost always out of place. "We can worry about it later," she said, pushing the stray locks back behind her shoulders. "You really should pay more attention. Today could be the day they finally decide to vote."

"Not likely," I muttered. "I'm sure Rufas will have a whole list of objections to get through before Jinale can even mention the subject." Raisa opened her mouth to speak, but before she could get a word out, the rest of the theater went silent. As one, all the liarre turned to look at the large platform in the middle of the circle. I could not help but follow their gaze, and as I had been seated in the second row up, I had an excellent view.

Four of the councilors were already in place. A lithe feliarre sat on the far left, her tail curled around her striped haunches. Sleek sheets of muscle covered her body, and the whiskers around her nose twitched with impatience beneath her slitted yellow eyes. Her name was Rachari, and she had been sympathetic to our cause from the beginning, despite the way her fur bristled whenever Larna or Cate drew too close for comfort.

Beside Rachari was another friendly face, though her appearance still frightened me if I didn't prepare myself. Jinale, the arachniarre councilor, was a fearsome sight with eight legs and a bulbous lower body. Although her upper half was human in appearance, her head was not. She had a nose and chin, but her lips and tongue were black, and her cheeks were covered in decorative eye tattoos. She was another ally of ours, and she had saved me and Raisa on two separate occasions during our journey to Ardu. Before her arrival in the city a few days prior, I hadn't been certain whether she survived my mother's attack.

"At least one of them understands the damage Mogra can do," I said to Raisa, nodding in Jinale's direction. "Jinale witnessed it firsthand. I don't understand why the others won't listen to her."

Raisa gave my hand a sympathetic squeeze. "You do understand. Remember how long you spent in denial about your mother's actions?"

Although she hadn't meant to hurt my feelings, Raisa's words cut the bottom from my stomach. Guilt and I had become fast friends over the past several months. If I was being honest with myself over the past several years. I didn't want to admit it, but Raisa was right. I did understand why Rufas and Weyshra, the other two councilors, wanted to remain in Ardu instead of sending troops to aid the Amendyrri rebellion. The kingdom was not their home. Until Mogra showed up at the city's doorstep, many of them were content to pretend everything was normal. It was not unlike the way I had behaved when my mother started to display the first signs of insanity.

Still, I couldn't help feeling resentful as my eyes shifted to Rufas, the caniarre councilor. He was large and muscular, with thick arms and heavy-set shoulders. His fangs jutted up from a severe underbite, and his jowls quivered whenever he spoke. He was currently whispering to Weyshra, who stood to his left. Although the tall, graceful equiarre councilor did not seem to have anything against humans or wyr, he was cautious by nature. While Rufas disparaged all of Larna's pleas for aid, Weyshra expressed at least some regret over his perceived inability to help.

The sound of a gong rang through the theater and I stopped brooding. The sick, swimming feeling in the pit of my belly eased a little. Chairwoman Maresth, the dracarre representative, slithered along the walkway leading up to the platform. Her scales shone in the sunlight, and the stadium was so silent I imagined I could hear the scratch of her giant claws and the rustle of her long, heavy tail dragging along the ground behind her. The other councilors bowed their heads and divided to make space for her at the center, Jinale and Rachari going one way, Rufas and Weyshra another.

Once she had taken her place among them, she turned in our direction to address the crowd. When she spoke, I shuddered at the soft hiss in her voice. "Though we are all different, we gather here as brothers and sisters, just as our ancestors did before us. Today, we debate a matter of great importance: whether the liarre will offer aid to the Kingdom of Amendyr in its time of need. Let us speak wisely, act justly, and make certain all voices are heard."

I leaned forward, listening carefully, but Maresth's flickering hiss revealed nothing. Over the past week, I had not been able to discern her opinion on the subject. While the other four councilors were all too happy to make their opinions known, Maresth acted as more of a moderator, making sure their arguments never got out of hand. Unfortunately, her conciliatory approach didn't do anything to speed up the proceedings.

My heart sank when Rufas leapt on the opportunity to speak first. "Madam Chairwoman, since I was the last to speak yesterday and wasn't given enough time to finish my remarks, I humbly request the opportunity to open today's debate."

While Maresth considered his request, Rachari rolled her eyes. It was strange to see such a human gesture on a feline face, but I reminded myself that the liarre had been human once. Lyr the shaper had created their ancestors centuries ago with his brutal magical experiments. Although they were friendly, it easily could have been otherwise. My mother's twisted creations were not so docile.

"I doubt more time to speak will help your cause," Rachari said. The sarcasm in her throaty voice was more than obvious, and Rufas' thick jaw bunched in annoyance. "We've been discussing our options for six days already. The time has come to make a decision. We owe our guests that much." She gestured at Larna and Cate, who were seated in the first row right at the foot of the platform. "The Farseer pack is a crucial part of the rebel army. An army, I might add, that is the only thing standing between us and the Queen's monsters."

"We have no reason to believe the Queen will invade Ardu," Rufas barked. His hands clenched into fists, and the short fur on the back of his haunches began to bristle. Of all the councilors, he was the most hot-tempered, and Rachari knew just how to rile him. "Our land hasn't been part of Amendyr for centuries. Sacrificing liarre lives on the slim possibility that the Queen might try and expand her borders is foolish."

"The foolish thing would be to wait until we have kerak and shadowkin at our doorstep." Jinale frowned, and even her eye tattoos seemed to narrow. "Believe me, Rufas, they will come. I have seen Mogra's creations myself. They are mindless killers, incapable of fear or sympathy. If we don't join the rebellion and strike first, they will wipe us out."

Weyshra gently cleared his throat and the other councilors turned toward him. "I believe your accounts of Mogra's creatures, Jinale, but if you encountered them only a few days from Ardu, why haven't they followed you here? You told us yourself you believed Mogra to be dead. Perhaps without their leader, they have already retreated?"

"I never said Mogra was dead. She's alive and well, I'm sure of it. An *Ariada* that powerful would never allow herself to be killed by something as insignificant as a rockslide."

In my heart, I knew Jinale was right. It was true I had seen no sign of Mogra after the avalanche that had nearly taken our lives, but that didn't mean anything. I could think of countless ways Mogra could have used her magic to survive the fall, and I had learned the hard way never to underestimate her. She would return at the head of the Queen's armies, and when she did, I would be waiting for her. She was my responsibility.

As the crowd murmured, I squeezed Raisa's hand. She was the only one who truly understood my feelings. Despite my hatred for my mother, despite the fact she had created monsters with corrupted magic and imprisoned Raisa in a cave, I did not hate her. In fact, I pitied her. On my worst days, I feared I might become her.

Rufas' gruff voice brought me back to the debate. "Whether the witch is dead or not isn't the issue. The facts are simple. We can't afford to sacrifice liarre lives for a human war."

"But it isn't just a human war," Rachari pointed out. "All manner of creatures live in Amendyr, some of whom are our brothers and sisters." She gestured at Larna and Cate, and though I could only see the backs of their heads, I could imagine their annoyed expressions perfectly. Larna's face would tense and twitch, narrow-eyed and fierce, while Cate's would remain a mask of long-suffering patience. "Wyr and liarre come from the same magic blood. You may be willing to dismiss the war as a silly human conflict, but the rest of us won't turn our backs on our kin so easily."

While Rufas fumed, Rachari turned toward the crowd, addressing them directly. "Liarre have always stood against the corruption of magic. Since our creation, we have fought back against *Ariada* who think they can shape living beings to their own purposes. Today, we have the opportunity to fight for freedom once again. A shaper has been practicing dark magic, just like Lyr did centuries ago, and creating an army of monsters. If you will not fight for your own safety, fight because our history demands it. The liarre cannot tolerate the abuse of magic in any form."

"You realize what you're implying, don't you, Rachari?" Weyshra said, looking at her with worried eyes. "The wyr are the result of shaping gone awry, just as we are. If we are to consider the wyr our kin, we must consider the kerak and shadowkin our brothers as well."

Rachari's lips pulled into a snarl, but Jinale spoke before she could unleash her fury on the equiarre councilor. "It is because they are our brothers that we must put them out of their misery. They are mindless, tormented desecrations of the dead. We cannot allow them to continue suffering under the hands of a tyrant like Mogra."

The sound of voices swelled around us, but the murmurs of approval from the crowd seemed to outnumber the shouts of protest. While Rufas fumed and Weyshra continued to fret, I remained focused on Maresth. Hers was the vote we needed, and hers was the only opinion I cared about. The councilor's reptilian face revealed little, but I thought I saw her second pair of eyelids blink and her tongue flicker. Perhaps Rachari's pleas had finally gotten through to her.

At last, she nodded to a crouched feliarre at the bottom of the platform. He struck the gong again, and the crowd went silent. Once she had the stadium's attention, Maresth addressed the audience in a dry, rasping voice. "This line of debate provides no satisfactory answers. We must make a decision quickly. The debate will continue, but I request the rebellion's ambassadors meet with us in private once we finish. Tomorrow, the five of us will announce our decision to the public."

I caught a glimpse of Cate turning around in the row below. She searched for my eyes, and I returned her look of disbelief. She, Larna, and I had been trying to meet with the council in private for almost a week, but Maresth had forbidden it. So far, only Jinale and Rachari had agreed to speak with us, but they were already sympathetic to the rebellion. The chance to meet with the rest of the council in private would prove invaluable. Perhaps when they were away from the eyes of the public they would be more concerned with listening to reason than posturing in front of the people who had elected them to office.

"See?" Raisa whispered beside me, clutching excitedly at my shoulder. "I told you things would be different today. We finally have a chance to convince the other councilors to vote our way."

"Don't get your hopes up," I muttered, even though I was already disobeying my own advice. "Until the council votes, we're just as bad off as we were before."

Raisa continued smiling. "Well, if you won't be optimistic, I will. One of us has to be."

I couldn't help but smile back. Raisa might not be *Ariada*, but she was far stronger than me. She had survived years of isolation and imprisonment with her sanity intact, and never once had she given up hope. If she could still have faith after enduring so much, so could I.

Chapter Four

Taken from the diary of Lady Eleanor Kingsclere

I JOLTED AWAKE TO the sound of a fearful hiss and a mild flash of pain. Sharp claws pierced the bare skin below my shoulder, and I blinked in surprise. Jessith's bright yellow eyes hovered an inch away from mine, almost overtaken by their dark pupils. "Ellie, wake up," she yowled, nudging me with her nose. "We have to leave. They're already gathering outside. Can't you hear them?"

I flinched away as Jessith's whiskers tickled my cheek. "Hear what?" I yawned, pushing her off my chest and into my lap. "Who's gathering?" Instinctively, I glanced over at Belle. She snored softly beside me, her face buried in her pillow and her glossy black hair tossed in a tangle around her head.

Jessith clambered over me and onto Belle's back, tail swishing in agitation. "You too," she said, butting against Belle's head. When her efforts proved useless, she extended her claws again, jabbing through the sheets.

That did the trick. Belle groaned and swung out blindly with one arm, trying to shove Jessith off the bed. "Tell that damnable cat to keep her paws to herself," she grumbled, her sleep-thickened voice muffled by the pillow. "It's the middle of the night."

"Wait," I said, scooping Jessith back into my arms. "She came here to warn us."

With a sigh of protest, Belle pushed up into a sitting position, sweeping her tousled hair back with one hand. "Warn us?" she slurred, blinking the sleep from her eyes. "About what?"

"About the monsters, you idiots." Jessith leapt to the floor, her fur bristling with impatience. "I already told you they're coming."

The last of my tiredness vanished. "What monsters?"

"The ones that smell of foul magic, of course." Jessith stared at me as if I was the greatest idiot alive. "There's an army of them headed straight for us. If we don't make our escape now, they'll have us surrounded."

Suddenly, I understood. The monsters from Cieran's letter had not confined themselves to Ronin. Some of them had made their way to Baxstresse, and I knew at once why they had come. "They're here for Neva," I said, groping for Belle's arm. "We have to get her to safety."

"What?" A furrow creased the middle of Belle's forehead. "But we aren't ready to leave for Amendyr yet—"

"Did you not hear the part about the army of monsters closing in on the estate?" Jessith snarled. "And to think I considered you intelligent for a human."

I didn't bother translating Jessith's insults. Instead, I leapt out of bed, searching for last night's clothes. "How much time do we have?" I asked as I pulled my dress over my head.

"Finally, a sensible question. A few minutes at best if the birds outside weren't spouting their usual gibberish. They kept shrieking about night-claws and burning eyes and giant dogs."

My fingers shook as I rummaged through the closet for my riding habit and shrugged into it. Cate had written to me about the horrible creatures taking over Amendyr in her letters. The kerak were lanky, twisted versions of what had once been men, and the shadowkin were the giant demon-dogs that accompanied them. If Mogra's army of undead monsters had somehow made its way from Ronin to Baxstresse...

"We need to go," I told Belle, slipping into my shoes. "Get dressed and grab everything you can. We have to evacuate the estate immediately."

Belle looked as though she wanted to protest, but after a moment's hesitation, she obeyed. Once the shock wore off, she was all business, rummaging through our wardrobe for her loosest clothes. "One of us needs to get Neva. The other should go warn the servants. If something really is coming."

"Somethings," I corrected her. "We're about to have an army at our door."

That made her move even faster. Soon, the two of us were racing through the manor, only half dressed but too frantic to care. Without consulting each other, Belle headed upstairs to the third floor while I headed downstairs. I had memorized the corridors long ago, and I didn't need light to find my way. I travelled the halls with sure feet, my mind racing just as fast. *What was it Cate wrote to me about the kerak? Fire. They're afraid of fire.* I veered off course, heading for the kitchens instead of the servants' quarters. *Mam always keeps a lantern burning there late at night. Saints, I hope she didn't forget.*

I let out a sigh of relief when I burst through the door and saw the tiny heart of flame pulsing inside the lantern's glass. Thank goodness for solid, dependable Mam and her habits. I snatched the lantern's handhold and raced back out into the hallway again, this time heading straight for Sarah's room. "Wake up!" I shouted, beating against the door.

Sarah came stumbling out a moment later, still in her dressing gown and looking disgruntled. "What in heaven's name?" she rasped, rubbing sleep from her eyes. She squinted at the lantern in my hand and winced. "It's not a fire, is it?"

"Worse. We have to get everyone out of here at once."

Thankfully, Sarah didn't question me. Like Belle, she was all action once she saw the concern on my face. With her help, we soon roused Mam, the other servants, and the remaining groomsmen. Most were displeased at having been woken, but when they saw me waving my lantern, their complaints petered out. No matter how unorthodox my behavior and dress could be, they had grown to respect me over the years. Once, I had been one of them.

"Everyone head for the stables," I ordered, catching Matthew's eye. "Gather torches and as much kindling as you can find. You're going to need fire."

The old stablemaster nodded once, and I knew he would make sure everyone obeyed. "Fer what, Miss?"

"Magical creatures are coming to Baxstresse. Fire and light are the only things that can harm them."

That pronouncement caused a wave of panicked whispers, but I ignored them. I couldn't show any fear even though my heart pounded frantically in the cage of my chest. Cate and her mate Larna might know how to fight these things, but I wasn't a warrior, and neither were most of the others at the estate. As much as I hated the thought of leaving, we had no other choice. Baxstresse wasn't nearly as important as making sure everyone survived.

"If they overwhelm you at the stables, don't stay," I told Sarah as all of us hurried out the front door and into the cold, wet night. Rain spattered my face, but I brushed it away and held Sarah's dark, frightened eyes with my own. "Saddle the horses and run as far and as fast as you can."

"But aren't you coming with us?"

"Belle and I have to take Neva to Amendyr. I need you to make sure Lady Kingsclere and the others get out of here safely." At that moment, three figures and several small shadows burst through the door, running across the field after us. I recognized Belle even from a distance, and relief washed over me when I saw that Neva, Lady Kingsclere, and a little army of Baxstresse tortoiseshell cats were keeping pace with her.

"Any sign of them yet?" Belle gasped as they caught up with us. I shook my head.

"Good. Here, take this." She shoved a pack into my arms, and I felt it squirm as I moved to loop the straps over my shoulders.

"Careful," Jessith hissed. "It's already cramped enough in here."

I had no idea why Jessith had elected to come with us, but there wasn't time to ask. An unearthly shriek split the sky, and a flare of lightning brightened the darkness. It highlighted several hulking shapes in the distance. They moved like sluggish mountains, all thick muscle, and I knew without a doubt I had been right. Those couldn't be anything but the shadowkin, and if there were shadowkin, that meant—this time, the sharp scream tore close beside my head. I lurched, swinging my lantern just as a dripping claw sliced beside my face. I caught a glimpse of row upon row of black, rotted teeth and an endless mouth before the hideous creature's long, twisted body erupted in flames. Its howls made my skull throb, I clamped my hands over my ears, hunching in on myself in terror.

"No, don't!"

My ears were still ringing, so I barely heard the small cry at my shoulder. I opened my eyes to see three more of the twisted husks standing before me, but unlike the first, they didn't move. They remained frozen, their eyeless maws turned directly on Neva. They seemed to be waiting for something, and gradually, I realized I was not going to die.

"Go away," Neva said, pointing into the distance. Her small hand shook, but her voice never wavered. "Leave and don't come back."

Shockingly, the kerak obeyed. They turned, loping off on their unnaturally long limbs and disappearing into the night. I stared at Neva in amazement. "How...how did you?"

But the girl didn't answer my question. "We have to go," she said, tugging on my hand. "The others are already running."

The Mirror's Gaze

I turned to see the rest of the servants hurrying toward the stables. Only Belle remained beside us, and her pale face looked just as shell-shocked as I was sure mine had to be. "Ellie, did she just—"

"She's a necromancer, you dolt," Jessith yowled. "I told you these things were undead. I can smell the rotting flesh. Now let's run before more of them show up. I'm not letting a barely-trained girl stand between me and an army."

Jessith had a point. The large shadowkin were drawing nearer, close enough for me to make out more of their shapes. Their heads alone were as large as a person, and I didn't fancy sticking around to find out how much bigger their bodies were. I grabbed Belle's hand in one of mine and Neva's in the other, hurrying to the stable.

A large fire was already burning by the time we got there. Mam and Lady Kingsclere directed the servants to feed it while Matthew and a few of the groomsmen saddled the horses. Even the cats were helping. I caught a glimpse of old Trugel batting some straw into the blaze and Ruficee carrying several sticks in his teeth. Unfortunately, the horses weren't nearly so helpful. They nickered in fear, thrashing and rising up onto their hind legs. I hurried over to help, soothing the nearest one I could find. "Sir Thom, no!"

Sir Thom stopped bucking as soon as I touched him. He settled back onto all fours, breathing heavily. "Thom, I need you to stay calm," I whispered, not caring whether any of the servants heard me. It was too late to worry about revealing my magical abilities. "You and the other horses have to get everyone away from Baxstresse."

"I can smell 'em," Thom huffed, bits of froth flecking from his mouth. "Smell the bad things."

"Right. We're going to help everyone out of here, away from the bad things."

"I want to help." I turned to see a familiar, narrow face in the stall beside Thom. Brahms wasn't panicking like the others, although his sides heaved with energy. "Ride me, Ellie. Let me take you away from here."

My inward debate didn't last long. Brahms was a racehorse, but he was sturdy. Nothing could run faster than him and his sister, Corynne. If Belle, Neva, and I made a sprint for the border on their backs, Mogra's army would never catch us. "You'll need to carry two," I told him. "Are you strong enough?"

Brahms whickered, almost as if he was insulted. "Of course I can. I'll take you faster than the wind."

I led him out of his stall and saddled him as quickly as I could, struggling to hold the reins in my clammy, trembling hands. He huffed as I helped Neva onto his back but didn't object. She was so small I doubt he would even feel her weight in addition to mine. Beside me Belle was already saddling Corynne. She was older than Brahms, but a champion in her own right. Her dark eyes fixed on me, and she gave me a small nod of acceptance. She was prepared to run as far and as fast as we needed to escape.

"I'll finish with her," I said, brushing Belle's hands aside and nodding pointedly in the direction of Lady Kingsclere. "Go and say goodbye."

A flash of pain crossed Belle's face, and I realized she hadn't thought this through. She had been so focused on preparing she hadn't realized what she would be leaving behind if we ran—her mother, her friends, and the only home she had ever known. But after a moment to digest the sacrifice, she let out a slow stream of air and headed toward Lady Kingsclere. They shared a whispered conversation while I finished preparing Corynne, and though I couldn't see much in the flickering firelight, I noticed tears streaming down Belle's cheeks as they embraced.

There wasn't enough time for me to make my own goodbyes. More howls came from outside the stables, and the ground beneath us trembled. The kerak were closing in, and the giant shadowkin shook the earth as they surrounded the stable. I leapt onto Brahms' back, swinging my leg over his side and perching behind Neva. I took the reins from her hands and dug in with my heels. "Run," I shouted as soon as I saw Belle mount Corynne.

We burst out through the door and into a swarm of monsters. The kerak swiped their scythe-shaped claws through the air, barely missing us as we hurtled through their ranks. I saw the endless pits of their mouths every time the lightning flashed, and I hunched further over Brahms' quivering body, trying not to look. The shortest glimpse sent a painful spike of fear through my chest. We sprinted over the fields, flying through the rain and leaving the stables behind.

"Ellie, look out!" Jessith hissed behind my head, and wet strands of hair whipped about my face as I whirled around.

The kerak and most of the shadowkin were a fair distance away, but a huge black shape was hurtling toward us. As it drew closer, another jagged fork of lightning cast a flashing picture. One of the shadowkin was running toward us, but it was no slow, lumbering beast.

It was moving almost as fast as we were, and something was perched atop its back. *No, someone,* I realized with the next flare. I caught a glimpse of pale, sloughing skin, but even though the person's face was indistinct, the banner of chestnut hair streaming behind was not. Some part of me knew instantly who it was despite the darkness and the blinding rain. I could feel it in my bones—Luciana had come for me at last.

Chapter Five

Taken from the letters of Cathelin Raybrook, edited by Lady Eleanor Kingsclere

RAIN STREAKS DOWN IN torrents, sliding over the twisted, dying flesh of the pale woman's face. Her eyes are snarled shut, sightless and scarred over, but her jaw hangs loose in a feral howl. Ribbons of matted chestnut hair stream behind her, lashing and whipping in the storm. Her clothes are soaked through, clinging to her frame. She's little more than bone, a living skeleton, but some kind of taut sinew holds her together as she gallops on the back of a giant, hulking beast. No, not just gallops. Chases. She's chasing the two shadows growing smaller and smaller across the fields.

Then—a flash. Smooth glass, the face of a mirror.

"You, my queen, are fair; it's true.
But the princess with the seven dwarves
Is still a thousand times fairer than you."

"No!" A shriek fills the stone hall. The mirror's surface ripples, threatening to splinter around a beautiful woman's face. Her lips are cut of red rubies and her crown gleams on top of her fair hair. "She's dead. You gave me her heart!"

Sharp nails dig into a sallow man's throat, piercing skin until blood wells out. His mouth moves, but the words are soundless. Hoarse attempts at breath rattle in his chest, but he can't take in air. His pupils fade, the whites swallow his eyes, and flecks of froth gather at the corner of his cracked lips.

"Since you lied to me, I will have to take yours as tribute instead."

Blood, twitching muscle, the cavity of a chest, ribs and yellow fat, sinew and clawing hands.

"Cate! Catie, be you all right?"

I opened my eyes to see Larna hovering over me. Her face was an instant relief, and I remembered where and who I truly was. *Larna. Larna's here. I'm safe.* I rose from the armchair I had been reading in before my vision, letting the abandoned book on my lap fall to the floorboards and reaching for her shirt instead. "It was terrible. I was at Baxstresse, and she was chasing me. Then the queen killed him." I knew I wasn't making any sense, but I couldn't seem to stop. The explanation tumbled out in a rush of mixed-up words that soon trailed off into dry, ugly sobs.

Larna folded her arms around me, holding me close through the spasms. "I'm here, little bird," she whispered against my hair, pressing kisses to my temple. Each one unraveled the tight knot in my chest a little more, and I sank back into myself instead of battering at the walls of my nightmares. As she rocked me, my breathing evened out. I closed my eyes and buried my face in her shoulder, inhaling her scent. *Sweet. Warm. Familiar.*

It was a long while before I could speak again, but Larna didn't rush me. She kept making soothing circles over my back until I found my words. "Another vision," I told her, although I was sure she already knew. "I saw Luciana. The new Luciana, the one in the mirror. She's been turned into something horrible, and I think..." I flashed back to the field I had seen in my mind. It had been dark in my dream, but I still recognized the landscape. "I think she was at Baxstresse."

My heart sank as I said the words. Some part of me knew they were true, and the implications were dreadful. If Luciana was at Baxstresse, that meant my friends were all in danger. I jerked out of Larna's arms, heading over to where my pack rested at the foot of the bed. I opened it up and started tossing things out: clothes, bandages, and several other bits and pieces until I found what I was looking for.

I pulled out the magical journal Cieran had given me. Its twin was with Ellie, allowing the two of us to write back and forth without the hassle of sending letters across the border. I had been the last one to write an entry, but as I flipped through the pages, I hoped Ellie had found the time to respond. The tears welling in my eyes streamed down my face when I saw that the final page wasn't in my handwriting. They dotted the paper, leaving a few smudges, but I could still read the blurry words.

Cate,

Belle and I are safe. Cieran has entrusted a young girl to us, a girl he claims is Neva, the Crown Princess of Amendyr. The night after she arrived, monsters attacked Baxstresse. From what little I saw, they are the same creatures Mogra makes for the Queen's armies. The three of us were forced to flee, and although we were given some warning, I don't know what has become of Lady Kingsclere, Sarah, Mam, Matthew, and the others.

There was no sign of Mogra among the monsters, but they did have a commander. It was Luciana, or something that was once her. She has been transformed into something so horrible I can scarcely begin to describe it. Belle, Neva, and I managed to outrun her on horseback, but I suspect she will try to follow us across the border.

We are coming to Amendyr as quickly as we can. Hopefully we will find the rebellion soon and deliver Neva to them for her own safety. Please, be careful. I fear Luciana and Mogra's Serian forces may find you if they do not find us first.

I love you,
Ellie

It took me another several minutes to compose myself as I read over the letter. *Transformed...something so horrible I can scarcely begin to describe.* Ellie needn't have tried. The images of the new Luciana's face were burned into my brain, and I wasn't sure they would ever leave. I closed the journal and hugged it to my chest, too overwhelmed to scrawl out a response. There wasn't much I could tell Ellie she didn't already know. She, Belle, and their strange charge were already on their way to Amendyr, and I doubted she would have much time to write while on the run.

"At least she's safe," I breathed as Larna knelt beside me.

She rested a hand on my shoulder, offering me a reassuring smile. "Who, Ellie?"

I nodded. "Her, Belle, and you're not going to believe this, but Ellie says she's escorting the Crown Princess of Amendyr across the border. Does the name Neva mean anything to you?"

Larna's concerned expression turned to one of shock. Her eyes widened, and she extended her hand for the journal.

"It won't do you any good to read it," I reminded her. "It's in Serian. Ellie didn't say much, just that a wizard named Cieran entrusted the girl to her. They're planning to meet up with the rebellion."

"I canna believe it." Larna lowered her hand and shook her head, still processing the news. "None of us were knowing where the princess was. Most thought she was long dead. I hoped, but I was never truly believing she could escape the Queen's reach. And you say Ellie is to be bringing her to Jett Bahari?"

"If Amendyr's princess is alive, the rebellion is probably the safest place for her. She can't keep hiding in Seria if Mogra's monsters are running loose at Baxstresse."

Larna seemed to agree. A hopeful look spread across her face, and she clutched my arm. "Surely the council must be listening to us now! We have a proper heir to the throne again. If all goes right, we will be having the liarre at our backs when we see the princess for ourselves."

My mate's optimism was infectious. I shook off the last of my lingering fear and returned her smile with only a little effort. The knowledge that Ellie and Belle had escaped had bolstered my spirits. "The fact that the council wants us to meet with them is a step in the right direction. How much do you think we should tell them about all this?"

"Everything," Larna said with unwavering certainty. "Even Rufas canna claim the rebellion is worthless with a princess to fight for."

Personally, I doubted Rufas would admit anything of the kind, but it didn't matter. "Let's not get ahead of ourselves. Ellie and Belle haven't even crossed the border with her yet. And besides, we don't need Rufas to agree with us. The only one we need to convince is Maresth. A three-two vote is still a win."

Larna nodded, and I busied myself with cleaning up the mess I had made. A flash of red and gold caught my eye, and I frowned, losing my train of thought. While Larna watched me curiously, I shifted some of the clothes I had unsettled to reveal the curved shape of a small hourglass. The past several days had been so busy I had almost forgotten about it.

My mentor Kalwyn had given the curious object to me before her death, but despite the morbid associations, it was fascinating to look at. The sand inside was a bright red, and the twisting golden seams that twined around its curves were the coiling bodies of dragons. No matter which way I turned it, the sand inside never moved. Kalwyn had told me it was supposed to measure the time of the dragons' return, although I had no way of knowing whether that was true, or one of her fanciful stories.

As I turned it back the right way, an answering heat blossomed against my chest. I set the hourglass down and pulled back my shirt instead, digging out a simple necklace. Threaded through the simple cord was a smooth, flat stone, and it too hummed with living warmth. It was a gleaming, polished black, and there was a hole straight through the center, large enough to set against someone's eye. Kalwyn had called it the deadeye, and along with the hourglass, I had carried it since her death. It was meant to be looked through, but I simply held it, taking some comfort in the warmth against my palm. A knock came at the door, and I hurried to tuck the deadeye back into my shirt and hide the hourglass away from prying eyes.

"Cate? Larna? It's Ailynn. I didn't see the two of you at lunch. Are you in there?"

I shoved the hourglass and my clothes back into my pack while Larna rose to answer the door. Ailynn stepped inside, but to my surprise, Raisa wasn't with her. The two of them were normally joined at the hip, especially since Raisa was expecting twins. Her condition only worsened Ailynn's tendency to hover.

"Sorry we missed lunch," I said, tossing the pack onto my bed. "We were getting ready to meet with the council, but we have some bad news. I received a letter from my friend Ellie. Mogra's creatures have made it to Seria. They're already invading the countryside."

A shadow fell over Ailynn's face. "New ones? I shouldn't be surprised. I already suspected she was alive, but..." I didn't object as she headed over to the bed and sat down on the edge of the mattress, resting her elbows on her knees and falling into a slump. "I suppose I was still holding out some hope the avalanche killed her."

Larna's eyes flicked over to the bed and both of us went to join her, one on each side. I put my hand on Ailynn's shoulder, trying to offer comfort. "She isn't your responsibility, you know." I could tell from my friend's face she didn't believe me. Her frown stayed firmly in place. "I have more reason to hate her than most, and I certainly don't blame you for what she did to me and the rest of the Farseer pack."

"I appreciate the kind words, but forgive me if I can't bring myself to believe them," Ailynn said with a sigh. "None of this would have happened if it weren't for me. I could have told her to stop her experiments. I could have interfered when I knew things were starting to go wrong. I could have tried harder—"

"You canna control your parents," Larna said, speaking with the force of experience. "Their sins and mistakes be their own."

Ailynn remained silent, obviously unwilling to argue, but also unwilling to accept what we were trying to tell her. "There's more news," I said, removing my hand from her tense arm. "Good this time, I promise. In her letter, Ellie claims she's traveling with the Crown Princess of Amendyr. She and her wife are fleeing for the border with the girl in their protection."

That got Ailynn's attention. "The princess?" Her brow lifted in surprise. "I barely even knew about her until I left home for the first time. Everyone in the villages I travelled through said she was dead, or at least in Shezad."

"Missing, not dead," Larna said. "No one was ever finding her body. Now we're knowing why."

"So, if she's alive, what does that mean for us?" Ailynn asked.

"It means our job is even more important than ever," I told her. "The princess will need our help to reclaim the white throne. Ellie and Belle are risking their lives to smuggle her into Amendyr. The least I can do is make sure they have an army waiting for them when they get here."

Ailynn gave me a skeptical look. "So, what's your plan? Rufas didn't seem eager to give you anything this morning, let alone an army."

I didn't want to be drawn back into the same circular conversation the three of us had been running through for days. I stood, heading over to the mirror on the other side of the room. My reflection was a little pale, and circles darkened under my eyes, but I didn't look as though I had been in the midst of a terrifying vision just minutes before. I wanted to appear at least somewhat presentable in front of the council. "Maresth asked us to meet with the council in private for a reason. Out of the three councilors who haven't thrown their support behind us, she's the least hostile. We need to convince her if we want to have any chance of success."

Larna and Ailynn both nodded. As they stood and headed toward the door, I stole one last glance in the mirror. I couldn't meet my own stare for long. Some part of me was afraid that a face other than my own might begin to creep in around the edges.

Chapter Six

Taken from the verbal accounts of Ailynn Gothel, edited by Lady Eleanor Kingsclere

WHEN CATE, LARNA, AND I arrived outside Maresth's private study, raised voices were already filtering out into the hallway. The three of us exchanged nervous glances, and my heart sank. I had allowed myself to indulge in a little optimism in preparation for our meeting with the council, but it quickly faded as I made out what they were saying.

"You're too reckless, Rachari," Rufas said in a gruff voice. The door did little to muffle his growl. "It's bad enough you want to go on a mad chase for Mogra outside our borders. Now you're demanding to take an army with you! You've got some of our people brainwashed into believing this is for their own good, but don't think you have me fooled. This will only end in more bloodshed."

I reached up for the high doorknob, but Larna shook her head. After a moment of hesitation, I withdrew. She was the rebellion's official ambassador to the liarre, and I was just a guest in Ardu. I didn't want to make things difficult for her, no matter how much I disagreed with Rufas.

Fortunately, another voice from inside the room said what I would have. "It is for their own good, and Rachari isn't fooling anyone," Jinale protested. "She's simply stating the truth, however much you might not want to hear it."

"She's more reasonable than I would have been," I muttered out of the corner of my mouth, glancing sideways at Cate. She snorted and nodded.

An angry yowl forced the three of us to focus back on the argument. "Not want to hear it? I'm surprised the idiot has ears,"

Rachari hissed. "He refuses to listen to sense even though you saw Mogra with your own eyes. What more proof do you need, Rufas?"

"Proof that going after her won't get good people killed," Rufas barked.

Jinale was slightly less aggressive in her approach. "Mogra is shaping an undead army. Her corrupted magic is already getting good people killed. I came back without half my scouts."

There was a moment of silence, as if the statement had finally given Rufas pause. Larna took the opportunity to open the door. I followed her in at Cate's side, scanning the room as I entered. It was a simple study, but large enough to comfortably fit the tall liarre. There were several platformed stools designed for their long bodies, but three of the five councilors weren't sitting. Rufas and Rachari were squared off in front of Maresth's desk with Jinale standing between them. Maresth remained coiled behind her desk while Weyshra watched nervously from the sidelines. The former seemed curious, the latter unwilling to interfere.

Rufas did not look pleased to see us. His sharp eyes locked on me like a hunting dog's, and his jowls quivered as he scented the air. "I didn't realize the human was coming," he said, ignoring Larna and Cate completely.

I sighed. "Apparently, we're not going to bother with formalities."

"Or politeness," Rachari added with more than a little sarcasm.

"Ailynn was invited," Jinale said, emphasizing my name since Rufas had refused to use it. "She has every right to be here. Her mother is the threat we're meeting to discuss. No one knows how dangerous Mogra can be better than she does." The comment made me nauseous, but I hid my discomfort. Everyone in the room already knew the shameful fact that Mogra was my mother and I had watched her descent into madness.

Rufas still looked as though he wanted to protest, but a surprising ally came to my defense. "We have good reason to question her," Weyshra pointed out. "Even if we don't choose to send our forces across the border into Amendyr, we need to know what the witch is capable of. If she truly has mastered more than one type of magic."

"She has," I said, meeting Weyshra's skittish gaze. "She was born a daughter of the First Son, but learned to shape and enchant as well. Her greed drove her to extreme lengths, and the extra power has corrupted her. When I faced her, she was no longer herself. She won't listen to reason, and she's a danger to anyone she comes into contact with."

"Aye, and so is her army," Larna added. "You worry about sending your people into another country's civil war, Rufas, but monsters dinna respect borders. Are you truly believing the undead will stop at your doorstep if you're after asking nicely? Kerak are'na exactly polite, Councilor."

"If your wicked queen does control Mogra and these monsters, she has no reason to send them here," Rufas said. "Her goal is to take over Amendyr, not to conquer other kingdoms."

Cate shook her head. "That isn't true. I received word from my friend, Lady Eleanor of Baxstresse, just today. She lives in Seria, and she's currently fleeing across the eastern border with a second army of monsters on her heels. They've attacked the royal palace and at least one estate. How can you know Ardu won't be next?"

"We can't," Rachari said before Rufas could get another word in. "That's why we have to act now, before the Queen's army comes for us. Our only chance is a united front. We need Jett Bahari and the rebellion as much as they need us."

"And what if we lose?" Weyshra asked. "Say we send our best soldiers to help the humans with their war. Who will remain to defend our people if they fall?"

My fists clenched with impatience, and my stomach began to twist itself into knots of anxiety. It seemed that this argument wasn't any more productive than the ones that had come before, and I knew all too well what would happen if they couldn't come to an agreement. It seemed that I was not the only one.

"Don't you two understand?" Rachari snapped. Even though her face was not human, I could see the anger in it. Her fur bristled and the edges of her fangs peeked out from beneath her upper lip. "If we don't join forces now, we're guaranteed to fall, every single one of us. Every kingdom, every border, every race." She and Rufas resumed glaring at each other, and Jinale and Weyshra shared an unhappy look. Meanwhile, Maresth watched the proceedings in silence, taking in everything with narrowed eyes.

"There is one more thing," Cate said, clearing her throat to get their attention. "My friend isn't fleeing Seria alone. Crown Princess Neva is with her."

Everyone whipped around to look at her, speaking at once.
"What?"
"I thought she was dead!"
"Are you sure?"

Cate nodded at the last question. "Yes, I'm absolutely sure. If Ellie says she has the princess under her protection, I believe her. If they move fast, it should take them a little over two weeks to reach Jett Bahari's camp from the eastern border."

"Enough time for us to meet them there," Rachari said. "This is good news, Cate. We'll have a united cause. Liarre, wyr, humans, and *Ariada* of all types, fighting to remove the pretender from the white throne and restore the rightful heir to her proper place."

"The white throne isn't our concern, Rachari," Weyshra said, objecting before Rufas could. "Our people's safety should be our first priority."

"And they'll be safest with Princess Neva as Amendyr's ruler," Rachari insisted. "What's it going to take for you to treat this problem seriously? Mogra flying in through the window?"

"No, but with the way you're talking, I'd like to send you through it instead," Rufas growled.

Cate, Larna, and I shared a worried glance. Our presence had done nothing to sway the councilors either way, and it seemed as if they would never agree to anything. Mogra could come flying in the window before they made up their minds. But my fears proved to be misplaced. Before the three of us could do anything, Maresth moved. She rose, unwinding gracefully from her seat and curling around her desk to join the other four councilors. Her heavy body slithered across the floor, with soft clinks of metal where her tail dragged, and the sound seemed to draw everyone else's attention.

"I suggest we put this matter to a vote," Maresth hissed. "A decision must be made."

"Will this be a public vote, or a private one?" Cate asked.

"I demand a public vote," Rufas said. "I won't be held accountable for sending my soldiers to die in a pointless war."

"The vote will be announced publicly in the Grand Theater tomorrow morning," Maresth said, "but we must choose now. Tempers need time to cool, and we should present a united front."

The room went quiet as everyone considered her words. I could see one more chance, possibly my last chance, to stop Mogra slipping away. The thought of standing by and doing nothing a second time was too much. "Please," I said after a beat of silence, looking straight at Maresth. Rufas and Weyshra seemed beyond convincing, but we didn't need their agreement. "I know Mogra, and I'm telling you she's merciless. Human, liarre, it doesn't matter to her. She'll use anyone, hurt anyone, to get what she wants. If her army crosses your border your people won't stand a chance."

Maresth's clear eyelids gave a slow blink, and she nodded once. "Your opinion has been noted. Rufas, Weyssshra, I assume you vote to remain out of this conflict?" Rufas grunted. Weyshra was more hesitant, but eventually he dipped his long muzzle. "Jinale and Rachari, do you wish to aid Jett Bahari and the rebellion?"

"With my life," Rachari said as Jinale nodded. "Protecting Amendyr protects our people, too."

Maresth heaved a hissing sigh. "Then the final decision is mine. I vote to send our forces to the rebellion's aid. I agree that if Amendyr and Seria fall to this false Queen, the liarre will fall soon after."

"Chairwoman," Rufas protested, but Maresth cut him off with a look.

"You will stand by the council's decision, Rufas. My vote is final. You can best serve your people by preparing them for the coming war. Turn your strength there."

Rufas remained still for a long moment. He looked as though he wanted to object, but at last, he lowered his gaze in deference. "As you say." He stormed past us, leaving the room without a proper dismissal.

Weyshra's exit wasn't quite as dramatic, but it was clear he wasn't happy with Maresth's choice, either. "As a member of the council, it is my duty to support any decision we make. But I fear this is one vote all of us will come to regret. Until later." When he received a nod of dismissal, he followed Rufas out into the hall and disappeared from sight.

"Well, that could have gone better," Cate sighed once the door had closed. "I'm sorry, Councilors. None of us wanted things to happen this way."

"It wasn't your fault," Jinale said. "This disagreement was brewing long before you arrived here. Weyshra is cautious, and Rufas is protective of his soldiers."

"To the point of blindness," Rachari added bitterly. She took in a deep breath, and some of her simmering anger cooled. "I apologize, Maresth. My temper got the better of me this afternoon. I'll try to be more cooperative with Rufas and his people now that we've made a decision."

Maresth gave Rachari a look of approval. "A united front is necessary. Apologize and concede however you need to. We announce our decision tomorrow morning, and we march in the afternoon."

For the first time in nearly a week, I felt the faint stirrings of hope. With the liarre on our side and Neva returning to Amendyr, perhaps the rebellion actually stood a chance against the Queen's army. Meanwhile, my own job was more than clear. Mogra was my responsibility, and I couldn't rest until she wasn't able to cause any more harm.

Chapter Seven

Taken from the diary of Lady Eleanor Kingsclere

TRAVELING LIGHT AND ON horseback, our party reached Amendyr far sooner than expected. The journey usually took over a week, but we arrived at the border in a matter of days. We moved as swiftly and silently as possible, constantly checking over our shoulders, but there were no further signs of Luciana or her undead army.

We only stopped long enough to rest the horses and feed ourselves, approaching inns after sundown and leaving before sunrise. Surely we must have been an odd sight, two furtive women guiding a small child and a tortoiseshell cat peeking out of a knapsack, but enough coin quieted the questions. It helped that the people we encountered were terrified. With war brewing just across the border, it didn't look like any of them were sleeping either.

Bringing Jessith along turned out to be a blessing. Nearly being eaten by kerak hadn't scared away her wit, and her dry commentary kept me sane during the long, tense days. She complained about the weather, the uncomfortable jolting of the horses, Belle's constant twitching, and Neva's disturbing silence, but I didn't mind. I was relieved to hear about something other than Luciana. It was a struggle not to think of her in my waking hours and impossible to forget her face when I slept.

"Cieran might have given us directions, at least," Jessith complained an hour past the final watchtower. We were a few minutes into Amendyr, but we still had no official destination, and we had not run into a single guard. All of the outposts had been abandoned. "A little more clarity could have saved us days of wandering around."

"Give it time. He said friends would find us once we crossed the border."

"I agree with Jessith," Belle said from a few paces ahead. She had become adept at filling in Jessith's portions of our conversations even though she couldn't understand them. "An explanation would be useful right about now. We can't just stop at someone's house and ask for directions to the rebellion, either. Remember what happened to Cate?"

"What a cheerful thing to bring up," I muttered. It was disconcerting to realize we couldn't be far from the place where Cate had been abducted and transformed into a wyr. The great Forest separating Amendyr and Seria had only one road, and travelers who left the path rarely found their way back again. It was so large and wild that it didn't have a name, and it had singlehandedly prevented Serian troops from conquering the western half of the continent centuries ago.

"She has a point," Jessith said. "It was stupid of him to be so cryptic."

"Cieran is far from stupid. I'm sure he had his reasons," I insisted. "Besides, the letter read like he scrawled it out seconds before Mogra's creatures stormed the palace. He might have run out of time."

Even Jessith didn't have a response. We travelled in silence for another few minutes, and my thoughts drifted to dark places. I hoped Cieran, his wife, and Prince Brendan had been able to escape the palace, but it wasn't likely. Brendan would never leave his home undefended, and Cieran was sworn to protect him. My friend's letter had read like a goodbye.

"Don't worry, Ellie," Neva said, jolting me from my thoughts. She was so quiet most of the time that I was always startled when she spoke, even though she was tucked into the circle of my arms. "Cieran will be fine."

"How did you know what I was thinking about?" I asked in surprise. "Are you a seer as well as a necromancer?"

Neva glanced back over her shoulder and shook her head. "No. But he promised me he would be, before he sent me away."

My heart clenched. "How long were you with him?"

"Almost a year. He told people I was his niece, made up a story about how his sister married a man from Shezad and sent me to Seria for an education." A soft smile crossed her dark face, one of the first I had seen. It made her look like a little girl instead of an exhausted miniature adult, and I smiled back. "He and Cassandra helped me with my training. They taught me about speaking the dead to rest."

"What do you mean?"

"I know what she means," Belle said. "Most Serian stories about necromancers are cautionary tales, but in Amendyr, not all *Kira'baas* raise the dead. Some of them use their powers to un-make creatures like the kerak. I read about it in—"

"the library," I finished for her with a sly look. "Is there a single book you haven't read?"

Belle sighed. "I'm going to miss it while we're gone. If I come back to find it destroyed, I'll make Luciana regret it."

"You'll have to fight Cate for the chance."

"Cate can help me. Having a wolf on my side against an undead monster would only help."

"Is your friend really a wolf?" Neva asked. "Can you talk to her like Jessith?"

"Not exactly. She can become one if she wants to, but she spends most of her time as a human."

Neva's face brightened with understanding. "Oh, a wyr?"

I shouldn't have been surprised. Neva had grown up in Amendyr, after all, where such things were unusual but not unheard of. "Yes, she's a wyr. She's also a member of the rebellion, and I think her pack might be the people we're looking for."

"Well, they're not the people we've found," Jessith said from behind me. "There's something moving in the trees, and it doesn't smell like dog."

I urged Brahms to slow his pace, scanning the Forest to try and spot the mysterious figures Jessith was talking about.

"You don't have to be so obvious," she drawled. "Perhaps you should read one of Belle's precious books once in a while. Maybe a dictionary? The word 'subtle' comes to mind."

I ignored her reproach and kept looking. This time, I saw something—a flash of movement, low to the ground like an animal. I almost spoke up to tell Jessith she had been wrong, but before I got the chance, rustling came from all sides. There was more than one of whatever was following us, and they didn't seem concerned about staying hidden.

"Ellie, should I run?" Brahms asked, haunches tensing.

My mind was made up for me as our pursuers left the cover of the trees and stepped into the middle of the road. They weren't animals, but they weren't human either, and the sight of them was so strange I stared for several seconds. Seven short, blocky figures stood shoulder to shoulder, wearing hoods that cast their faces in shadow. From the little I could see from their bare hands and feet, their flesh was a pallid grey color. Although they were small, their shoulders were thick and broad, and they seemed muscular. Their feet were abnormally large and flat, sticking out awkwardly from beneath their robes. All of them were armed, although they made no move to attack us.

"Dwarves," Belle whispered beside me, barely able to contain her excitement. She stared in fascination, wearing the same expression that came upon her in the middle of a good book.

"How do you know?"

"I've seen illustrations, but why are they here? They almost never come to the surface."

One of the dwarves lowered his hood, revealing his face. His eyes were smaller than coppers, black and beetle-like, and they blinked against the faint sunlight. The rest of his face was almost all mouth. It was wet and large, with several rows of teeth and two giant tusks. His tongue threatened to poke out as he spoke in a scraping voice. "You. Sun-hair. Off thing." He pointed at Brahms, who canted back a few nervous steps. Corynne tossed her head, whickering, and Belle had to stroke her neck to calm her.

I wasn't prepared to leave Brahms' back. The dwarves hadn't drawn their weapons, but that didn't mean they were friendly, either. While I stayed perched in relative safety, Neva scrambled to the ground, leaping down before I could hold her back. She let out a cry of joy and ran forward, arms open.

"Ulig, you came!" She squeezed the dwarf in a tight hug, smiling gleefully.

To my shock, the creature hugged her back. His enormous mouth warped into something like a smile, and he lifted her a few inches off the ground even though they were the same height, twirling her around. "Neva! Back, you!"

"Well, I guess that means it's safe to get down." Belle slid off Corynne and approached the group cautiously, hanging a few yards back. I followed her example, and as we watched, all the dwarves took a turn hugging Neva. It was strange, seeing the withdrawn girl we had spent the past few days with so exuberantly happy, but also touching. These people were her friends, and they seemed just as relieved to see her as she was to see them.

One of the dwarves turned toward us, and it, too, pulled back its hood. Its features were slightly different, with smaller tusks jutting out from between its thick lips, and it took me a moment to realize that this one was female. Up close, I could tell her grey skin was actually covered in soft, downy fuzz. "Hello," she said. "My name is Lok. That's my husband Ulig, and this is our clan. I believe you must be Eleanor and Belladonna?"

I nodded dumbly. Considering the first dwarf's rough, broken speech, I hadn't expected one of their number to speak such good Serian. She had a bit of an accent, but I had no trouble understanding her.

"Good! The three of us have a mutual friend. I'm the one who sent Neva to stay in Seria with Cieran. We hated to let her go, but we all agreed she would be safer among her own kind."

"Wait," I asked, "Neva stayed with you before she came to Ronin?"

"Yes," Lok said.

"Why didn't she tell us?"

Lok continued staring. "Did you ask her?"

"No," I said, a little hesitantly.

"I didn't realize we specifically needed to ask her if she used to run around with a band of wild dwarves," Jessith muttered. Yet again, I was grateful no one else could understand her.

The other dwarves had stopped hugging Neva, and they all turned to study us. Some looked wary, but Neva hastened to reassure them. She spoke to them in Amendyrri, and her lilting voice seemed to put them at ease. They stared up at us from beneath their hoods, shuffling forward on their large feet and studying us with unconcealed curiosity. I did not blame them. Surely they found me just as interesting as I found them.

"They can't understand Serian, I'm afraid, and they don't speak much Amendyrri either," Lok said. "Ulig knows a bit of both, but I'll have to be your translator."

"That's all right," Belle said, smiling. "It's nice to meet you. Cieran told us we would find friends across the border, but I wasn't expecting dwarves."

Ulig frowned around his tusks, and Lok cleared her throat a little awkwardly. "Actually, we prefer to be called dwellyn. That's the name of our people. 'Dwarves' are a Serian invention."

Belle's face fell, and she seemed horrified by her mistake. "I'm so sorry," she began, but Lok brushed her off.

"You didn't know. Anyway, we should hurry. There are eyes and ears everywhere in the Forest, and we need to get underground before they find us."

"That might be a problem," I said, eyeing the horses.

Lok's big, messy grin grew wider. Her velvety face crinkled around her tiny eyes. "You've never seen a dwellyn warren, have you? There's plenty of room for the horses. We might be smaller than humans, but we work big." She nodded at Ulig, and he spoke to the others in a gurgling sort of speech I couldn't understand. It wasn't Amendyrri, and I suspected it was the dwellyn's own language.

The dwellyn stopped staring at us and formed two ordered lines, with Ulig at their head. He nodded at us. "Sun-hair. Night-hair. Come, you. And things." He pointed at the horses with a stubby hand, and I grabbed Brahms' reins while Belle took Corynne.

"I object to being called a thing," Jessith said from my knapsack.

I sighed. "Isn't this what you wanted? To find the friends Cieran was talking about?"

"I didn't expect them to be so...earthy. The dirt's staining my whiskers from here."

"Well, you don't have a choice." I started off after the dwarves, ignoring Jessith's grumbling and falling into step beside Neva. For once, she wasn't silent. She chattered away to the dwellyn in long, flowing Amendyrri sentences, skipping up and down the line to speak to them all.

"How do you think she came to be with them?" I asked Belle.

She offered a shrug. "No idea. We'll have to ask later. From what Lok said, it sounds like they took her in after she left Kalmarin. However she ended up with them, it must be an interesting story."

"It's about to get more interesting," I said. Some of Belle's enthusiasm was running off on me. "How big do you think a dwellyn city is, exactly?"

"Huge," Belle said. "Dwa...er, dwellyn live in colonies. There can be hundreds of them in one place."

"Good thing they're friendly. If there are so many of them, and they're friends with Neva, do you think Jett Bahari and the rebellion could use them?"

"Let's not get ahead of ourselves," Belle said. "For now, it's enough that they want to help us."

We fell into comfortable silence as the dwellyn led us off the path and into the Forest. Eventually, Neva drifted back to us, and I was surprised but pleased when she reached out for my hand. We walked with our arms swinging between us. "You're going to love them, Ellie. I know they look scary at first, but they're really sweet. Gurn makes the best deeproot pies, and Rup knows how to forge swords, and..."

I couldn't keep track of all the names and professions, but I was happy for her happiness. It was a blessed relief from the constant tension and strain of the past several days. I smiled and let my shoulders relax. For once, I would have something positive to write in my next letter to Cate. I had no doubt that she would find the dwellyn as fascinating as Belle and I did.

Chapter Eight

Taken from the letters of Cathelin Raybrook, edited by Lady Eleanor Kingsclere

The ghostly woman with the golden crown stands before the mirror. She runs her hand along it, lips parted, sipping shallow breaths. She can feel its hunger. Can feel it seeping through her skin, burrowing into the pit of her stomach, clawing out a screaming ache. It burns hot to the touch, fire against her icy hands, but she can't pull away. She needs this pain. Needs it like food or water or air.

"Mirror, mirror, on the wall. Who is the fairest of them all?"
The glass ripples like a living thing. It flashes. Her eyes are caught.

You, my queen, are fair; it's true.
But the princess beyond the Forest
Is still a thousand times fairer than you.

Her anger blazes within her, ripping out through the scream that tears her throat. The girl must die. Must die so that she may satisfy the never-ending hunger, so that she may serve her purpose.
The mirror grows large, devouring everything. It swallows the woman, the room, the castle, the entire world. Inside its depth, the sliver of a white dress flutters. A girl with dark skin is running. She stumbles through the forest on bare feet, face streaked with tears. Shadows scurry around her, closing in, forming a circle.
Another face, already dying. Beauty decaying, reeking of sweet rot, cracked strips of black-grey flesh crumbling away. The cruel tilt of its mouth is chillingly familiar. Matted chestnut hair, burning eyes—

I jolted awake, drenched in sweat, clawing at the covers beneath me and shivering all over. For a moment, I was certain she had come for me. Certain she was hovering over me, just as she had so many times before. I waited for pain, but it never came. There was only the burning of my lungs as I struggled to breathe and the aching hammer of my wild heart.

I didn't come back to myself until Larna stirred beside me. She reached out, eyes blurry with sleep, and stroked a hand along my tense stomach. "Little bird?" I tried to speak, but my words stubbornly refused to come. I could only manage a strangled sort of sob that broke somewhere in my stopped-up throat. Larna sat up and folded her arm around my shoulder. "Her again?" she asked, her soft voice not demanding an answer.

It was an effort even to nod my head, but I didn't have to say anything. Larna held me until the shaking ceased and the knot in my chest stopped hurting. My body was completely drained, but my mind raced in circles. The Queen. The dark-skinned girl. Luciana. The visions were of the past, but they were also happening now. The Queen was using Luciana to hunt the girl, but for what? I had felt her drive, a hunger so strong one person could scarcely hold it.

"Cate, sweetling," Larna whispered, her lips warm against my temple, "is there anything to be doing now? At this moment?"

The sound of my *Tuathe's* voice brought me back to myself. I wasn't in the dark room. Luciana and the Queen were nowhere to be found. We were still safe in Ardu, in the room the liarre had given us, as far away from danger as possible. "No." My lips were thick around the word, numb as I moved them. "There's nothing I can do right now."

"Then sleep." Larna began to stroke my hair, and the steady petting slowed my frantic heartbeat. "Sleep until the sun comes, at least."

As exhausted as I was, the thought of sleep terrified me. My visions didn't only happen at night, but that didn't matter. If I closed my eyes, they might come flooding back. "I don't think I can," I whispered. The nightmares in my head were all twisted up in black memories, and I struggled to tell them apart. I flinched, remembering a bookcase digging into my back, the tear of fabric.

Once again, Larna brought me back. "How can I be helping you?" she asked, and when I looked up into her face, Luciana's faded. I couldn't stand her presence in my mind. I had kept her safely tucked away for so long, and despite the chaos around me, I had never been stronger. Now, I threatened to buckle under the weight. I gripped Larna's hands tight and leaned further into her, blinking back tears. The nights in Ardu were frigid, but her body was hot against mine where we touched, and it banished some of the cold.

Suddenly, I remembered her offer. *"If you want to forget her touch with mine, I will be helping you. If you are needing anything..."*

The shred of normalcy I felt as I imagined Larna against me, over me, in me, was an instant relief. She was my anchor to the present, to the person I had grown into. With her love surrounding me, the past couldn't touch me and the future couldn't frighten me. "Larna." She held my eyes, searching them for answers, waiting for me to tell her what to do. "I need you to help me forget."

Larna cupped my cheek, searching my eyes for any signs of doubt. "Be you sure?"

"Yes. Her face isn't the one I want to see when I close my eyes." My memories of Luciana had faded almost to nothing since my arrival in Amendyr, and I was resentful that my visions had dredged them up again. It wasn't fair that she still held so much power over me. I was supposed to be free.

Larna nodded. "Then guide my hands. I will be giving you whatever you need."

The thought of Larna's hands made me smile. They were large, rough-textured and square-shaped, but gentle when I needed them to be. The touch resting on my face was feather-light. I threaded my fingers through hers again, bringing her hand away from my cheek and guiding it toward my lips. My eyes drifted shut as I brushed a kiss across her knuckles. "I love you," I murmured into her skin. "I love you so much, *Tuathe*. I love you endlessly."

"I love you, too."

Words fell away as Larna's mouth took the place of her fingers. It was a careful, cautious kiss, a request instead of a demand. I savored its sweetness at first, allowing Larna's lips to rest on mine. But I had grown to adore the demands Larna made of me, and I had learned to enjoy placing demands on her. She had asked me to guide her hands, and I could think of nothing I needed more.

I brought our linked fingers down, sliding Larna's hand down until her palm rested on the bare skin of my stomach. It hesitated there instead of moving, and I wasn't sure whether to be grateful or frustrated. I hadn't realized Larna's offer to let me lead had been quite so literal. "I'll show you what I need, but I don't want you to be passive," I murmured, nipping at her lower lip. Her fingers twitched along my abdomen, but otherwise, she remained perfectly still. "I want you to take me until there isn't room inside my body or my head for anyone else."

Larna's lips fluttered into a smile against mine before she took them in an even deeper kiss. Her tongue teased forward, and the flat palm on my belly curled around my hip instead. The hold was still more tentative than I would have liked, but it made me shudder with want. Soon, I reconsidered how I felt about her careful pace. It was yet another difference to cling to if my mind wandered to dark places.

We sank back onto the mattress together, her body on top of mine, a perfect fit. Our mouths found each other again and again, but I didn't mind the burning in my lungs. I needed Larna and her slow, hot string of kisses more than I needed to breathe. I clutched the back of her head, toying with the light wisps of hair at the base of her neck as my other hand continued guiding hers. I drew Larna's palm up along my abdomen, past my shivering stomach until it cupped over my breast.

She hesitated again, but only for a moment. When I arched my spine, she began squeezing, dragging the tip of her thumb back and forth across the point of my nipple until it ached with hardness. A low, familiar throb began to grow between my legs, and I gasped, rocking forward in search of an answering pressure. Thankfully, the firm muscle of Larna's thigh was there to meet me. It was a perfect surface to rub against, and I sighed into her mouth. The hand on my hip went away, and I started to protest until Larna shifted more of the covers away. "I am needing to see you," she said, staring at me with dark, pleading eyes. "All of you, *Tuathe*. All of you that belongs to me."

I nodded, clutching her tighter. My hands were slightly frantic, but hers lingered, stroking every inch of my skin. She lavished attention on my stomach and breasts before moving on to my shoulders, tracing the line of my collarbone one moment and the vulnerable column of my throat the next. The deliberate purpose behind each touch threatened to drive the wolf in me mad, but the human part of me longed for it. I trembled, torn between indulging my swiftly growing desire and surrendering to her slow pace. "Larna," I hissed, "I...this isn't what I wanted." I had wanted her possessiveness, and I wasn't prepared for tenderness instead.

Larna drew back a few inches, still smiling at me. "Perhaps not. But it is what you are needing."

There was an unspoken question in her voice, a plea for me to listen to her. She wasn't asking for my submission this time, not exactly, but she was asking for my trust. She was asking me to believe she knew what I needed better than I did. And I did believe her. We were *Tuathe,* two souls living as one. I closed my eyes, stretching my arms over my head and spreading my legs.

My acceptance pleased her. She groaned into the place where my neck met my shoulder, sucking a tender spot there. I felt her inhale as she scented me, and I couldn't resist doing the same, nuzzling into her hair. Larna always smelled so good, like sweetly burning wood. I pressed a kiss there as her teeth took my throat, holding just enough to assert her claim, but not enough to leave a mark. Her restraint was maddening. I had wanted bruises, bites, and stinging scratches, but she would only give me softness.

As I shook with need, Larna began her achingly slow descent. Her hands and lips remembered every inch of me, lingering far longer than I wanted. I whimpered and sighed, but the sounds didn't encourage her. Her hands traveled along my sides, tracing the grooves in my ribs, spread wide to cover as much skin as possible. I tensed as her mouth followed the slope of my breast, stopping short of the hard tip. "Larna, please." I grasped the back of her head, trying to push her lower. "Your mouth."

To my surprise, she did as I asked. Warmth folded around me, and my hips bucked forward. The muscles of her stomach were wonderfully firm, and the thought of running my own hands over them made my clit pulse. Larna laughed, sending ticklish vibrations through my skin and bringing a flush to my face. She could feel everything, how wet I was for her, how slick, open, and ready her steady pace had made me. She released my nipple with a light pop and pursed her lips, blowing cool air across its edge.

"How," I panted, raking my fingers through her hair. "How do you do this to me?"

"Easily." Her mouth wound a trail over to my other breast, trapping the tip with the edges of her teeth. She let go as a surge of heat shuddered between my legs, sliding across her abdomen. She laughed again, louder this time. "Your body is telling me exactly what you are needing."

I let my nails scratch along her scalp as she continued her way down. Without her firm stomach to grind against, the ache inside of me returned, twice as fierce as before. The small slips of wetness came faster, heavier, and I hissed as her fingertips traced along my thighs, never delving between them. "Sometimes I hate that you know me better than I do."

"Aye?" She nipped a patch of skin above my navel, but when she released it, the flesh was only a light pink. The only permanent marks on my body were old ones from other nights, most of them already healed. "What are you hating about it?"

"I hate that you know just where my limits are." I let go of her and twisted the sheets instead, struggling not to move. All my instincts urged me to search for the mouth I knew I wouldn't find. "It means you can walk right up to them and push until I can't think."

"Then dinna think, little bird." Larna guided my legs over her shoulders and brought one of her hands between them, peeling back the hood of my clit with the edge of her thumb. The warmth of her breath washed lower, teasing me with the promise of her tongue. "Just feel."

Feeling was about all I could manage when the heat of her mouth wrapped around me. She sucked gently, tongue painting over me in maddening circles. I throbbed in the tight seal of her mouth, torn between sinking my fingers back into her hair and bunching the covers harder in my fists. It was a battle I quickly lost. I gripped her head again, not forcing, but making sure she couldn't leave.

The mistake only made Larna draw out my torment. She released the swollen bud of my clit and wandered lower, intent on driving me insane. The press and swirl of her tongue around my entrance made my hips hover off the mattress. If my knees hadn't been hooked over her shoulders, I might have floated into the air. She growled against me, a low vibration that made it clear I shouldn't move. This was hers—I was hers—and the possessive sound finally gave me the rest of what I had been missing. I didn't need her roughness, at least not this time. All I needed was to belong to her, as she belonged to me.

I let her taste me for as long as she liked, chewing at my lower lip and squeezing her shoulder whenever she did anything close to unbearable. She never stayed in one place for long, pulling me into the silk of her mouth one moment, pushing inside me the next. The sensations blurred into a steady burn, and although I wanted nothing more than to watch her, I couldn't keep my eyes open. They fluttered shut, and I surrendered, barely able to take in air. All I could manage to say was her name. "Larna."

She pulled back far enough to whisper without touching me. "Catie. My little bird."

The pet name rekindled the tears I thought I had banished. Before Larna, I had never known this was possible. Love, trust, a joining of bodies that didn't bring pain. It had seemed too incomprehensible to me then, and the woman I was now was overwhelmed with gratitude. I had made this. I had built this. I wasn't broken. Instead, I was whole enough to give half of myself to someone else. I didn't have to be afraid anymore, because I would never be alone.

I cried out as two of Larna's fingers pushed inside me to take the place of her tongue. The stretch stole what little breath I had, and I bowed, eyes snapping open. She knew just how to find the swollen, full place inside of me and exactly how hard to hook against it. I knew I wouldn't be able to last if she continued, but I couldn't bear to ask her to stop. I wanted to come for her—because of her.

Larna seemed to understand. Her lips closed back around my clit, and with her hand and mouth working together, she managed to draw out a river from deep within me. I squeezed tight around her fingers, spilling into her palm and down her wrist. I felt my release flooding over her chin as well. I gave her everything I had without holding back. The warmth, the ripples, the blissful release of pressure was too perfect. They lined up with each soft tug of her mouth, and I wept openly, this time for joy.

My peak seemed to last forever. Whenever the waves started to calm, Larna pushed deeper or lashed her tongue, and I broke for her all over again. By the time I was spent, I had wept an ocean of tears, and the sheets were damp beneath me. Larna kissed up along my belly, nuzzling into me every time I whimpered. "Happy crying," I gasped, smiling when I saw her dark eyes peer at me with concern. "Promise. I feel relieved."

Larna ran her tongue over her lips, looking pleased. "Then I was after doing my job."

I stroked her messy hair, urging her to rest her slick cheek on my stomach for a while. We relaxed together, breathing as one while I regained my strength. The silence wasn't uncomfortable, but after some time passed, I felt the urge to speak. I wanted to thank Larna for what she had done, or perhaps explain some of my intense emotions. But I didn't need to explain anything. Larna brushed one last kiss across my stomach and climbed over me, caging me in the safe circle of her arms.

"Larna, do you need me to..."

She shook her head and silenced me with a kiss, one that tasted like both of us. "I love you, little bird," she murmured against my mouth. "You are my mate, and I will always be here. When you be hurting, when you be happy, and when you be somewhere in between."

I smiled and closed my eyes, welcoming her weight on top of me. Perhaps later I would wake her in the middle of the night and return the pleasure she had given me, but I was content to accept her comfort. She had offered it with all the love in her heart, and I was happy to take it with all the love in mine.

Chapter Nine

Taken from the verbal accounts of Ailynn Gothel, edited by Lady Eleanor Kingsclere

THE NEXT SEVERAL DAYS were a flurry of activity. It took the liarre surprisingly little time to prepare an advance party, and I had to give the council credit. Once they actually made a decision, they threw themselves into it with everything they had. We were marching within two days, partially thanks to the efforts of Rufas. As promised, he had ordered his own warriors into the ranks leaving for Amendyr, and he had decided to join them. Although I didn't look forward to spending more time around him, I had to admire his principles.

Jinale and Rachari were also among the liarre who traveled with us. Rachari seemed relieved to be doing something productive, while Jinale's mood remained sober. They were almost always together, and I often saw them whispering to each other. However, they weren't the only familiar faces. My old friend Hassa had also decided to come along for the journey. I hadn't been able to see much of him during my time in Ardu, and I was grateful for his presence.

"You've been a stranger lately," I panted as we made our way up to the valley's edge. It had been easy enough to climb down and enter the city, but going the other way was tiring, especially since the lush green hills were secretly dotted with traps. There were few obvious paths, and we had to follow our guides closely or risk stumbling into one of them.

Hassa was kind enough to slow down for me. Larna and Cate had no trouble keeping up—I often caught sight of a pair of red and black wolves trotting at the edges of the group—but I was left breathless and practically sprinting thanks to the liarre's quick pace, and the glare of the early morning sun was surprisingly hot on my face. "Hello to you, too, Ailynn. Where is Raisa?"

"Riding on Jinale," I told him. "She can't keep up in her condition without help."

Hassa flared his nostrils in what I assumed was amusement. "I'm sure Rufas loved that. Would you like a lift as well? You don't seem to be doing much better."

The offer was tempting. Hassa had carried me once before, on our wild flight away from Mogra to take refuge in Ardu. His swiftness had saved us, and we had formed a bond while escaping death together. "Actually, I could use a break," I admitted. He stopped to kneel down, ignoring a few disapproving looks, and I scrambled onto his broad back. My legs had to stretch to wrap all the way around his powerful sides, but his tawny coat was surprisingly soft beneath my hands as I searched for a place to hold on. "Thank you. I know you didn't have to do that."

"I enjoy your company, Ailynn. The only reason I've made myself scarce this past week is because of Weyshra. I'm his cousin, and most people expect me to take his position once he abdicates. I had to be seen as impartial."

"What about now? Are you still worried people will disapprove of your friendship with a human?"

"I don't care what they think anymore. A decision has already been made. I'm relieved the council saw things our way."

"It wasn't easy. I was there when they cast their votes. Rufas and Weyshra were anything but happy about it."

Hassa sighed. "A surprise to no one. I understand Weyshra's caution and Rufas' loyalty to his soldiers, but now isn't the time to be hesitant. Sometimes hard decisions have to be made."

"You sound like Rachari, but less angry. I wish you'd been on the council, too. We might already be with the rebellion by now."

"The important thing is we're going. And now that you're not lagging behind, we should make good time," Hassa said with a laugh. He caught sight of Raisa, Jinale, and Rachari a little ahead of us, and he quickened his pace to join them.

Raisa smiled when she saw us, and I gave her a wave. To my relief, the lines of weariness on her face didn't run too deep, and she looked to be in good spirits. "Look who I found, *Tuathe*. I bet he's glad he doesn't have to carry both of us this time."

"You shouldn't make comments about a pregnant woman's weight, Ailynn," she teased. "I can barely fit into my largest shirts anymore. Hello, Hassa. It's nice to see you again. I didn't know you'd decided to join the advance party."

"You're joking," Jinale said, black lips peeling back over her fangs in the spider version of a smile.

Rachari answered the look with a sly grin of her own. "Hassa loves trouble. He wouldn't miss it."

"Don't listen to her," Hassa huffed, although he didn't sound displeased. "The three of us had a few adventures growing up together, but we're respectable now. I have a mate and children, and the two of them are on the council."

"It should have been the three of us," Rachari said. "Weyshra was only elected by the hair of his mane."

Hassa tossed his head. "I don't need a council position. Besides, I don't envy your jobs. Having to deal with Rufas every day? I'll leave that to the two of you."

The three of them kept us entertained with banter until we stopped to rest and eat during the hottest hour of the day. Even though I hadn't made much use of my legs thanks to Hassa, I still found myself tired. Raisa and I joined Cate and Larna when they motioned us over, and I sat down gratefully beside them.

"You look as exhausted as I feel," I said when I noticed Cate's pale complexion and the purple shadows beneath her eyes. "I didn't know shifting took that much out of you. Or is keeping up with the liarre hard in your wolf forms?"

Cate tried to answer, but it ended in a yawn instead. "She's only tired," Larna said. "She hasna been sleeping. Her visions be troubling her."

I hesitated, unsure whether to ask questions or offer comfort, but Raisa knew what to say. "Is there anything we can do?" She placed a reassuring hand on Cate's arm, brow knitted with concern.

"I'm not sure," Cate said. "There's almost too much to keep track of. I keep seeing fragments of something important, but I don't know how they fit together." She hesitated, as if considering how much to tell us. "Have either of you ever wondered why the Queen is evil? What drove her to kill her husband, drive away her stepdaughter, and conquer Amendyr?"

"I didn't even think to ask the question," I admitted. "Then again, I watched my own mother go insane. Maybe that normalized it for me."

"The Queen is one of the people in my visions. Every time I see her, she seems to be communicating with a mirror. It's hard to describe, but the mirror almost behaves like a living thing. It has emotions. It talks to her." Cate shuddered, as if reliving an awful memory. "It feels hungry, and almost familiar."

"Familiar?" Raisa asked. "What do you mean?"

"I haven't told you much about my life before becoming a wyr,"

Cate said. "When I lived across the border in Seria, I was a servant. One of the ladies of the house, Luciana, was horribly cruel to me." She hesitated, pain now written across her face.

"I remember," I said. Cate had revealed snatches of her life before, although only in small pieces.

"What I didn't tell you is how it ended. Her sadism only stopped when my friends Ellie and Belle broke the sorcerer's chain she wore. It belonged to a *High Ariada* named Umbra centuries ago. Its magic was so strong that even Ellie heard it speak to her, and she isn't a shaman or a seer."

Raisa's eyes lit up in recognition. "Umbra. I know that name. From the story of Feradith and her hatchling, isn't it, Ailynn? You've told me that one."

I nodded. It was one of the Amendyrri legends I had recited to Raisa as a child, and also one of my favorites, probably because of the dragons. Although there was often a kernel of truth in such tales, I couldn't help being skeptical. "Please don't take this the wrong way, Cate, but that seems very unlikely. How would a magical object belonging to one of the High Ariada end up with a Serian noble? It would have had to travel a long way and pass through many hands to get there."

"It had centuries to position itself," Cate said. "It sounds strange, but it seems like these objects have minds and intentions of their own." She hesitated, drawing her lip between her teeth and regarding me with a surprising amount of caution. "I think the mirror might have done to the Queen what the sorcerer's chain did to Luciana. I've often wondered if the magic twisted her, or if she was already twisted enough to use it."

A sudden thought occurred to me, an explanation for Cate's uncertain looks, and it burst from my lips before I could hold it back. "Do you think that's what happened to my mo...Mogra...too? She had a whole room full of strange treasures while I was growing up. One of them might have belonged to Umbra."

"It's possible," Cate said. "You told me she wasn't always evil."

My stomach churned at the thought. The words weren't as comforting as I had hoped, and I wasn't even certain whether I wanted them to be true. If Mogra had been corrupted by an ancient magical object that meant all the horrible things she had done weren't really her fault. But it also meant my mother had been stolen from me, and she wouldn't fully deserve the end I intended to make of her.

"Maybe it only takes a small crack to let the evil in," I murmured.

"Pretty things were always her weakness."

Warmth folded around one of my hands, and I looked down into my lap to see Raisa's thumb stroking the ridges of my knuckles. The wordless gesture brought me some comfort, and I gave her hand a grateful squeeze.

"Cate, are you thinking these objects could be helping us?" Larna asked, ever the practical one. "If they were after corrupting the Queen, Luciana, and Mogra, destroying them might end this."

"Luciana was a shell of herself once the sorcerer's chain was broken," Cate said. "Perhaps destroying the mirror will lessen the Queen's power as well. It's worth a try, at any rate. I'm going to tell Jett Bahari everything I know when we arrive. I respect his opinion a great deal."

Raisa nodded, giving the party a small smile. "In the meantime, if we find ourselves standing in front of any cursed magical objects, we'll be sure to smash them. Right, Ailynn?"

"Right," I said, although I couldn't match her enthusiasm. Although Cate was the one with nightmares, I feared I wouldn't sleep much better in the coming days. The more I discovered about the evil in my mother's heart, the more my guilt grew.

"There's one more thing," Cate whispered, so low I almost missed it. "The Queen isn't the only one I see in my visions. When her army invaded Seria, Mogra did something to Luciana. She must have found her in Prince Brendan's dungeon and shaped her into some kind of monster on the Queen's orders. That's the reason I think all three of them are connected to Umbra."

My eyes widened in alarm. "You're saying my mother brought back the monster that hurt you? Cate, I...this is my fault. I'm so sor—"

"Don't say you're sorry," Cate insisted. She straightened her shoulders, and some of the life returned to her eyes. "You didn't do this. Besides, she was a monster long before Mogra got hold of her. Now she just looks the way she always was on the inside."

"Do you think she'll come after you?" Raisa asked.

"Right now, she's chasing Ellie, Belle, and the princess. That should keep her busy for a while. Ellie might not be a trained fighter, but she's surprisingly resourceful."

"She'd better not be coming after you," Larna said with a low growl. The fire in her eyes was frightening, and I could tell she had shared a great deal of Cate's pain, fear, and rage. If Luciana ever did come after Cate and Larna was anywhere nearby, I suspected both of them would make sure she met a grisly end. "She willna lay a hand on you. Never again."

The camp around us began to stir, and I took that as our cue to leave, sensing Cate and Larna needed a moment. "It looks like everyone's getting ready to leave," I whispered, standing and offering Raisa my arm. She groaned a little as she stood, and I massaged the tense muscles at the base of her spine on instinct. "Do you want to ask Hassa if you can ride him instead of Jinale? It might be easier on your back."

Raisa shook her head. "I don't think so. Jinale and I enjoy each other's company." She looked back over at Cate and Larna. They hadn't left their seats, and they clasped each other's hands tight, faces hovering close. "Do you think Cate will be all right?"

"I'm sure she will. I remember the first time we met. She saved me from a whole pack of kerak all by herself. If Luciana comes within a mile of her, her visions will get a lot quieter afterward."

"And what about Mogra?" Raisa asked, reading my unspoken thoughts. "If she's one of Umbra's victims as well, are you still prepared to deal with her?"

I shook my head and sighed. "It doesn't matter. She's my responsibility. I'll do whatever I must to make sure she doesn't hurt anyone else."

Raisa didn't reply. She simply nodded and took my hand in hers, leading me over to where Hassa, Jinale, and Rachari waited for us. Although I wished I could be alone for a while longer, I was grudgingly grateful we would be traveling as part of a group. While they talked among themselves, I wouldn't be expected to speak.

Chapter Ten

Taken from the diary of Lady Eleanor Kingsclere

THE DWELLYN'S WARREN PROVED just as magnificent as Lok promised. Considering their size, I had expected a narrow network of tunnels, but the road leading down into the city was enormous. It was more than wide enough for us to walk abreast, and the high ceiling disappeared into darkness. The bones of the buildings were hewn from stone, almost like the inside of a giant castle, and the place was just as busy as any thoroughfare on the surface. By the light of the torch Lok had given me, I saw scores of dwellyn scurrying to and fro, going about their business.

"This definitely isn't what I expected," I whispered to Belle as we merged with the crowd. Most of them didn't even seem to notice our group despite the fact that we were human and leading a pair of horses. In fact, aside from a tinge of damp earth, it didn't smell any different from the other marketplaces I had been in back in Seria. Even the sounds were the same, footsteps and turning wheels and the sound of merchants hawking their wares. If it hadn't been for the dimness, I wouldn't have realized we were underground at all.

"It's magnificent!" Belle said, her blue eyes wide with awe. She lifted her own torch higher, trying to look everywhere at once. "It has to be as big as Ronin at the very least. I think this is the trade market. There are vendors everywhere." I saw that she was right, and I was even more surprised to notice we weren't the only humans in attendance. A few other torches passed by from time to time, illuminating taller figures as they wandered between the various stalls and buildings.

Lok laughed, pleased by Belle's enthusiasm. "I'm glad you're impressed. We don't let many humans come here, but the ones who receive trading permits are usually taken aback. Most people have no idea that some of Amendyr's finest cities are underground."

"I need to update my library when I get home, or write a book about Amendyr myself," Belle said. "I know Serians like to pretend your country is primitive, but the books I read about the dwellyn made it sound like you lived in holes in the ground. This is absolutely amazing. Did you use magic to help build the city?"

"Of course not," Lok said, sounding almost offended. "The dwellyn don't need to hire human *Ariada* to build for us. Our engineers do fine work without magic, and they're a lot more reliable than mages."

While Belle and Lok continued talking, I heard small footsteps scurry beside me. I looked down to see Neva hovering by my side, still grinning. "This is where Ulig and his clan brought me after they found me. One of the palace servants was supposed to kill me, but he couldn't do it. He smuggled me to the Forest instead and left me there. They saved me from a group of kerak I couldn't fight on my own."

Her pleased delivery was a complete contrast to her awful story. I had known Neva's stepmother wanted her dead, but hearing it from her lips was still horrible. "I'm so sorry, Neva," I said, reaching out to clasp her shoulder after a brief hesitation to make sure the touch was welcome. "That must have been terrifying for you."

Neva continued smiling. "Don't be sorry. I'm not afraid of the dead anymore. Cieran has taught me a lot since then, and I have friends here."

"I wish I could be as optimistic as you," I said, shaking my head a little in awe. I was swiftly growing attached to this side of Neva's personality. Since reuniting with the dwellyn, she had been bubbly instead of sullen and withdrawn, full of energy and positivity.

Ulig, who had been walking nearby and listening to our conversation, nodded. "Friends, you, princess," he said, speaking in his limited Serian for my benefit. "Help home."

I looked at him curiously, and my earlier conversation with Belle came back to me. "Wait, you want to help Neva return to Kalmarin?"

Ulig nodded, grunting. He said something in Amendyrri, and Neva translated. "He says his clan is going to escort us to the rebellion, and some of the other clans want to fight."

"Jett Bahari will be happy to hear that," Belle said. "You should write to Cate, Ellie. She'll know how to contact him."

"There's no need for that," Lok said. "We're already in negotiations with the rebellion. In fact, we were just waiting for your arrival. Our army should be prepared to march in a week, but the ten of us will be leaving in another day. We think it best to keep Neva apart from the main group."

"Ten?" an unhappy voice purred from behind me. Jessith rustled inside my pack, waking from one of her many naps just in time to be offended.

"Thirteen," I said. Brahms huffed in approval and lipped the side of my head.

Belle smiled. "Of course, we can't forget the animals. Thirteen might be unlucky in Seria, but in Amendyr, it's considered a number of power. Maybe our luck is turning around."

"I hope so. After the past week, we could definitely use some."

A shadow fell over Belle's face, and after a moment's thought, she turned to Lok. "I've read that the dwellyn are skilled at forging and using swords. Is that true?"

"Of course," Lok said with pride. "We're the finest in the world. Why? Are you interested in buying a sword?"

"I'm interested in learning how to use one," Belle said. It wasn't at all what I expected to hear from her lips. Although she was fairly fit for a noble, my wife had never shown any interest in fighting before. The idea certainly didn't appeal to me. Coming face to face with the kerak at Baxstresse had been more than enough danger for one lifetime. Their faces still gaped at me from my nightmares, making it hard to forget.

Apparently, Belle's mind had turned back to the same night. When I gave her a questioning look, she mentioned it as well. "Watching the kerak and the shadowkin take over Baxstresse was difficult for me. I felt helpless. We might have died if Jessith hadn't warned us and Neva hadn't been able to stop some of them." Her face furrowed into a look of determination. "Next time, I want to be able to do something."

Her pronouncement gave me mixed emotions. I understood her urge to protect what she cared about, but my mind flashed back to years earlier, when her bravery had almost killed her. She had fought with Luciana to save me, and the scuffle had left her on the brink of death for almost a week. A pit formed in my stomach at the thought of seeing her like that again. "If that's truly what you want," I said in an uncertain voice.

Belle held my eyes for a moment, and I knew she could read my thoughts. "I need to try. I wish it wasn't true, but I'm certain we're going to end up fighting for our lives again. When it happens, I'd like to have a weapon in my hand and know something about how to use it."

"A wise opinion to have," Lok said. "Rup is a master smith, so if you want something better than the tin sticks the rebellion has on hand, we might be able to accommodate you. We usually charge a fair price for our finest work, but considering the circumstances, I think we owe you." She gave Neva a fond look, which the girl happily returned. "You brought our princess back to us. I think that's worth a sword, at least."

***

That evening, after our hosts fed us, the animals were tended to, and Neva had been put to bed, Belle and I finally made it to a set of guest rooms with human-sized furniture. The stone walls didn't look all that different from Baxstresse's, and I could almost fool myself into thinking we were visiting another Serian noble's manor. Only the decorations were different. They had a definite theme—metal and weapons of all types. In fact, two crossed maces with spiked heads hung directly above our bed.

While Belle unpacked our meager supplies and Jessith found a place to sleep by the fire, I took the chance to curl up in one of the plush armchairs and check my journal. There had barely been time to read or write while on the run, so I was relieved when I opened to the latest page and saw a short message in Cate's familiar handwriting:

Ellie,

You have no idea how relieved I am to hear that you are alive. I had a vision of you being chased by a monster before your message came, and somehow, I knew it was Luciana. She is under the Queen's power, and I am certain she has been sent to capture Neva. The Queen wants her desperately—or, at least, her body. My visions haven't revealed why, but I hope they will soon. I am certain that understanding the Queen's plans is the only way to protect Neva and help the rebellion succeed.

The more my Sight reveals, the more confused I become. Luciana's face isn't the only one that haunts my dreams. I see a pale woman with a golden crown, staring into a giant mirror that feels alive. The mirror's hunger is palpable, and its energy reminds me of Umbra's sorcerer's chain. If the two objects are related, as I believe they are, it could explain how the Queen, Mogra, and Luciana are connected.

I do have some good news, however. The liarre have finally seen things our way. Two of the councilors were not happy about the decision, but we managed to convince Chairwoman Maresth to vote in our favor. We left to join the rebellion two days ago with an army at our backs. There have been no signs of Mogra or her creatures here, so I suspect she is still near Seria, but Ailynn and Raisa are traveling with us. Ailynn's conscience is weighing on her, and she blames herself for the evil her mother has done.

Please, hurry to meet us as fast as you can. I doubt I will truly believe you are all right until I can hold you in my arms for proof.
   Be careful,
Cate

   I studied her signature for a long time, my heart filled with worry. The letter held more information than the words scribbled on the page, and because of our close friendship, I could read between the lines. If Cate was having visions of Luciana, she had to be frightened. The dark days we had shared as servants at Baxstresse under her power seemed a lifetime ago, but I had not forgotten. She had lived in a constant state of terror, flinching like a kicked dog whenever anyone so much as spoke to her. Her transformation since then was astounding, but I knew Luciana haunted her still.
   "Another love letter?" Belladonna teased, causing me to look up from the journal. She wasn't truly jealous, but I could tell she was a little disappointed I hadn't come to bed with her straight away.
   I closed the book, marking the page with my finger. "You know better," I said, giving my wife a smile as well as my full attention. "But if you're asking for a little reassurance..."
   Belle's eyes flashed at that suggestion. "Perhaps I do need some reassurance. That is, if you aren't wrapped up in other things."
   I knew she wouldn't be too upset if I chose to write instead of retiring with her, but I decided that responding to Cate's letter could wait until morning. Even though I was eager to tell her all about the dwellyn and their offer of help, the note of promise in Belle's voice was too tempting to resist. The week we had spent scurrying around the Serian countryside hadn't offered many opportunities for "reassurance," especially with Neva in our charge.
   "Not too wrapped up to spend a moment with you." I set the journal aside, allowing my eyes to roam up and down Belladonna's figure. Before our flight from Baxstresse, I had hardly ever seen her in casual clothes. Her station came with certain expectations, and she normally wore fashionable dresses. However, she had purchased three plain shirts and two pairs of practical pants on the second day of our journey to make riding easier, and they suited her far better than I had imagined.
   She noticed my admiring glance and gave a little spin, laughing as she did. "I'm surprised you enjoy seeing me in men's clothes," she said with a smirk. "I miss a few of my dresses, but I have to admit, these are

comfortable. I might have a pair tailored for me when we get home."

"I would like that," I said, standing up from the chair. It only took a few steps to reach her, and I slid a hand around the back of her neck, teasing my fingers through her long dark hair. "But I know for a fact you'll look even better without the pants, or a dress, or anything else."

A pleased flush rose at the points of her cheeks, and her arms folded around me, drawing me against her body. She felt even warmer than usual with fewer layers between us, and I caught a slight hint of sweat—not altogether unpleasant, and in fact rather pleasing. All in all, it was a miracle she still smelled as good as she did after traipsing across the border with me. "I wouldn't object if you wanted a pair of pants as well," she whispered. Her hands began folding up the skirt of my dress, searching for the hem so she could lift it higher. I gasped when soft fingertips skimmed the side of my thigh. "But I do appreciate the easy access of your current outfit."

"No clothes," I insisted, pulling back and turning around before she could kiss me and change my mind. "Here, undo my dress?"

She stepped up behind me, pressing close again and placing a kiss behind my ear as her hands went to work. "Of course, my Ellie. Anything you desire."

Part Two

Taken from the accounts of Lady Eleanor Sandleford, Cathelin Raybrook, and Ailynn Gothel. Edited and summarized by Princess Rowena, Keeper of the Royal Library.

Chapter One

Taken from the verbal accounts of Ailynn Gothel, edited by Lady Eleanor Kingsclere

THANKS TO OUR FAST pace, the next week was a blur. The network of narrow sandstone cliffs all seemed the same, and the longer we walked, the more they started to smear together. Although I had been happy to be on the move when we first left Ardu, the atmosphere among the advance party was tense. Rufas and his men clearly did not want to be there, and Rachari and Jinale's followers had taken notice.

"How long do you think this stand-off will last?" I asked Larna one evening as we prepared dinner. The evening was warm, especially beside the fire where we had chosen to sit, but the atmosphere amongst our party was much frostier. Rachari and Rufas were glaring daggers at each other again from opposite sides of camp, sharpening their claws and their respective weapons in between murderous looks. Even Jinale and Hassa, the reasonable peacekeepers, had decided to avoid them.

Larna prodded a loose bit of kindling with the toe of her boot, kicking it back into the fire pit. "'Isna a stand-off. And dinna be so obvious about staring."

I glanced away before either of them could notice me. "If it's not a stand-off, then what?"

"Rufas is already knowing he's lost," Larna said. "He willna leave the group."

I heard what she didn't say as well. "But he won't stop being unpleasant about it, either."

"Aye. He'll be obeying, but grudgingly."

"I'm not sure that's the kind of ally we want," I muttered. "If we're going to march on Kalmarin, we'll need everyone at their best. We're bound to fail if we have discord in our own ranks."

Larna paused, holding a moment of thoughtful silence. When she raised her dark eyes to mine, I was taken aback by their intensity.

"Exactly. I've been seeing this before, Ailynn. A broken pack canna take down a bear."

There wasn't much more to be said about the subject. Larna and I spent a few more minutes conversing about other things and finishing our meal before we returned to our *Tuathe* and our separate bedrolls. Raisa was still awake by the time I joined her, struggling to get comfortable on the hard ground. "Oh good, you're here," she said, brightening as soon as she saw me. "I can never fall asleep without you."

"Do you want me to rub your back first?" I asked, sitting beside her.

She grinned and sat up, sweeping her long braid aside. "Please?"

I heaved a fake sigh before lifting the hem of her shirt, revealing the naked skin of her lower back. "You feel tense," I murmured beside her ear as I dug into the firm bands of muscle with my thumbs. She groaned, and I pressed harder. "Are you sure you're all right? If I didn't think the rebellion was the safest place possible, I wouldn't want you wandering about the wilderness like this."

Even though Raisa was facing away, I could tell she was smiling. "You worry too much, Ailynn. Besides, I want to help. I might not be able to fight or cast spells, but I'll find a way to make myself useful."

"That's what I'm afraid of. Your version of 'making yourself useful' is probably going to put all of us in danger someday soon." I paused, placing a kiss on the back of her neck. "I almost watched you die once already. I don't think I can bear to do it again."

"Fine." Raisa leaned away from my hands and turned around, taking me by surprise. "Then let's go. Right now. We can take enough supplies to last a few days and find a safe place to hole up until the war is over. If it's ever over."

I stared into her eyes, looking for anger, but I found only a calm. "You're serious, aren't you?"

"Just tell me yes or no. Do you want to leave?"

I did want to leave. I wanted to run away, wrap Raisa in my arms, and protect her from everything until the storm passed. But we would never truly be safe until Mogra was dealt with and a proper ruler was on the white throne. She knew it, and so did I. "I see your point," I said, grudgingly. "I have an obligation to see this through."

"*We* have an obligation to see this through," Raisa insisted. "For all intents and purposes, Mogra was my mother, too, and Amendyr is my country. This isn't something you have to bear alone."

I smiled. There would be no arguing with her. Raisa had already spent far too many years under someone else's power, trapped and alone. If this was how she wanted to spend her freedom, even at risk to her safety, I couldn't deny her. "Who am I to tell you what you can and can't do? If you're crazy enough to want to stay by my side while I fight for the rebellion, I suppose I'm crazy enough to let you."

"Wise words. Now, help me trim my hair before bed," she said, holding up her braid.

"Of course, *Tuathe*," I said, summoning wisps of flame between my fingers. "Anything for you."

***

We arrived at our destination sooner than anticipated. Our party came upon the rebels a few days out from the sandstone cliffs, only a short journey from the southwestern edge of the Forest. Jett Bahari's army was smaller than I expected, but my hopes soared when I saw how well prepared they were. Everyone seemed to have enough food, and I noticed plenty of weapons and supplies as we made our way through camp.

"They're far more organized than I thought," I said to Cate and Larna as we wound our way between the tents. The bulk of the advance party had remained behind, but Jinale, Rachari, and Rufas had elected to join us. Many of the humans had never seen liarre before, and the three councilors drew stares and whispers wherever we passed.

"Organized, yes, but numbers are a problem," Cate said. "Jett Bahari kept the rebellion small before to weed out traitors, but if we're going to march on Kalmarin, a guerilla force won't do. We need an army to take back the city."

Rachari purred in approval. "That's where we come in. The liarre will give you the numbers you need. Just point and we'll shoot."

"You're a fool if you think arrows will solve everything, pussycat," Rufas grunted.

Rachari's tail lashed in anger, but before the low growl in her throat could become a rebuke, Jinale stepped in. "Let's try and conduct ourselves in a dignified way now that we're here, please. The two of you can fight about this later. We need to make a good impression."

"Why?" Rufas asked. "The humans are the ones asking us for help."

"Because we are supposed to be good allies and worthy representatives of our people," Jinale said coldly.

That kept him quiet until we arrived at the middle of the camp. The crowd gathering around us grew larger and more suspicious, but a smile spread across Cate's face as she caught sight of someone she knew. "Kera," she said, hurrying to meet a slender woman with high cheekbones. The two of them embraced, and I got a better look at the stranger's face from over Cate's shoulder. On second glance, she did look familiar, and I was fairly certain we had met before in passing during my first encounter with the Farseer pack. Her hair was pulled back in a tight bun, but her dark eyes were soft.

"Cate, you're home." The woman caught sight of Larna, and instantly, her demeanor changed. She let go of Cate and dropped her shoulders, inclining her head respectfully. "Most of the pack is out fetching dinner, Larna, but I'll be telling them of your return as soon as they come in. We've been working hard to earn our keep here while you were away."

"Good," Larna said, nodding. The single word of praise was enough to brighten Kera's face again. If she'd had her tail, I suspected it would have been wagging. "Where be Jett Bahari?"

Kera started to answer the question, but then her eyes fell on the liarre waiting behind us. Despite being a wyr, she seemed just as fascinated by them as any human. She stared outright. "You found them," she said, with more than a little awe in her voice. "Then you were successful? Will the liarre be helping us?"

"Aye," Larna said with a grin. She seemed almost amused by Kera's amazement.

"Some more reluctantly than others," Cate muttered under her breath, and I caught her eyes darting toward Rufas as he rejoined our group. He seemed to be growing more impatient, a fact that didn't escape Larna's notice.

"Kera, Jett Bahari?"

"Oh! Of course," she said, a blush staining her cheeks. "I'll just be going to announce your arrival—"

"No need for that," said another, much deeper voice. A burly giant of a man with a rough grey beard pushed his way through the crowd, getting several of them to back off with his sheer bulk. "I've already told him to expect you."

"Jethro," Cate said, smiling. I was certain I had never met him during my first encounter with the rebellion—surely I would have remembered someone so huge—but he was clearly her friend. "I hope you didn't miss us too much."

"Only a little." He took in the liarre, obviously impressed and a little awed. "But I see you've brought something back to make up for it."

"Indeed we have," Cate said. "The start of an army is waiting for us at the edge of camp, and more are coming soon. Where is Jett Bahari?"

"Waiting on you, I expect." Another figure pushed his way through the crowd and stepped forward from the onlookers. He was barely half Jethro's size, and bent beneath his cloak, but I recognized him immediately. This time, I let out a cry of joy.

"Doran," I said, hurrying over to hug him. "What are you doing here?"

Although I was shocked to see him, Doran didn't seem surprised by my arrival at all. "The same thing you are, *Acha.* These old bones are still good for something. And besides, the two of us have unfinished business."

I knew at once that Doran was speaking of Mogra. He hadn't told me all the details, but I had gleaned some of their history during our conversations. I often wondered if he was my father despite his age, although I had never asked. I wasn't sure he even knew for certain. Mogra had never told me my father's identity, and I suspected that if Doran was my other parent, she wouldn't have told him either.

"Mogra was besieging a palace in Seria the last I heard of her," I said. "I have no idea where she is now, but I'm sure she'll find us before too long."

"Mogra?" I looked over to see Jethro staring at me. His dark eyes burned with such intensity I couldn't stammer out a response. Although he had seemed nothing but friendly before, the mention of her name had transformed his face into a mask of anger, and his size only made the look more terrifying. "How do you know the witch?"

I hesitated, unsure how to explain, but Cate stepped in. "Ailynn fights against her, just like we do. You couldn't ask for a better ally."

Jethro studied me for a long time, but eventually, he nodded. "I'm sorry, Ailynn. I have a score to settle with Mogra as well. My wife died during one of her experiments."

A lump of guilt formed in my chest. "I'm sorry. I was her daughter. She's hurt a lot of people, and I blame myself for not trying to stop her sooner. That's why I'm here. I can't rest until she's been dealt with."

I waited for an angry outburst, but it never came. Instead, Jethro held out his enormous hand. I shook it, wincing a little at the strength of his grip. "I don't care how you're related. If you fight against her, I'll consider you a friend." I sighed with relief. I definitely didn't want this large, angry stranger to consider me an enemy.

Before we could speak further, movement came from the large tent in the center of camp. The front opened, and another stocky man stepped out, raising his hand to our party. Although he wasn't a giant like Jethro, he was still tall and broad-shouldered, with cropped hair and a sword strapped to his back. His dark skin marked him as a man of Shezad, from far across the sea, but his clothes were Amendyrri, and his speech had no trace of an accent as he called out to us. "Larna, Cate, we were just told you'd come back. My father's ready to meet you."

"Jett Markku, Jett Bahari's son," Larna whispered to me and the three liarre. "Please, dinna fight in front of him."

Rufas gave an annoyed grunt, but also a subtle nod of his head. Rachari responded with a silent blink. Jinale plastered on a needle-filled smile that had only become a little less terrifying in the time I had known her. "We'll be on our best behavior, Larna." She glared at the other two councilors, and even her eye-tattoos seemed to narrow in warning. "I promise." We approached Jett Markku together, and he led us inside.

Despite our numbers, the tent was big enough to hold us, although it quickly became warm with so many people pressed close together. There was a table inside, its surface covered with maps, and several crates of supplies doubled as chairs. Behind it stood a man who was almost a double of Jett Markku, although he looked to be several decades older. He wore a sword across his back, and his eyes glinted like metal as he studied us.

"Larna, welcome back," he said, nodding in greeting.

She did the same. "*Arim dei,* Jett Bahari. Cate and I are bringing good news, as you can see."

I waited in silence, unsure what to expect. This setting was far removed from the grand theater in Ardu, and I didn't know how serious or formal the situation was supposed to be. I didn't even know what I was supposed to call Jett Bahari. *Does he have a title? Am I supposed to bow or something? How do you treat the leader of a secret rebellion?* I needed these people to accept me, and though Cate, Larna, and Doran would vouch for me, I was at a disadvantage as Mogra's daughter.

Jett Bahari didn't stand on ceremony, much to my relief. He stepped out from around the table, standing tall before the liarre even though their long bodies were far larger. "We're honored by your presence, friends. I know it isn't often liarre agree to work with humans."

As usual, the levelheaded Jinale took over. "These are desperate times. My name is Jinale, and my companions are Rachari and Rufas. The liarre stand ready to fight with anyone who seeks to remove the Queen from power. Our people have agreed that she represents a threat to us as well as Amendyr."

Rufas snorted, but for once, he didn't say anything offensive.

"Then we have a common goal," Jett Bahari said. "How many have come here with you?"

"Threescore with our party," Rachari told him. "Six times that many are following us to Kalmarin. That should bolster your numbers enough to stand against the witch's army."

Jett Bahari nodded. "It will certainly help. Our own ranks keep growing as we travel south, and our other allies, the dwellyn, are also preparing to join us."

I smiled. That was good news indeed. A third army to fight alongside the liarre and the humans would certainly help. I had never met one, but I knew the dwellyn were expert fighters and swordsmiths. If they were anything like they were in the old stories, perhaps we had a chance with them on our side.

Rufas was not so enthusiastic. "Please tell me you have some kind of plan to go along with our people. Not all of us were in favor of coming here, and it would be reassuring to know what you expect us to do when we arrive at Kalmarin."

If Jett Bahari was offended, it didn't show on his face. He seemed to take Rufas' concerns seriously as he returned to the table. "Kalmarin's strength is also its weakness." He placed his hand beside one of the maps. We all crowded around, and I peeked between Rachari's flank and Larna's shoulder to see. "The city sits high on a cliff, with no way to enter or leave aside from the great bridge."

"Will a siege be working on an army of the undead?" Larna asked. "I dinna think kerak and shadowkin are needing to eat."

"Kerak and shadowkin are only one part of the Queen's army. She has human forces, too. It only takes one starving soldier to open a door."

Rufas frowned. "Are you prepared to risk everything on that chance?"

Rachari returned the expression with a scowl of her own. "Everyone knows the gates are the only way past Kalmarin's walls. If you can think of another way to bring them down, by all means, enlighten us."

There was a moment of silence, but Rufas had nothing else to say.

Eventually, Cate spoke up, breaking the tension with a note of optimism. "It seems like our only option, if not our best. At the very least, the Queen will run low on forces if she sends them out to fight us. According to my sources, Mogra isn't with her to make more creatures."

Yet, I added silently. I had no doubts that when we launched our attack on Kalmarin, she would appear at precisely the wrong moment, as always.

"Assuming we can match their numbers, we could eventually scale the walls," Cate continued.

Jinale smirked. "Scaling walls isn't a problem for an arachniarre, no matter how high. If your forces can clear out the bulk of the Queen's army, Jett Bahari, this plan might work better than you think."

"What if Mogra returns?" I asked.

Everyone turned to look at me, surprised I had spoken, and I began to doubt myself. I had no forces at my command and no rank to speak of. In fact, I wasn't even sure why they had allowed me to take part in this private meeting. I swallowed as Jett Bahari's gaze fixed on me at last, wishing I hadn't said anything.

"And you must be Ailynn Gothel. Cate and Doran have told me a great deal about you."

I held my chin high even though shame burned my cheeks. "Then you know why I'm here. My mother is the most dangerous weapon the Queen has. If you plan on outlasting the Queen's army, she needs to be eliminated. Otherwise, she will shape more undead to throw at us."

"Can she be killed?" Jett Bahari asked. "Many people have tried and failed."

I nodded. "As far as I know, she's only a very powerful *Ariada.* She can shape and enchant and control the elements, and I suspect she's studied the way of the *Kira'baas,* but she isn't immortal. I almost managed to kill her once before."

"Almost is a long way from dead," Rufas muttered under his breath.

I looked at him, face set into a determined frown. No one knew my own mistakes better than I did. "I know. And believe me, the next time I see her, I plan on fixing my error."

Chapter Two

Taken from the diary of Lady Eleanor Kingsclere

I JOLTED AWAKE TO the sound of shouts and clanging metal. My eyes snapped open, and it took me a moment to remember where I was—in a shallow cave, resting on the sleeping pallet the dwellyn had lent me. Although I had been gone from Baxstresse for two weeks, and travelling for most of that time, I still expected to wake up in my own bed each morning.

After stretching my arms above my head to work out some of the early-morning stiffness, I glanced at the empty pallet beside me. That wasn't a surprise. Belle took her commitment to learning seriously, whether it was history or literature or her latest attempts at swordsmanship. I still wasn't thrilled she had chosen to train with the dwellyn, but I couldn't think of a logical reason to stop her, either. The two of us were supposed to be protecting Neva, and we couldn't rely on her to save us again.

My eyes flicked to the other side, checking to make sure the princess was still asleep. The morning light filtering in through the cave's mouth only showed the top of her head. The rest of her body was buried beneath a blanket, and Jessith was curled up in the crook of her knees. I couldn't bear to wake them. Although Neva had been much happier since the dwellyn had joined us, she often looked sad and exhausted. I couldn't blame her, since I frequently felt the same.

Grudgingly, I got up and began a modified version of my morning routine. I couldn't take a bath—there was no suitable place by the river—so I settled for splashing my face with some of the water from my side-pouch. It helped wash away some of my frustrations, and by the time I had pulled on a fresh set of clothes I managed to force a smile. It wouldn't help anything to start the day depressed.

Outside, I came upon the same scene I had observed for the last few mornings. Belle and Ulig stood opposite each other, trading blows back and forth. The clanging rang through the air every time their blades clashed. They repeated the same series of motions over and over again, pausing so Belle could fall back into a defensive stance in between each strike. Lok stood beside her, commenting every time she returned to position.

"You're swinging too wide," she said, one hand on Belle's arm. "Blocking is about speed and efficiency of motion. Try to get your sword into the same position with the least amount of effort. You'll move faster."

Belle nodded, but even from a few yards away I could see lines of weariness around her eyes. She slept even worse than I did, and the extra hours she spent training each morning sapped her energy. Despite my disapproval and my fear that her determination in regards to learning this skill would endanger her in far more danger than necessary, I couldn't help being proud of her. My eyes followed a rivulet of sweat as it ran down from her temple and across the side of her face, and my heart fluttered. Only my wife could make sweating and swinging swords about in the middle of the wilderness look attractive.

"I think that's enough for today," I said, noticing the wobble in Belle's legs. "You need to be able to walk later."

Belle looked to Lok for an opinion, and to my relief, she nodded. "You're making improvements. Soon, we should be able to move on to forward strikes."

My brow furrowed. "You mean you haven't taught her anything offensive yet?"

Lok shrugged. "What's more important? That she knows how to stab someone, or how to prevent someone from stabbing her?"

"A fair point," I said, trying not to picture what she was describing. Between Luciana and Mogra's army, I already had enough unpleasant images in my head to last a lifetime. Thankfully, Belle offered me a distraction. She strode over to me and I smiled. "Once again, I find myself surprised at the depths of my attraction to you," I murmured under my breath so only she could hear. "Your clothes are already ruined, and I suspect you only put them on a few hours ago."

Belle returned my teasing with a half-lidded look that was all seduction. "Admit it. You're enjoying the rugged clothes and the new muscles."

I prodded her arm with one of my fingers. I wasn't sure if it was any bulkier, but it was certainly stiff and likely sore as well. "It takes more than a little over a week to build muscle. And the clothes have nothing to do with it at all. The woman in them, however..." I let my voice trail off with a sigh. It was a good thing we had stolen a night together at the dwellyn's city, because I didn't foresee any more opportunities for privacy coming our way in the near future. "I suppose you're proud of the fact that you look like a character from one of your horrible romance novels."

One of Belle's arms folded around my waist, pulling me close enough to feel her lithe body against mine. "Only a little. But don't worry. I'm no different than I was before. When this is over, it's back to my books and library."

The words should have comforted me, but instead, my heart sank. I hadn't said so aloud, but part of me feared "when this is over" wouldn't mean a happy ending. We were two foreign civilians trapped in the middle of a magical kingdom's war, and every day brought constant reminders we were in way over our heads. Still, the best I could do was follow Belle's example. She was fighting hard to manage despite everything, and I admired her fiercely for it.

"Neva's still asleep," I said after a while, although I made no move to leave the safe circle of her arms. "We should go wake her." The rest of the dwellyn were already packing up camp, and Brahms and Corynne looked restless at the prospect of moving. They had held up better than I would have expected of racehorses, especially since they no longer needed to carry us.

"Do you want to fetch her, or shall I?" Belle asked. "She seems to have attached herself to you."

"She's attached herself to Jessith," I said with a smile. Although the two of them couldn't speak with each other, they had formed a bond. I was only a little put out that Jessith had taken to sleeping between us instead of on top of me.

As if speaking her name had summoned her, Jessith came bolting out of the cave a split second later, tail raised high. She darted straight for us, and Belle let out a short laugh of surprise. "What in the world has gotten into that cat? She's running like she has pack of dogs on her heels."

I was not amused. Despite being a cat, Jessith wasn't easily startled. Something had frightened her, and badly. When she reached us, she launched herself at my feet with wide, terrified eyes. "Ellie, come quick," she yowled. "Something's wrong with Neva!"

"What?" I gasped, but Jessith didn't wait for me. She streaked back toward the mouth of the cave, moving so fast she became a blur. I ran after her, and Belle followed.

When we burst into the cave, Neva was still lying on her pallet, but she no longer looked peaceful. Her head lolled to one side, sending her dark hair spilling across the ground, and her face was pale as death. I stared at her chest, but there was no steady rise and fall. "Neva? Neva! Oh Saints, she isn't breathing! What happened?" I knelt beside her, pulling back the blanket. She didn't even twitch.

"I don't know," Jessith said. "I was half asleep when she came in."

"Who?" I pressed my fingers to Neva's throat, feeling for a pulse. Her heartbeat was faint, but still there.

Jessith's tail lashed. "The old woman. I opened my eyes and saw her hovering over Neva's head."

My eyes flicked back up to Neva's face, and this time, I noticed something else abnormal. Her hair hadn't simply washed to the side on its own. The teeth of a dark, gleaming comb were snared in her locks, digging into her scalp. I had been so concerned for her I hadn't even noticed, but as soon as I saw it, the warm hum of magic washed over me. Whatever had happened to her, this was the cause.

I tried to rip the comb away, but as soon as I touched it, fire throbbed in my palm. My vision began to swim, and the biting scent of magic flooded my nose. I tore the comb free, but not before my hand was cracked and aching as if I had been burned, and my head felt like it wanted to split in half. Darkness crept in around the edges of my eyes, and I bent forward, bracing my good palm against the ground as my heart thudded sluggishly.

"Ellie?" I recognized the sound of Belle's voice, but it was muffled and fuzzy, like someone shouting underwater. "Ellie, are you all right?"

"Neva," I said, struggling to lift my head. My lips moved, but forming any other words was too much effort. They would have been drowned out by the loud hum echoing through my head.

A warm hand stroked worried circles between my shoulder blades, and I sagged further under the touch. "Neva's awake. She's getting up. See?"

I tried once more to look up, and this time, I managed to raise my eyes a few inches. The wave of magic had begun to wear off, its vibrations a softer warmth rather than a searing burn, and Neva was stirring at last. She yawned and stretched as if she had been woken from a deep, restful sleep. "Good morning," she said, giving us a cheerful smile. "Is it time to get up yet?"

I used my returning strength to pull her into a tight hug. Seeing her sleeping like the dead had terrified me, and I trembled as I embraced her. Thankfully, Belle steadied us both. Without her arm around my waist, I might have fallen over again.

Neva allowed herself to be held for a moment, but soon grew uncomfortable. She squirmed away from me, a furrow forming in her brow. "What's wrong? Why are you looking at me like that?" As I drew back, she caught sight of my injured hand. "What happened to your palm? It's all blistered."

I stared down at my hand in surprise. It still seared and ached, but I wasn't expecting the raw mess I found. My vision began to blur again at the awful sight, and Belle helped me lie down on Neva's pallet. "Stay there and don't move," she ordered. "I'm going for help."

As it turned out, she didn't have to. The dwellyn were already crowded at the entrance to the cave, and Lok and Ulig hurried inside. "There's magic here," Lok said as soon as she reached us. "I can sense it. What happened?"

I pointed at the comb with my good hand. It had skidded a short distance across the cave floor, but I could feel where it had gone. Lok's tiny, beetle-black eyes flashed when she saw it, and a serious expression crossed her face. "Whoever enchanted that is a powerful *Ariada*. How did it get here?"

"Mogra," I told her, absolutely certain. Surely there couldn't be two evil, cape-wearing witches hunting us through the forest. "Jessith saw an old woman hovering over Neva while she slept. When we came in, she was barely breathing."

Lok's expression grew terrified, and Neva hastened to reassure her before she could be pulled into another concerned hug. "I'm all right, but I don't remember anything about a woman."

"She didn't respond when I shook her, but then I noticed the comb in her hair," I continued. "I tried to pull it out."

Lok clicked her tongue. "You should have found one of us right away." She turned to the other dwellyn, rattling something off in her own language. Three of them headed back for the mouth of the cave, drawing their weapons and heading out into the forest. "My people will look for Mogra, but why don't you show me that comb? Dwellyn know how to deal with enchanted objects."

"How?" Belle asked. "Your people don't have *Ariada*."

"That doesn't mean we don't know how magic works. Many named weapons carry magic. Dwellyn have worked with human enchanters for centuries." Lok headed over to the place where the comb had fallen and held out her hand to Ulig, muttering something else I couldn't understand.

Ulig nodded his blocky head and reached behind his back, withdrawing his sword from its scabbard. He passed it to Lok, who dropped to her knees and raised the blade above her head. When it came crashing down, I felt a heavy jolt rush through the air. The singed smell of magic burned in my nose again, and then suddenly, the faint hum was gone. I gasped and tried to sit up for a better look.

"Don't," Belle said, placing a hand on my chest. She urged me to lie back down, and I obeyed grudgingly. "Lok, we need some kind of healer. Ellie almost passed out, and she hurt her hand when she tried to touch the comb."

Lok nodded, turning back toward the cave. "Gurn?"

One of the other dwellyn scuttled forward. He knelt beside the cot as well, pushing back his hood to look at me. When he saw my hand, the fuzzy wrinkles around his eyes grew deeper. He said something I assumed was sympathetic as he reached into the deep pockets of his robes and started rummaging around.

"Can you help her?" Belle asked, watching him.

"Gurn help," Ulig said. "Sun-hair fine."

The words did little to reassure her, and she continued hovering over me while Gurn dressed and bandaged my hand. Jessith offered comfort by curling up on my legs, and Neva sat by my shoulder, as silent and worried as I had ever seen her. "Are you all right?" I asked. "The comb didn't hurt you, did it?"

Neva shook her head. "I don't feel any different." She fell silent for a long moment, and her lips trembled. "You got hurt because she's trying to capture me again. This is my fault."

"Of course it isn't," I insisted. "Mogra was the one who did this."

"No, not Mogra," Neva whispered. "My stepmother. She's the one who wants me dead."

Belle circled around to my other side and placed a reassuring hand on Neva's shoulder. "That still doesn't make any of this your fault. If your stepmother ordered Mogra to do this, then she's the one who hurt Ellie. Do you understand?"

Neva nodded, but she still didn't look convinced. "Maybe if I wasn't *Kira'baas*, she wouldn't need me so much. She might have just let me run away without chasing me."

Although I knew little of the Queen's motivations, it sounded plausible. I had only witnessed Neva's powers for myself once, but I had to admit that they were remarkable. Surely if it had been a simple matter of taking the white throne, the Queen wouldn't have troubled to send Mogra after us. She wanted something else with Neva, something we did not yet understand.

"Neva," I said, not wanting to ask, but knowing I had to. I had tried not to pry into her past, sensing it carried a great deal of pain, but with Mogra's involvement, the situation had grown more urgent. "What do you think the Queen wants with you? Why is she trying so hard to find you?"

Neva's eyes fell into her lap. "I don't know. I'm not even fully trained yet. I can tell small groups of undead what to do if I concentrate hard, but she has a whole army. She doesn't need me to control them."

"Well, hopefully we won't find out," I said. Gurn had finished bandaging my hand, and I looked down at his handiwork. It didn't hurt nearly as much. "Thank you," I told him, and he seemed to understand.

"You should be thanking me, too," Jessith said from my lap. "I was the one who rescued Neva, after all."

I rolled my eyes, but I had to admit she was right. "Thank you, Jessith," I said, reaching down to scratch beneath her chin with my good hand. "You saved Neva's life."

That brought a smile to Neva's face. She crawled forward and pulled Jessith into her lap, cradling her like a baby. It was a position Jessith usually wouldn't have allowed anyone but me to hold her in, but this time, she looked almost pleased with herself as Neva kissed her head. "Good kitty."

"It's true," she purred, eyes narrowing to slits. "I am a very good cat."

Chapter Three

Taken from the letters of Cathelin Raybrook, edited by Lady Eleanor Kingsclere

PALE FINGERTIPS STROKE THE flickering surface of the mirror, stirring the swirling mist within. It gathers like storm clouds, growing larger and darker. Through the fog, a pale reflection shines, the Queen, her golden crown on her head, ruby lips pulled into a chilling smile.

"Mirror, mirror, on the wall,
Who in this land is fairest of all?"

The mirror pulses and the hum of magic grows louder.

"You, my queen, are fair; it's true.
But the princess beyond the plains
Is still a thousand times fairer than you."

The Queen's smile vanishes. Her long fingers clench, bleaching the spikes of her knuckles as her blood-red nails dig into her palm. A shriek of rage fills the dark hall, and she slams her fist against the glass. "What? Show me!"

Light flashes, and the mist solidifies. The thin, dark-haired girl takes shape, but this time, she is fast asleep. Her face is peaceful, and a blanket is tucked under her shoulder. A shadow swishes above her. The ragged edge of a cape flutters. A gnarled hand reaches out, threading the sharp teeth of a comb through her hair.

Slitted yellow eyes pierce the darkness, and the yowl of an angry cat makes the hand falter. The shadow vanishes, and voices float through the mirror from far away. "Neva? Neva! Oh Saints, she isn't breathing! What happened?"

The voice cuts off, and the image vanishes. Only the Queen's reflection remains, pulled stiff with a cold sort of rage. "So, the princess has a pet?" she says, caressing the mirror's gleaming frame. "Well, so do I. And if the witch can't take care of her, my other pet will."

The mirror flares again, and someone else appears from within the dark clouds: a familiar face of peeling flesh, sweet rot, and stitched-shut eyes.

I jerked back to reality, gasping for breath and blinking to banish Luciana's image from my mind. Whether my eyes were open or shut, her face still lingered behind them, flickering between dead and alive. "Ellie," I muttered, sucking in air through my teeth. My lungs ached even though I was breathing at double speed. "The Queen is sending Luciana after—"

"Cate, are you all right?"

I suddenly realized I was not alone. I had fallen to the ground right outside my tent, and Raisa was crouched beside me, her brow knitted. The worry on her face helped reestablish my connection with my body. My leg started to ache beneath me, and I suspected I would carry several bruises. Gingerly, I pushed myself up into a sitting position, brushing away dust and dead leaves. "It's not myself I'm worried about," I said while Raisa stared. "I had another vision. Where is Ailynn?"

Raisa's eyes widened. "Ailynn? I thought you'd want Larna. That fall looked painful."

I hesitated. I did want my mate's comfort, but the visions had become more bearable over the past several weeks. They were trying to impart a message, and it was my duty to deliver it.

"No, Ailynn," I insisted, still fighting the shivers coursing through my body. "I know where her mother is."

Raisa rose at once, although she stroked my arm as she stood. "I'll be right back. Try not to move until I bring help. Do you promise?"

"I'm fine," I lied, sitting up straighter. "The fall didn't hurt."

"All right." Raisa was far from convinced, but she went to fetch Ailynn as I had asked. I watched her go, breathing deep to regain some of my strength and stop my trembling. My leg still throbbed with pain, and the vision had left me dizzy, but a few bruises were the least of my problems. My Sight hadn't been this physically demanding in a long time. Since studying with Kalwyn, my visions rarely carried me away from my body without my consent, especially in the middle of the day while in a public place. Their frequency and intensity was disturbing, and some part of me knew they wouldn't stop until the mirror was gone.

"Cate, what happened?" Sooner than I expected, Ailynn came rushing out of a nearby tent, looking just as alarmed as Raisa. She hurried to my side, leaning in nervously. "Raisa told me you fell. Was it another vision?"

I gave a reluctant nod. Although I didn't want to cause Ailynn any unnecessary distress, she needed to know what I had seen. "Yes. I know where your mother is."

Ailynn hesitated. Her worry turned to anger, and her eyes narrowed. "Where is she? What was she doing?"

"Chasing Princess Neva, under the Queen's orders. She's enchanting more magical objects as well. I think she tried to kill the princess with a comb."

"She didn't succeed, though," Ailynn said, willing me to give her the answer she wanted to hear.

"No. She was interrupted. I heard a cat hissing, and Ellie's voice." I shook my head, sorting through my memory for the truly important details. "They were in darkness, some distance away. A cave, perhaps?"

"Caves and beautiful enchanted objects," Ailynn muttered, rolling her eyes. "That certainly sounds like my mother. Do you know where I can find her?"

"I don't think you need to. The Queen has sent her and Luciana to kill Neva. If Ellie and Belle bring the princess to the rebel camp, both of them will come to us."

Ailynn's frown deepened. I could see she wasn't pleased with waiting, although she didn't say so. "Let's hope you're right. I'd rather face her on her own in the Forest than at Kalmarin with an army at her back."

I began picking myself up off the ground, and both Ailynn and Raisa extended a hand to help me. "Thank you," I said, accepting their help. "Please, don't tell Larna about this. My visions haven't been this persistent since I watched her die over and over again. They'll only get worse, and I don't want to worry her any more than necessary. She has a pack to lead and a battle to fight."

"We won't say anything," Raisa promised. "Right, Ailynn?"

Ailynn looked as though she wanted to object, but a look from her lover had her nodding. "You still look pale. At least let us get you something to eat."

"Would you do me a favor and bring it to my tent? I need to rest for a minute." In reality, I was itching to open my journal. Although I didn't think Ellie, Belle, or Princess Neva had been harmed, I wanted to make sure.

Raisa began to agree, but Ailynn objected. "I'll do it. I don't want you handling raw meat."

"I'm not made of glass, Ailynn," Raisa protested. "I've been helping some of the other civilians prepare food almost every day. Next, you'll be taking the cooking knives away from me."

As they continued to bicker, I slipped away on quiet feet, retiring to my tent before they could notice. It was simple, but spacious enough for two, with room for two bedrolls and our packs. Once I was alone, I sighed and sank down beside my pack. Ailynn and Raisa had become good friends, but they couldn't truly understand what I had seen. No one but an oracle or another shaman could.

I suddenly found myself missing Kalwyn with bitter fierceness. Even though I had only trained with her for a few months before her death, she had been my mentor. She had taught me my history, put me in touch with my powers, and shown me how to control the most frightening of my visions. At least, I thought she had. These new visions were some of the most detailed—and the most horrible—I had ever suffered through. On impulse, I reached beneath my shirt, folding my fingers around the deadeye.

"I wish you were here," I whispered to the empty tent, staring sadly at my pack. "You would know how to help me."

To my surprise, the pack tipped over, falling against my thigh. I opened it, and I wasn't sure whether to feel sad or wistful when I saw the gleaming hourglass on top of my supplies. Perhaps it was my imagination, but the golden dragons twined around its body almost seemed to glow as well. I picked it up, twisting it in my hands and letting the subtle heat of old magic blossom against my palms. It felt much like the deadeye, and I felt an answering hum against my chest.

It took me several moments to realize what about the hourglass had captured my attention. The sand inside moved, draining into the lower half. I blinked, shaking myself to make sure I hadn't been imagining things. The sand continued to slide, just a trickle, but enough to clear my doubts. Every single time I had looked before, the sand had stayed frozen, remaining stationary even when I turned the hourglass over. I flipped it upside down, but the sand didn't fall back to the bottom. It kept climbing the wrong way, flying into the top.

It seemed impossible, but there could be no mistake. If Kalwyn's magic hourglass had begun to move again, and the deadeye had responded to it, that meant the dragons had awoken from their centuries-long slumber. No one had seen them in recent memory, and even written accounts of the beasts were scarce. They were legends now, passed down through stories and songs, and most people believed them to be extinct. I had doubted their existence myself until Kalwyn taught me otherwise. But after all I had witnessed since coming to Amendyr, the return of the dragons didn't seem fantastical. In fact, the timing seemed strangely appropriate, and even exciting. My mother had told me stories of dragons before I had gone to live in Seria, and the thought of such giant beasts made of pure magic had always amazed me.

"Cate? I brought you something to eat." I looked up with a start, tucking the hourglass back into the open bag. Raisa stood at the entrance to my tent, but instead of looking worried, she seemed almost curious. "What was that?" she asked, staring at my pack.

I hesitated. There was no reason to conceal the hourglass's existence, but for some reason, the thought of sharing it made me nervous. After a few moments' thought, I withdrew it and held it up for her to see. Raisa gasped, setting aside the bundle she had brought and dropping to her knees for a closer look. "It was a gift from my teacher," I explained as she studied the hourglass. "She told me it's supposed to mark the time of the dragons' return to Amendyr. Before she gave it to me, the sand inside never moved, no matter which way you turned it."

"Well, it's moving now," Raisa said. "When did it start?"

"Just now. Here, watch." I turned the hourglass upside down, but the sand continued flying the same way, filling the upturned bottom chamber.

Raisa scooted closer. "But the dragons have been gone for centuries. Most people think they're extinct. Why now?"

I shrugged and set the hourglass down between us. "I wish I knew."

A thoughtful look came over Raisa's face. "You know, dragons have shaped Amendyr's history and legends from the beginning. Perhaps this is a little insane, but what if—"

She never got a chance to finish. Moments later, Larna and Ailynn both burst into the tent, one looking worried and the other guilty. "Cate," Larna said, hurrying to kneel by my side and folding an arm around my shoulder. I relaxed at the comforting weight, but felt guilty Ailynn had fetched her. "Be you all right? Ailynn was telling me—"

"I specifically told her not to tell you," I said, aiming a sour look in Ailynn's direction. Ailynn bit her lip, while Larna started to protest. I silenced her with a finger to her lips. "You watch me endure enough. You don't have to know every detail."

Larna didn't argue, but she didn't look happy, either. She kept her arm around me, pulling me against her chest for comfort. Once she stopped fussing over me, straightening the front of my shirt and checking my visible skin for bruises, her eyes fell on the hourglass.

Ailynn noticed where she was looking, and her eyes narrowed. "What is that?" she asked, almost suspicious. "It's enchanted. I can feel it from here. Where did you get it?"

"Not from Mogra," I assured her. "My old mentor gave this to me. It's supposed to mark the time of the dragons' return to Amendyr."

"Do you believe that's what it does?" Ailynn knelt with the rest of us, studying the hourglass closely without touching it.

"I do." Raisa's enthusiasm had returned, and her face almost glowed. "In fact, I just had an idea I wanted to run by the three of you. Who was the last dragon to appear in the old Amendyrri legends?"

I frowned. "Feradith and her hatchling, but—"

"Exactly," Raisa continued. "And who was her greatest enemy?"

"Umbra and the High Ariada," Ailynn said. "I told you that story when you were just a girl."

"So, doesn't it make sense that if some shadow of Umbra has awakened and possessed the Queen, Mogra, and Luciana, the dragons might awaken as well? Perhaps they can sense Umbra's presence in them."

Her theory made a startling amount of sense. "But why would they awaken now?" I asked, even as I became more and more convinced. "Umbra possessed Luciana years ago through the sorcerer's chain."

Raisa wasn't discouraged. "I imagine waking from a centuries-long sleep doesn't happen overnight. Or perhaps his presence simply wasn't strong enough to alert them until now. But if the dragons have awakened because of Umbra's return, they might be our allies."

"You're crazy," Ailynn said, shaking her head. "You want us to ally with dragons? If we could even find them, how would we manage to ask them for help before they ate us? You're conveniently forgetting what Feradith did to the rest of the High Ariada after Umbra's death."

Raisa only smiled. "Actually, I had some thoughts about that, too."

Chapter Four

Taken from the verbal accounts of Ailynn Gothel, edited by Lady Eleanor Kingsclere

THE BLAST OF WIND took me by surprise, buffeting my legs and threatening to steal my footing. I skidded backwards, struggling for balance as I scrambled to summon a cushion of air. *"Secutem!"* The Word of Power worked, but barely. Doran's next attack didn't send me sprawling, and I searched for cover before he could strike again.

There were few options. The open plains south of the forest had no trees, and even rocks were scarce. When a bright ball of fire flew too close to my cheek for comfort, I had no choice but to make my own. I braced myself, reaching through my feet to the earth beneath and calling it up. *"Erets!"* A wall of rock jutted up from the ground, protecting my face from the next flurry of flames.

"You can't just defend yourself forever," Doran called out as I ducked behind my makeshift shield. "Mogra won't give you time to figure out an attack."

I knew he was right, and hearing my mother's name sent a flare of anger through me. I summoned another gust of air, vaulting myself over the ridge of rock and calling to the heat that always lived in my hands. I had no need for Words of Power now. Fire was my element, and I could call it with nothing but my mind.

The attack was fast enough to put Doran on the defensive. He summoned his own shield, but he wasn't quite fast enough. A few of the sparks singed the edge of his wild white hair, and he smiled. "Better," he said, returning fire with a volley of earth. The plume of dust stung my eyes, and I couldn't see well enough to aim.

"That's cheating," I said, blowing aside the dirt with a swipe of my hand. Threads of fire wove through the wind I called, but I didn't suppress them. Calling the other elements was always easier when I added my favorite.

More earth showered on top of me, and I had to summon another shield to protect my head. I didn't need to shout the word, but the barrier was weaker. It soon shattered under the larger rocks, and I was forced to return to cover.

Doran chuckled. "And you think Mogra won't cheat?"

"Stop bringing her up," I begged, panting. Fire lashed out from my arms, whipping toward Doran through the wind that blustered between us. "I don't want to talk about her."

"You don't have a choice," Doran said. Unlike me, he wasn't even out of breath. However, I was gratified to see that his barriers of earth crumbled beneath the heat of my flames. "She's had decades to master the elements, as well as forbidden magic she should never have touched. You need to be prepared."

I lost my temper. The earth beneath my feet began to quake, and I reached deep within, calling up all the heat I could. The rock bubbled and cracked, melting under the force of my will. A sea of glowing, red-gold earth and fire flowed toward Doran, sweeping up into a giant wave.

"Ailynn!"

His cry startled me, and I pulled the wave back before it could crash. I didn't know whether the blow would have hit or not, but when Doran circled the molten puddle to rejoin me, he smiled. "Much better, *Acha*," he said, giving me a nod. "You're still too reliant on your Words of Power, but you're faster and more consistent than I've ever seen you."

Despite my annoyance, I was flattered. "That's your doing, not mine."

"Be that as it may, you might stand a chance against Mogra now."

"I would stand a better chance if you helped me," I suggested hopefully. "I still think we should fight her together."

Doran shook his head, although he seemed regretful. "No, Ailynn. I am much older and weaker than you know. Too old to fight against someone of her power, and too weak to kill her even if I won."

I understood what he meant. While my guilt drove me to stop Mogra, the thought of killing her was still painful to contemplate. Doran had been her lover once. Surely he felt the same. "You're not that old," I mumbled, trying to ignore the familiar burn of guilt in the pit of my stomach. "Actually, you've never told me your age."

"My real age and the age of my body are two separate things," Doran explained. "One of the magical adventures in my youth stole more years from me than I like to admit."

I sensed there was more to the tale, but also that Doran did not want to explain it. I couldn't help but wonder if that was what had ended his relationship with my mother. It might have been his mysterious magical accident, but it could have just as easily been some toxic part of Mogra's personality. Although she had possessed some good qualities before her corruption, she had never been an easy person to deal with, and she was kind only when she felt like it.

"You don't have to explain," I said as the two of us headed back toward camp. Afternoon was fading into evening, but there was still plenty of light for us to find our way. "And you're right. Killing her is my job. I'm the one who let her slip into madness. I'm the one who should put her out of her misery."

A frown tugged at Doran's weathered face, and when he fixed his gaze on me, I noticed sadness in his eyes. "You don't have to kill anyone, *Acha,*" he said, squeezing my arm with one of his gnarled hands. "I didn't train you because I think killing Mogra is your sole purpose, or the only way to atone for your perceived sins. I trained you because Mogra will come after you whether we like it or not, and I want you to be prepared."

"But the offensive attacks," I protested. "You were telling me I shouldn't just defend myself."

Doran gave me a small smile. "Defeating your enemy is part of defending yourself. That doesn't mean I want you to seek your enemies out, whether it's Mogra or anyone else. Fight when you need to, but don't throw your life away to save your soul."

I was saved from searching for a response by the arrival of another figure near the edge of camp. His height and the broad shape of his shoulders gave him away from a fair distance, and I smiled "Don't let Jethro hear you say that. I promised him I would help hunt Mogra down to avenge the death of his wife."

Doran sighed. "Then you're both idiots," he mumbled, tottering off and disappearing between a pair of tents before I could stop him. There was no time to follow even if I wanted to. Jethro approached me, swinging his enormous axe up to rest on his shoulder.

"How do you even lift that?" I asked, peering up at him in amazement. Looking at Jethro always put a crick in my neck.

"Easily," he joked. "I've been looking for you, Ailynn. Cate has someone she wants to introduce you to."

It took me a moment to put the pieces together, but when I did, I began beaming. "Did Ellie, Belladonna, and the princess finally arrive?"

"Aye, with seven dwellyn in their party and a pair of fine horses. Cate was weeping all over a short blonde woman before she sent me to fetch you. They're just past the Farseer cookfires if you want to join them."

I nodded my thanks and hurried away, passing several other people headed in the same direction. Apparently, news of the princess' arrival had spread throughout the camp. A sizable crowd stood around Jett Bahari's tent, whispering excitedly amongst each other, but I wove my way through and passed to the other side without stopping. Surely Cate and Ellie wouldn't want to have their reunion in front of curious onlookers.

It didn't take me long to spot them. A smaller group was gathered around the Farseer fire pit, just where Jethro had said. As I drew closer, I noticed Cate holding a short, blonde woman's hands. The stranger—surely Ellie, judging by Cate's numerous descriptions—had bright green eyes, and her cheeks dimpled as she smiled. Despite the generous scattering of freckles across her face, she didn't look Amendyrri. She was Serian, although I could tell she was *Ariada* before I even reached her side.

Next to her stood a tall woman in traveling clothes. While Ellie was charming enough to look at, Belladonna was uncomfortably beautiful. Her face was almost too perfect, and her black hair gleamed like a raven's wing. Her pale skin added to the illusion of a carefully carved statue instead of a human being. I was intimidated before I even spoke to her.

Before I could figure out how to introduce myself, Cate noticed me standing awkwardly on the sidelines. "Ailynn, come here," she said in Serian, motioning me over. "Ellie and Belle just arrived a few minutes ago. I sent Jethro to bring Larna, but it seems he found you first."

I shuffled forward when summoned, forcing a smile. Although I did want to meet them, I wasn't much for social niceties. Living alone in a forest with only my mother and Raisa for company hadn't given me many opportunities to practice. "Hello," I said, sticking my hand out for an awkward handshake. "I'm Ailynn."

"Oh good, you speak Serian," Ellie said, squeezing my hand in a surprisingly strong grip. "That saves Cate the trouble of translating. I'm trying to learn some Amendyrri, but I don't have much more than the basics down yet. I'm Ellie, by the way. It's a pleasure to meet you."

"I grew up in the Forest, right on the border," I explained. "I've been fluent in both languages since I was a child. I could help you learn, if you like."

"That would be very kind," Belladonna said. She took my hand when Ellie let go, and though her shake was also strong, it wasn't overly enthusiastic. "So, you're the one I lent my copy of *Elementary Magicks* to. Did you find it useful?"

A blush heated the points of my cheeks. Although Belle had lent the book to me to help free Raisa from her prison, I hadn't been able to return it. For all I knew, it was still lost somewhere in the middle of the Forest. "I'm so sorry about that," I said, pulling back a little in dismay. "There were...extenuating circumstances."

"So we were told," Belladonna said. "But there's no harm done. I was able to secure another copy for the library, although God knows what state I'll find it in when we get home."

"It was exactly what I needed. Without it, I never would have been able to break the enchantment keeping my *Tuathe* imprisoned."

Belladonna smiled. "Then I'm glad it was sacrificed to a noble cause."

While I groped for some other way to express how grateful I was to a woman I had never met before, another familiar figure approached. Larna joined us, grinning as she slung an affectionate arm over Cate's shoulder. "Here they be," she said in Amendyrri, "and early, too."

"Oh! Ellie, Belle, this is Larna."

Larna moved to greet the newcomers, but before she could, an unhappy yowl came from inside Ellie's knapsack. I stared in surprise as a small, furry head peeked out through the top, led by a twitching pink nose and a set of long whiskers. "Is that a cat?" I blurted out. "Oh my goodness, don't show Raisa, or she won't leave it alone. She still misses hers."

Ellie sighed and took the cat out of the knapsack, setting her down on the ground. Instantly, it wove between her legs and adopted an arched position in front of Larna, hissing and baring its teeth. "Don't be like that, Jessith," Ellie said, speaking to the cat just as she would have to another human. "You know Cate, and Larna isn't going to hurt you."

"What did she say?" Cate asked as Larna took a hesitant step back. She eyed the cat with suspicion, and Jessith growled.

"Something impolite that I shan't repeat," Ellie said. She nudged Jessith with her foot, and the cat took that as a signal to leave. She darted off toward Jett Bahari's tent, fur bristling as she streaked away. "I'm sorry about her. She isn't fond of dogs. Or wyr, I suppose, or the way they smell."

"Aren't you worried, letting her go off on her own?" I asked.

Ellie shook her head. "Jessith can fend for herself. I think she went looking for Neva and the dwellyn. She's taken a liking to them."

"Neva," I repeated. "The princess. So, you did bring her here?"

Belladonna nodded. "It took some doing, but we managed. And we had plenty of help." She turned to Larna and extended her hand. "Let's have a proper introduction, without interruptions this time."

I hung back as Larna introduced herself in halting Serian. It was only a little better than Ellie's limited Amendyrri, but with Cate helping them, they almost managed to have a proper conversation with a mixture of both languages. As the four of them talked, I once again felt like an outsider. I hadn't had many opportunities to make friends in my life, and Cate was one of the only ones I had. Her bond with Ellie and even Belle was obviously strong, and I wasn't sure where I fit in.

"Ailynn?" To my surprise, Belle was looking at me, her forehead wrinkled with concern. "Are you all right?"

I was surprised she had noticed my silence. "To be honest, I feel like I'm intruding on a moment that isn't mine. Cate and Ellie look so happy to see each other, and it doesn't help that I'm not much for conversation."

Belle gave me a reassuring smile. "I understand. I'm a noble back in Seria. You wouldn't believe how many conversations have rushed by without me while I floundered to catch up. Fortunately, standing still, looking attentive, and nodding can get you far at court. Everyone thinks you're just agreeing with them."

"Really?" I asked, unable to hide my skepticism. "You, floundering in a conversation?" Belle sighed, and I realized how my comment had probably come off. "I mean, you're just so..."

The look on Belle's face told me she was finishing my sentence in her head. "Looks don't always accompany a charming personality." Her eyes slid to the side, where Ellie, Cate, and Larna were still chattering away. "I'm lucky Ellie tolerates me."

I laughed. "I know exactly what you mean. Perhaps the two of us can be awkward together sometime."

"I think I would like that," Belle said. Then, to my relief, she drew us both back into the conversation. "Cate, Ellie tells me you saved Ailynn's life the night you met."

Instead of blushing or deflecting, Cate gave a proud nod of her head. "Actually, I did. She fainted as soon as she saw me, though, so she might not remember much."

"I do remember," I insisted, feeling much more lighthearted now that I had been included. "I remember a giant red beast with huge teeth tearing through a pack of undead monsters right before they chopped me in half. Then I fainted."

Ellie's face blanched, and Cate hastened to reassure her. "The shift isn't always frightening, Ellie. I promise. Do you want to see?"

"That wasn't the part of the story that frightened me," Ellie muttered, but Belle's enthusiasm overshadowed her.

"Really? Oh, please! I'd love to see. So, it's true that you can change even without the full moon?"

Larna nodded. "Aye. We change whenever we wish. Our half-shape is just stronger then, and sometimes we are being called to mating runs."

Ellie frowned in confusion, and a blush spread across Cate's cheeks. "I'm not translating that," she muttered in Amendyrri, then switched back to Serian. "Come with me. I'll need to take off my clothes so I don't ruin them, and I'd rather not be naked out in the open."

As Cate led us away, explaining the difference between her wolf form and her half-shape, I followed along behind, content to listen instead of feeling as though I had to. Perhaps there was room in my life for friends other than Cate and Larna. Ellie and Belle might be an excellent place to start.

Chapter Five

Taken from the diary of Lady Eleanor Kingsclere

THE DAYS PASSED QUICKLY once we arrived at the rebel camp. There was always plenty of work to be done and plenty of company as well. I scarcely had a moment to myself, but instead of exhausting me, the constant activity bolstered my spirits. It had been easy to slip into a fearful depression while wandering the dark, claustrophobic paths of the Forest, and the wide-open plains gave me hope.

Although Belle, Cate, and the others were excellent company, it was Neva who had the biggest impact on my mood. The two of us spent a great deal of time together, and she took an interest in almost everything I did. At first, her watchful eyes and silent feet were a little unsettling, but gradually, I grew used to having her as my shadow. She didn't speak often, but when she did, her soft questions usually led to interesting conversations—almost like Belle when we first met.

"What are you doing?" she asked one day as I sat on an abandoned log at the edge of camp, my journal open on my knee. The afternoon was grey and overcast, but after spending my morning hard at work, I had decided to take a moment for myself to write. Even in the privacy of my tent, the interior of the camp had been too noisy and crowded for me, and I appreciated the distant purple silhouette of the Rengast Mountains during my pauses.

"Journaling," I said, raising my eyes from the page. Although Cate and I had been reunited, it was hard to break the habit of writing whenever I could. Instead of informing her of my activities, I recorded them for myself, hoping I would be able to look back on them fondly later. Perhaps in the future, I would view my journey through Amendyr as a grand, exciting adventure instead of the dangerous reality it was.

"What are you writing?"

I finished my last sentence, closed the journal, and faced Neva. She stood behind me, hands folded behind her back, rocking on the balls of her feet. Her eyes were large and curious, and I decided I didn't mind the interruption. "I'm writing about everything that's happened to us. We've seen and done so much, and I want to remember it all later."

Neva frowned. "You want to remember all of it? Even the scary parts?"

"Even the scary parts. They aren't all bad. Being chased by the kerak at Baxstresse was terrifying, but I do like remembering the way you saved me."

A little of Neva's confidence returned. "There are things I wish I didn't remember. Things that happened before I met the dwellyn and Cieran and you. After my mother died, and she came to live with us." She lowered her eyes, but I could see the struggle on her face.

I felt a wave of empathy for her. "That must have been difficult," I said softly. "I lost my mother, too. She was a gardener, and I brought some of her plants with me when I came to Baxstresse, to help me remember her."

"I don't have anything left of my mother's," Neva said. "She had some things she brought with her from Shezad, dresses and jewelry and some musical instruments, but they're all at the palace."

"Do you want to know another reason I write everything down?" Neva peeked up at me through the curtain of her hair and nodded. "Because then the bad memories have another place to go besides my head, and the good ones I've written are there to fill it up again. It helps me remember important things and important people."

"And it helps?"

"More often than not." I opened my journal again, turning to an empty page. "Here, why don't you try for yourself? I can give you some paper to write on and one of my spare quills." With a quick rip I tore out several blank sheets and folded them in half, holding them out for her.

Neva took them as if she had been given the most precious gift in the world. When she looked back up at me, the hope in her eyes made my heart clench. "You didn't have to tear your journal for me. I know it's important."

I gave her hand a soft squeeze. "So are you."

That night, when I found another free moment to finish writing, something else was waiting for me instead. Careful, blocky words had appeared on the page after my last entry, and they weren't in Cate's handwriting:

Today, Ellie showed me how to write down what I remember. She says it might help stop the nightmares. I hope she's right.

I remember my mother. I remember the dresses she had in bright colors and her big smile. She used to sit with me, and sometimes she would play her jali and sing. I tried, but my fingers wouldn't fit on the strings, and the gourd was too big for my knee. She had to sit behind me and help me hold it. I still miss her.

I remember when the Huntsman took me away from the palace. We rode far away. One night, when it was dark, he left me alone. He said he had to. I know she told him to kill me. He never told me why he didn't. It means he's probably dead now. I never knew his name.

I remember when the dwellyn found me. I was so hungry it felt like knives in my belly. There were dead things in the forest, but I was too tired to put them back to sleep. I ran until my legs stopped working. That's when I saw them. They killed the dead things then they took me underground and gave me food. I slept for a week.

I remember when I found out Papan died. Lok and Ulig and the others came into my room. When they told me, I didn't cry. Then I started sobbing without tears because I thought maybe I forgot how. Ulig gave me a hug. He gives good hugs. He told me I wasn't alone.

I remember when I met Cieran. I didn't want to go. I remembered how to cry then. But Lok said I needed to be with humans. She said a girl can't spend her whole life underground, and I needed to learn how to control my powers. She said Cieran could help me. She promised I would be safe with him. He told me I was a Daughter of the Sixth Son. It was the same thing Papan used to tell me, so I went with him.

I remember when I had to leave again. The kerak and the shadowkin came to the palace. She didn't make them, but they were hers. I told Cieran I wanted to help them sleep, but he wouldn't let me. He said I had to go before it was too late. He gave me a letter and put me in a carriage. I saw why on the way out. There were hollow bodies on the grounds outside. They were clawed to pieces. The dead were eating them. I tell myself Cieran didn't get eaten. He didn't become one of them.

I remember when I met Ellie and Belle and Jessith. It was raining. The sky was close to the ground. Ellie caught me when I came out of the carriage. She took me inside. When she touched me, I knew she was like me. She could talk to the horses and the cats. I gave her the letter, and she got scared. Just like me. Belle whispered to her, and I knew something else. I knew someone wanted to hurt her, like She wanted to hurt me.

I shut the journal and closed my eyes. I hadn't realized just how many people Neva had lost—her parents, the dwellyn, Cieran, and Cassandra. Her grief reminded me of what I had felt after my mother died. For a moment, I pictured the hazel sapling I had planted at Baxstresse. I had been alone, frightened, and friendless then, before Belle became my lover and Cate became my friend. I didn't want the same for Neva.

When I opened my eyes again, I was determined. I had rebuilt a new family after the death of my old one, and it was my everything. Perhaps I had been brought into Neva's life for a reason. Maybe I was meant to show her that she could make a new family, the way I had.

***

The sound of terrified screams shattered my sleep. Within moments, I was wide-eyed and upright, heart hammering against my ribs. I reached off to the side, but Belle wasn't lying next to me, and Neva's cot was empty. They had disappeared without disturbing me. I groped in the dark, searching for a candle. Bright flashes of light streaked past the tent, and I heard running footsteps beneath the shouting. I threw a blanket around my shoulders and hurried outside.

The entire camp was in chaos. Torches blazed everywhere, and the smell of smoke burned in my nose and mouth. I tried to catch a glimpse of Belle or Neva, but I didn't see them among the figures rushing by. Most of them raced for the fire pits, and I followed them, hoping I had chosen the right direction.

As I was jostled along, I realized several of the warriors around me weren't human. I had seen liarre wandering the camp from a distance, but by torchlight, they were terrifying. They towered above me, three times as large as I was, fur bristling and weapons drawn. I tripped backwards in fear when a huge spider scurried past me on legs as high as my chest.

Unearthly, high-pitched shrieks pierced through the rest of the din, and my blood turned to ice. I knew that noise. It was the same call I had heard at Baxstresse the night of our escape. Mogra's undead forces were here.

Luciana. I wasn't sure if she had followed us, or if this was a different army, but I couldn't take the chance. I had to find Belle and Neva. I regained my balance and ran for the fire, calling out their names. It didn't do any good. My voice wouldn't carry over the horrible screeching.

Suddenly, the sound was right behind me. It sent sharp spikes of pain stabbing through my head, and I whipped around. The endless, gaping pit of a kerak's mouth was inches away from mine, filled with rows of dripping teeth. Flecks of spit and the smell of death hit my face, but my body refused to move. The kerak raised its hooked hands.

Before the kerak's scythes came slicing down, a red blur darted between me and the blow. A giant creature stood before me, tall and brimming with muscle. It snatched the kerak's knotted arms, yanking them apart with a sickening rip. The kerak howled. Black blood burst from the stumps, and its sucking mouth contorted with agony, letting out a shrill wail as it dissolved into dust.

It was over before I could even scream. I was breathless. Shouts and bobbing torches still surrounded us, but I couldn't tear my eyes away from my terrifying savior. Its face was mostly wolf, but it held itself on two legs. "Cate?" I searched the creature's long, pointed face, and as soon as I looked into its soft eyes, I knew I was right. This was Cate's half-shape, and she had saved my life.

Cate only held my gaze for a moment. Shadows converged around us, and she hunched over with a low, rumbling growl, readying for another fight. What happened next could only be described as a massacre. She moved faster than I had imagined possible, leaping at a second kerak before it could charge her. One snap of her powerful jaws, and its head jerked at an awkward angle. She shoved it toward the fire pit, and it thrashed in agony as the flames ate through its peeling, slick-grey flesh.

While she was turned, a third kerak leapt for her vulnerable back. I yelled and tried to rush forward, but there was no need. Cate whirled around, and her sharp claws stabbed through the kerak's stomach. It stopped when her hand was halfway buried in its abdomen, twitching in death, teeth still snapping. She withdrew with a rough pull, tugging out a mess of steaming entrails. It slumped to the ground with a wet squelch, and she kicked it into the fire with the others.

"Ellie," she said in a low, rasping growl, hardly even a human voice. "Where is—"

Darkness stretched over us, blotting out the light of the fire. I stared up, but there was no sky—just a pair of hot-coal eyes set amidst the darkness and dripping jaws four times larger than Cate's. The ground beneath me shook at the shadowkin's roar, but I couldn't move. Surely even Cate couldn't kill something this massive alone. Both of us were going to die.

"Cate!"

A hulking black shape hurtled between the pillars of the shadowkin's legs, flying faster than an arrow. It was another wyr, larger than any I'd seen. As I stared in awe, it launched itself at the shadowkin's underbelly, tearing with flashes of white teeth. Something sailed over my head, and I glanced up just in time to see Cate leaping for the shadowkin's throat. She latched on and didn't let go, even when it thrashed its enormous head from side to side.

Working together, they managed to bring the shadowkin down. The earth quaked as it fell, and a lake of blood soaked the ground beneath its corpse. The black wyr shook its matted coat before standing on its hind legs. Cate bounded forward, and the two of them rested their muzzles together. I recognized Larna's eyes.

"Cate, Larna, we have to find Belle," I said, tugging at Cate's rippling arm. My hand came away sticky from her fur, but I didn't care. "She and Neva are missing!"

That got Cate's attention. Her ears perked, and she and Larna shared a moment of silent communication. They bounded off, and I did my best to follow, stumbling over rocks and severed limbs and other disgusting things I didn't want to think about. I was so busy trying to keep up I almost ran straight into a hissing wall of fire. It devoured everything around it, and only Larna's powerful arm prevented me from toppling headfirst into it.

Through the flickering flames, I made out the shape of a woman. Auburn hair spilled from beneath her hood. Ailynn was scorching the battlefield, burning a path through the carnage. When she saw us, she parted her hands, and the wall split in two. "They're behind me," she shouted before I could even speak. "Hurry!" I raced by without answering, relieved to hear she had seen them alive.

There was much less fighting further on, but we passed several piles of blackened bone and ash. Ailynn's flames could probably devour an army of kerak all on their own. We ran across the charred ground, away from the fire pits and deeper into the darkness. The shouts behind us faded, but they picked up again further on, coming from the direction we were headed. Cate and Larna bounded off with a fast, loping gait, leaving me to scurry after them as best I could.

At last, they stopped, and I managed to catch up. The sound of clashing swords rang out, and I saw a flashing ring of silver, shining beneath more torches. The dwellyn had formed a circle, slicing through everything that came near them. Their blades dripped with black blood, and over a dozen bodies lay strewn at their feet, but I scarcely noticed. A much taller figure stood in the center of the wheel, and I melted. *Thank the Saints, she's alive.*

"Belle!"

Belle turned toward me, and I noticed her sword was drawn as well. The relief on her pale face when she saw me mirrored mine, and she lowered her arm.

Before she could move, Ulig called out, beady eyes wild above his bristling beard. "Behind!" Belle whipped back around, and another wave of kerak exploded out of the darkness, shrieking. They launched themselves at the dwellyn's circle, trying to tear their way through to the middle.

At first, the dwellyn cut them down. The unlucky few at the front of the pack screeched in agony as they met the line and quickly crumpled before it. The ones that didn't met Cate and Larna's claws as they rushed to join the fray. But the kerak kept coming, mindless and fearless. As the pile of corpses grew, one of the creatures clambered past the others. It clawed its way over the twisted pile of grey limbs, flying straight for Belle.

I screamed. She swung. Her sword came up to block just in time, and the kerak's scythes glanced off the blade. Its mouth gaped howling-wide, and while it struggled to find an opening, Belle lunged. Her sword went straight between the kerak's jaws, piercing through the back of its throat. The kerak gnashed its teeth, snapping uselessly, and Belle had to use her foot to dislodge her weapon. By the time she freed it, the rest of the kerak were dead. The circle fell apart, and I caught sight of Lok standing atop one of the countless bodies. "Belle, is she still breathing?"

That was when I noticed a small, huddled form at Belle's feet. Neva was sprawled on the ground, clad only in her thin white shift. She was still and unmoving, and a foul cloud of magic surrounded her. It tasted sharp and smelled of fire sparks, and it rushed into fill my head. I rushed forward, but Belle was already on her knees. Her hands roamed over Neva's body, as if searching for something. "I don't know what she did this time," she rasped. "I can't."

"I can," Lok said. "Hold her."

By the time I reached them, Lok had taken her sword to the laces on Neva's nightgown. They sliced open, and a rush of air filled her small body. She started shivering, and Lok ran a hand along her back as Belle held her. "It was Mogra," she explained as I crouched beside them.

"When I woke and noticed Neva's cot was empty, I went looking for her."

"It's a good thing you did," Lok said. "Otherwise, we might not have found her in time."

"Did we?" Belle asked, letting Neva's cheek rest against her shoulder. "She's breathing properly again, but she isn't moving."

Before any of us could panic, Neva began to stir. Her blurry eyes shifted from Belle to Lok, then focused on my face. "Ellie? Why is it so cold?"

Everyone smiled. Relief flooded through me, banishing the fear. The dwellyn huddled around us, and Gurn gave up his coat, draping it over Neva's shoulders. "Everything's fine," Belle said, although I knew she didn't believe it. "The witch tried to take you, but she's gone now."

"So this was Mogra's army?" I swallowed, trying to hide the waver in my voice. On top of almost dying several times over, watching Belle fight off the kerak had shaken me. I scarcely knew how to process it. Remembering the monster leap for her and Neva seemed like something out of a nightmare. "Luciana isn't here?"

Belle shook her head. "I know it was Mogra. I saw an old woman in a black cloak talking to Neva near the edge of camp. She ran when she saw me, and by the time I caught up, Neva was unconscious." Ailynn's fury and her unwillingness to follow us suddenly made sense. She hadn't just been defending the camp, but chasing after Mogra.

Cate growled beside me, and her nostrils flared. Her form began to bunch, and she curled in on herself with the sickening crunch of bone. Her fur disappeared, and she lost several inches of height. Soon, she had regained her human form. "Wonderful," she said, disgusted. "Now we've got three evil villains and two undead armies trying to kill us."

"Not just trying to kill us," Lok pointed out. "Mogra came here with a specific goal in mind."

Though Lok's words were vague, Neva understood immediately. "She wants me back. That's why she sent the woman with no eyes to take me, and the witch to put me to sleep. She needs me to wake the dead for her."

"But why?" Cate asked. "Mogra is already supplying her with an army."

"Because," Neva whispered, her eyes wide and dark with fear. "If she didn't need me...or part of me ...she would have killed me."

Chapter Six

Taken from the letters of Cathelin Raybrook, edited by Lady Eleanor Kingsclere

THE MOOD WAS TENSE when Larna and I entered Jett Bahari's tent. Everyone else was already gathered around the table, and no one smiled. Rachari and Rufas exchanged icy stares, only breaking eye contact to spare us the briefest of glances. Jinale sucked steadily on the tip of an arrow, and Hassa's flanks shivered. Jett Bahari and Doran stopped their whispered conversation, and Jett Markku busied himself with the large map spread between them. Ellie still seemed pale from her brush with death the night before, and Belle didn't look much better. Only Ailynn's brooding didn't seem out of place. She wasn't normally cheerful to begin with.

"Oh good," Raisa said, breaking the awkward silence. I was surprised to see her among the war council, and even more surprised by her chipper tone of voice. "You're finally here."

"Aye, and so are you," Larna said, frowning slightly. "I might be asking why?"

Rufas grunted. "A reasonable question, wolf. I don't see the need for so many humans here, especially those without rank or command."

I bristled, angry on Raisa's behalf, but before I could argue, Ailynn stepped in. "Raisa, Lady Eleanor, and Lady Belladonna are here on my invitation. Raisa has a plan to deal with the Queen's armies, and as Princess Neva's guardians, Lady Eleanor and Lady Belladonna are involved in that plan."

Her words did little to pacify him. Rufas turned to loom over her, lower jaw jutting out, jowls quivering. "I still don't see the need—"

"Then it's a good thing you aren't in charge." Rachari shot him a disdainful glare before gesturing toward Jett Bahari. "The leader of the rebellion himself approved Ailynn's request. Who do you think you are to question his authority here?"

"We are guests in his camp," Jinale agreed, ever the voice of diplomacy. I couldn't help but admire her patience. Rufas' aggressive behavior was the last thing we needed, especially after last night's attack, and I doubted I would have been so reasonable had I been in her place. "We have no right to dictate who he invites to his war councils."

Jett Bahari nodded in thanks. "I agree. We have more important things to discuss than the make-up of this group. Mogra knows our location, and we suffered heavy losses in last night's attack. We need a better way to deal with her forces. Waiting for them to pick us off while we march for Kalmarin is unacceptable."

"Quite right," said another voice low to the ground. I glanced down, trying to find its source, but all I could make out was the top of someone's forehead. It was one of the dwellyn that had arrived with Ellie, Belladonna, and the princess. I recognized her as the one who had sliced through the laces of Neva's gown during the chaos of the previous night. Despite her tusks, her Amendyrri was perfect, without a trace of an accent. "The dwellyn army will meet us at Kalmarin, but until then, your forces are vulnerable. You have few means of defense against a horde of the undead, especially while traveling south across the plains."

"What would you have us do until then, Lok?" Rufas huffed. "The liarre's main forces won't be able to help before then either. We're stuck with what we've got."

"Not necessarily," Raisa said. To my surprise, she waved me closer. "Cate, I don't suppose you brought your bag with you?"

I had, though I was uncertain as I set it on the table. The threads of Raisa's plan were starting to weave together in my mind, and I wasn't sure whether it was crazy or impressive. Without being asked, I drew out the hourglass Kalwyn had given me. The river of red sand flowed steadily no matter which way I turned it, and more than half of the grains had settled in the bottom portion.

"Cate came into the possession of this enchanted hourglass through her mentor, Kalwyn," Raisa explained. "Supposedly, it predicts the return of the dragons to Amendyr."

"Dragons?" Jinale repeated, eyes alighting. "Are you certain?"

Rufas scoffed. "That's foolishness. No one's seen a dragon in hundreds of years."

"Just because you haven't seen one doesn't mean they don't exist," Raisa continued, undaunted by his doubts. "I believe they do, and I also believe the unrest throughout Amendyr has woken them up. If we can find them and convince them to join our cause, Mogra's forces won't be a problem. And it wouldn't hurt to have a little wing-power on our side while trying to get past Kalmarin's walls, either."

"Just how are you planning to convince these nonexistent dragons to join us in our fight, human?" Rufas growled.

I rolled my eyes, but Raisa merely stared at him. "'Human'? I have a name, Rufas, and I'd appreciate you using it. But to answer your question, I'm not going to convince the dragons of anything. Ellie is."

Ellie perked up at the sound of her name, and I hurried to translate. As I explained what Raisa had said, they grew even larger. "You want me to go looking for dragons? Why?"

"Why not you?" I said. Part of me still thought Raisa's plan was crazy, but I did have faith in my friend. If anyone could convince a flight of dragons to fight on our side, Ellie could. "You're a druid. You can speak to them in their own language."

"Besides, you've had a first-hand encounter with Umbra's sorcerer's chain," Raisa added in Serian, eyes glowing with excitement. "According to all the old legends, the dragons hated him. If we tell them Umbra's magical artifacts have corrupted the Queen, Mogra, and Luciana, they might decide to help us."

"No." Belle's face set into a determined frown, but her blue eyes remained terrified. "Absolutely not. You can't possibly—"

I smiled. I knew Ellie, and there was no faster way to convince her to do something than to tell her she couldn't.

"I'll go," she said, resting her hand on Belle's stiff arm. "I'm not much good to the rebellion here anyway. I can't fight like the rest of you. If there's any way I can use my powers to help, I'll do it."

"Did you not hear the part about dragons?" Belle's voice rose in alarm. "Being caught in the middle of a war is bad enough. Now you want us to leave the safest place we could possibly be to go chasing the most dangerous creatures imaginable!"

"Jett Bahari's camp isn't safe, Belle. Nowhere is." Ellie gazed up at her, fingers curling tight around her sleeve. "You know it's true. That's why you took up a sword. You can't ask me not to use the only weapon I have."

Belle pulled Ellie in her arms, chin resting on top of her head.

Raisa cleared her throat, redirecting all the stares back to her so they could have their private moment. "Good news," she said in Amendyrri. "Our resident druid has agreed to go. Any other volunteers?"

"Ulig and I would be honored to accompany her," Lok said. "Princess Neva has become rather attached, and we believe it's best to remove her from camp as quickly as possible, considering the incident last night."

"An incident?" Rachari said. "I suppose that's one way of putting it."

Jett Bahari cleared his throat to cover her rudeness. "Lok, do you believe Princess Neva was the reason for Mogra's attack on our camp? Could the witch have used her to find us?"

"It's a likely thought," Lok said. She glanced toward Ailynn, who nodded.

"I'm certain of it. According to Ellie and Belle, Mogra was tailing them before they arrived here."

I agreed with her. I knew all too well how cunning and devious Mogra could be, always working from the shadows. It wasn't outside the realm of possibility that she had been following Neva all along, or had used her magic to track the princess down.

"You can't possibly be considering this, Commander," Rufas said to Jett Bahari. "Sending the heir to Amendyr's throne out into the wilderness on a mad hunt for dragons is the definition of insanity."

Despite Rufas' anger, Jett Bahari's smooth expression didn't twitch. "If Mogra is trying to abduct Princess Neva and bring her back to the Queen, none of us are safe. Last night's attack proved that. Things will only get more dangerous as we approach Kalmarin. A small group headed for the mountains might have a better chance of hiding Neva from the witch."

"This might sound cold, but Neva has already done all she can here," Rachari said. "She's given the human rebels a name and a face to fight for. I hope for her safety, but if she dies a martyr, she can still serve her purpose."

It did sound cold, and I glanced over at Larna to see if she shared my disapproval. Although I could see the logic in Rachari's thinking, it had been a callous thing to say. My mate looked similarly uncomfortable. Neva was under our protection, and we all needed to take the responsibility seriously.

"Tell the troops she's under guard during the march south and send her north into the mountains for her own safety," Jinale said. "If all goes well, she and her escorts should return just in time to take the city."

That's not good enough. I exchanged a silent glance with Larna. Pain welled in her dark eyes, but I saw acceptance there, too. She knew exactly what I was thinking, and she nodded once, bangs falling over her forehead. Though she had given her permission, she couldn't keep looking at me.

My heart clenched, but instead of taking her hand the way I wanted to, I stepped forward. There was no other choice I could make. "I volunteer to go with them," I said around the lump in my throat. "Ellie and the princess are going to need protection, as well as someone with a good nose to find the way."

"Actually, you have to go," Raisa said, staring at the hourglass sitting on the table. "You're the only one with the map."

"Map?" I studied the hourglass, but it looked the same as always. "What sort of map?"

Raisa's face brightened. "That thing you wear around your neck. It lets you see magic, doesn't it?"

"You mean the deadeye?" I withdrew the stone from beneath my shirt, feeling it hum in my fist. "Yes, it does. But I don't see how—"

"Look at the hourglass. The enchantment has to lead to something. How is it supposed to know when the dragons have awoken if it isn't connected to them?"

The others murmured with a mixture of surprise and disbelief, but Ailynn spoke up in support. "It's a sound theory," she said, giving Raisa a smile. "I learned something about enchanting from Mogra after our falling out. Those kinds of connections exist."

With her encouragement, I lifted the stone and set it against my eye, peering through the gap in the middle. Instantly, the air around me came alive. Energy hummed through the tent, and my skin began to glow with warmth. Magic shimmered everywhere, curling like smoke and gathering in clouds. It pulsed around Ellie like an excited heartbeat, and Ailynn's deep auburn hair almost looked like it had been set aflame. The whipping streams around Doran seemed as though they might carry his frail body into the air.

I turned away from them, focusing on the hourglass. It shuddered, curling like a living thing as I reached out to touch it. The tiny dragons coiled around the smooth glass body, ruby eyes blazing, stretching their jaws to show sharp golden teeth. Their tails flicked aside, and I noticed something else. A long, shimmering line was tied around the narrowest part of the hourglass, unraveling like a spool of crimson thread. It travelled in a straight line, disappearing through the wall of the tent.

"She's right," I said, my voice rising. I lowered the stone. "I can see the magic stretching out somewhere, like it's reaching for something. Why didn't I think to use the deadeye before?"

Raisa grinned. "Sometimes it takes an outsider to come up with a plan instead of an expert."

"Fascinating," Lok muttered, peering eagerly over the table. "I'm even more certain in our party's decision to accompany you now. Our people always welcome opportunities to study ancient enchantments and magical objects. If this hourglass is literally tied to the dragons through magic, it has to be several centuries old at least!"

I wasn't sure how I felt about letting the dwellyn study Kalwyn's last gift to me, but I didn't have much time to worry. Jett Bahari commanded the room's attention once more. "Then it's settled. A small party will leave tomorrow to enlist the aid of the dragons. The rest of us will march on Kalmarin to meet our reinforcements."

"Jett Bahari, you must listen to reason," Rufas said, almost imploring instead of angry. "If the wyr, the human, and the dwellyn want to go chasing dragons, I see no reason to stop them, but you can't possibly think sending the princess away is a good idea? There are no other heirs to the throne. The entire reason my people agreed to fight in your war was to stabilize the kingdom, for our own sake if nothing else."

Darkness clouded Jett Bahari's face, and he held Rufas' gaze despite being half his size. "The kingdom will be stabilized, Rufas, with or without Princess Neva. Our primary goal must be removing the Queen from power. Until we do that, the princess isn't safe in camp. She's made an appearance and rallied the troops to our cause, as Rachari said. Now, we need to get her as far away from the fighting as possible."

"And what if the fighting follows her?" Jinale asked. "Mogra's tracked the girl this far. Who's to say she won't notice her sneaking off into the mountains and follow her again?"

"She might," Jett Bahari said. "That's why she'll need a guardian. Someone who has fought Mogra before." His eyes settled on Ailynn, and the entire room fell into a heavy silence.

It took Ailynn several moments to realize that Jett Bahari was talking about her. Her eyes widened, and she tapped her chest in surprise. "Me? Jett Bahari, I can't. My *Tuathe* is carrying twins." She wrapped a protective arm around Raisa's waist, as if she feared someone might physically part them. "She's due in just a few months!"

"Ailynn," Raisa murmured, her voice dropping to a whisper not meant to be shared, "you don't need to worry about me. I'll be fine until you get back."

But Ailynn's eyes blazed, and she grew increasingly frantic. "You will be fine, because I'm not going anywhere without you. I abandoned you once before. I won't do it again."

Jett Bahari made as if to speak, but a look from Doran silenced him. The old man circled the table, coming to stand before Ailynn. *"Acha,* it isn't safe for Raisa to go with you." Ailynn's lips trembled as she tried to form an objection, but no words came out. "You know the pain Mogra causes. She destroys everything she touches. You are one of the few people in the kingdom capable of stopping her."

"I don't care about a stupid princess," Ailynn shouted. She let go of Raisa, hands bunching into fists. "I have my own family to protect!"

Larna stepped beside me and took my hand. I knew my mate was just as terrified, although she hadn't said a word. Our fingers laced together, locking painfully tight. "Ailynn."

Ailynn whipped around to face us, furious at the interruption. "What? Not you, too! You might be willing to let Cate go off into the wilderness on her own, but at least she can defend herself. Raisa isn't a wy*, or even an *Ariada,* and she's pregnant!"

Larna didn't rise to the bait. "Aye. And is this the world you're wanting your pups born into? I am having a responsibility to my pack. Cate is having a responsibility to Ellie and to Amendyr."

"My responsibility is to my wife and children," Ailynn said through clenched teeth. Steam billowed from her fists, and her pale face flushed red.

"So fight for them," Larna said, pleading with her eyes. "Give your mate a future. Give your pups a kingdom to grow up in. That's what I be doing. It's what we all are needing to do."

Ailynn didn't respond for several seconds. She stood stock still, frozen with fear, unable to respond. Then, she stormed out of the tent without another word, flinging herself past me and pulling her hood up around her face.

I turned on instinct. "Ailynn, wait."

"Don't, Cate." Raisa gripped my shoulder, the lightest of touches. "I need to talk to her alone. Please, finish the meeting without me." She turned to Jett Bahari, bowing her head in apology. "I'm sorry, Commander Bahari. Ailynn will be ready to go with the others tomorrow. I'll make sure of it."

Chapter Seven

Taken from the verbal accounts of Ailynn Gothel, edited by Lady Eleanor Kingsclere

THIS ISN'T HAPPENING. I raced back toward my tent, strands of hair whipping against the wet tears on my face. *This isn't happening.* People moved around me, but I didn't pay them any notice. I blazed a path right through them. *This isn't happening.* There was no way I was going to leave Raisa, no matter what Jett Bahari and the others told me to do. She was my everything. My reason for existing. Leaving her the first time had nearly broken me, not to mention the scars it had left on her. We wouldn't...couldn't be parted again. I refused to allow it. *This isn't happening.*

    At last, I reached our tent. I burst inside still seething, looking for something to burn or break. But the tent was sparse, and aside from our bedrolls and traveling packs, there was nothing to destroy. There was barely even enough room to pace. I felt trapped, caged, even worse than when I had run from Jett Bahari and the rest of his war council. Before I could figure out what to do next, the tent flaps parted. Raisa entered, but seeing her face didn't improve my mood. I knew why she had followed me, and it wasn't just to see whether I was all right.

    "I don't care what you say to me," I snapped, hands throbbing on the edge of flame. "I'm not leaving you." If she tried to convince me otherwise, I couldn't promise that the tent would stay standing.

    "Ailynn."

    She only spoke my name, but her voice held so many other things I couldn't sort through it all. In the end, I didn't even try. I didn't want to have this conversation, didn't want to think or feel. I was sick and tired of letting my fears consume me while the same doubts circled through my head. In desperation, I latched onto the only thing that made sense. The only thing I could trust to stay solid while everything else fell apart. Raisa and I hadn't always been strong, but now, our bond was all I had. I gripped the back of her head and tugged her in for a fierce kiss.

Raisa's first response was surprise, but after a moment of stiffness, she melted into me. Her lips parted, and she let out a gentle sigh into my mouth. I threaded my fingers even tighter through her golden hair, finding a firm grip on the back of her neck. I didn't know why the intense desire to claim her had struck me, but I couldn't think about anything else. While I was focused on Raisa, I couldn't be afraid. There was only her taste, her sweetness, the soft, coaxing glide of her tongue against my bottom lip, a wordless plea for more.

It was all too much. I needed the rest of the world to go away, and for that, my world had to shrink until there was only room for two. *Maybe this is what I need. And maybe...maybe I should let myself have it. Have her.* I held Raisa tight, staring into her eyes to make absolutely sure my touch was welcome. The acceptance I found there sent cracks splitting through my heart. Raisa knew exactly what I was asking, and when her well-kissed lips curved up into a sad but heartfelt smile, I knew she was more than willing to let me be selfish with her.

I unlaced her bodice with shaking hands, and the next kiss I stole was interrupted by a growl of frustration when it didn't loosen fast enough. Eventually, I got fed up with my own fumbling. I connected with my power and lit the tips of my fingers, burning through the fabric I couldn't untie or tear. I was careful not to touch her skin, but she still gasped as smoldering strips of her bodice and the dress beneath fell away.

I made sure to stifle the flames before I got anywhere near her stomach, leaving my hands warm but unlit. I cupped my palms over the curve of her abdomen before moving down to her hips, groaning at the bare flesh I found. Raisa was made up almost entirely of smooth lines, and I treasured the rare places where her body veered into sharper angles. Her mouth was too tempting to resist, and I took it again as her smallclothes met a similar fate to the rest of her outfit.

"Ailynn," Raisa whimpered when we broke apart to breathe at last. She rocked forward in the cage of my arms, searching for more contact. I couldn't tell exactly what she was begging for, but the plea wrapped around my name was unmistakable. My gaze flicked down, taking in the hard tips of her breasts, the rapid rise and fall of her breathing, the blotchy, uneven flush spreading across her smooth skin. She needed this as much as I did, perhaps simply because I did.

I dragged her down onto my bedroll and rolled on top of her, careful not to put pressure on her stomach, and raked the edges of my nails along one of her thighs. The muscles there flinched, quivering beneath my touch, but her hiss wasn't one of pain. "I'm not going to stop," I breathed an inch away from her mouth. "I'm going to take what I want until I'm finished with you, unless you tell me to stop."

Her eyes met mine again, and the blush at the points of her cheeks deepened as she nodded her understanding. Both of us knew she wouldn't tell me to stop. She cried out when my hand cupped between her legs, slickness spilling over my fingers at the first contact. Her warmth snapped my final thread of patience. I had caused this response in her. Me. It gave me a sense of power and a sense of purpose.

My explorations were short, but thorough. My teeth latched onto the tender place at her throat that always made her shake, and my fingers found the right spots. Her clit was already hard for me, with the hood pulled halfway back. It only took a few passes to discover a pressure and speed that had Raisa biting her lip, trying to muffle a shout. I was determined to make her release it. I needed every part of her, all the proof of her desire.

But bringing her pleasure wasn't enough. I wanted to make her mine. Wanted to take back some of the control constantly slipping away from my grasp. I abandoned the stiff point, ignoring her unhappy whimper as I shifted my focus. It turned into a loud moan of approval as I settled at her entrance instead. The river I found there was more than enough encouragement. There was some resistance as I slid in with two fingers at once, but soon she was squeezing down around my knuckles, and I was buried all the way inside her.

For a brief second, I was still. I needed to savor this. Savor her. Her silk, her heat, the way her inner walls rippled to draw me deeper. Such possessive, entitled thoughts usually frightened me, considering the example I had learned from, but I couldn't help it. She was mine, and it felt wonderfully right to have her. I formed a hook, searching inside her until I hit the swollen spot that always made her scream. This time was no different. The sharp, needy sob that broke in her throat was the sweetest sound I had ever heard.

"Ailynn!"

Hearing Raisa cry out my name was even better than hearing her whisper it. I increased the pressure, curling and thrusting until my forearm burned, encouraged by the way she shuddered against me. Each reaction she gave me was an affirmation. Proof I was giving her what she needed. Proof she had given herself to me.

"Ailynn, please," she gasped, panting. "I...if you don't slow down, I'm going to—"

"No," I said, a little harshly. I wanted to make her come, wanted it more than anything in the world, but even that wasn't enough. I needed more. I needed her. I needed to know we wouldn't be torn apart. "Tell me you're mine first." The words came tumbling out before I could stifle them, but Raisa barely seemed to be listening. Her eyes were glazed over, and her inner muscles fluttered wildly around me as more wetness poured into my palm. "Tell me...tell me you belong to me. Only me."

For a moment, some clarity returned to Raisa's face. Surprise and what could have been a flash of hurt shone there, and I felt wretched for asking. I began to withdraw my fingers, threatening to crumble under the guilt. *I shouldn't have done this. Haven't I learned anything? Haven't I grown beyond treating her like some beautiful prize to be claimed? Disgusting. Just like—*

Before I could pull out, a soft hand cupped over mine, keeping it in place. My eyes locked onto Raisa's lips, unable to look away. "I belong to you, Ailynn. I'm yours."

It took me several moments to speak. "Raisa, you don't have to...not when I'm like this."

She gave my hand another squeeze, making sure it stayed just where it was. Her face was still flushed, and her breathing came fast and heavy. "I like you when you're like this, you idiot, as long as you're not always this way."

I stared at her in disbelief. *Can it really be that simple? I just let her compensate for my flaws and insecurities and baggage?* But something in her eyes told me that it was. If *Tuathe* were truly two halves of one soul, perhaps there were places within her that matched up with my bad parts as well as my good parts. She was still so warm and tight around me, pulsing even with the small, unintentional motions of my fingers. If she still wanted this, so did I.

"Again," I rasped, raising myself over her again so that my lips moved against her temple. I braced one forearm to keep my balance as the other resumed thrusting. "Tell me again."

"I... Ah!" Her voice trailed off into another cry as I started moving, but I could hear the need in it. "I'm yours. Only yours."

With the broken parts of me satisfied, I focused my attention on Raisa's pleasure. I added a third finger, stretching her even further, and swiped my thumb over the swollen bundle of her clit. It was already slick and straining, and she trembled whenever I rolled over it. I kept giving her more—more pressure, deeper thrusts, faster movements—until she couldn't bear any more. Her entire body seized up, and she froze, forgetting to breathe.

"Come for me," I murmured, kissing her one last time.

My permission was enough. Raisa's hips gave an unsteady jerk, her inner walls drew impossibly tight, and a flood rushed through my fingers and past my wrist. She screamed into my mouth, but I swallowed the sound, not even pulling away when her teeth sank into my lower lip. The slight pain only made me prouder. Her clit throbbed beneath my thumb, and I kept it trapped through her contractions, trying to follow the frantic movements of her hips so I wouldn't lose the right spot. My arm ached, but I didn't care. She was mine, and she loved me.

After an eternity, but all too soon, it ended. Raisa's lips went slack against mine, and she slumped backwards. Once I returned to myself, my first instinct was to check on the twins. I tried to lean back, but was surprised to find that Raisa's arms were in the way, holding me fast. I hadn't even noticed before that she was clutching my shirt for dear life. I reached down between our bodies to caress her stomach, waiting for the reassuring taps, and breathed a sigh of relief when they came. Logically, I knew treating her roughly wouldn't harm them. But my feelings where my children were concerned weren't logical at all.

Neither are your feelings for Raisa, I reminded myself. I stared down at the place where my other hand remained buried between the dripping mess of her thighs. I withdrew my fingers as gently as I could, reluctant to part from her but unwilling to make her uncomfortable. I tried my best to ignore the ache between my own legs. My lover could barely keep her eyes open, and even I wasn't selfish enough to ask her to return the favor in such a state.

To my surprise, I didn't need to ask. Raisa reversed our positions, which took some effort, considering her condition. I began to protest, but I couldn't get the words out before she started tugging down my leggings. "Raisa."

"I thought we agreed you were going to stop being an idiot?" she said, shaking her head at me with a mixture of fondness and exasperation. "I know you need my mouth after claiming me like that. Don't lie and tell me otherwise."

Of course, I couldn't lie to her. When she pulled my leggings and smallclothes down to my knees, the ache within me doubled in a matter of seconds. My thighs parted instinctively, and my inner walls gave a sharp throb. Taking Raisa had left me on edge, and I was afraid I might come the moment her tongue touched me. Still, I couldn't help watching as she leaned in, holding my hips for leverage. I tensed, bracing myself for the warmth of her mouth.

The first brush of her lips was nearly as shattering as I feared. They were still a centimeter high, but I felt the wet, open kiss all the way to my core. I buried my fingers into her hair without thinking, desperate for something to grab onto. *I can't lose this again. I can't lose you.*

Raisa formed a seal around my clit, and I let out a strangled cry. She started easy, with slow pulls and soft circles, but her enthusiasm was still almost too much. I could feel the purpose in her every motion. She wanted my release, was hungry for it, and that thought would have sent me sprawling if I hadn't gripped her hair with one hand and braced the other against the bedroll. The thought that she craved some part of me so badly was almost as intense as the hot, sliding silk of her mouth around me.

Each time I thought I couldn't take another sweet tug of her lips, her tongue slipped down to tease somewhere else. If I tilted my hips toward her, it pushed past the pulsing ring of my entrance, sliding deeper than I would have expected. If I jerked them away in an overwhelming moment, she found a hundred other sensitive spots instead. In the end, she always returned to where I needed her most. Whenever I suddenly found myself wrapped back in the blissful heat of her mouth, part of me was certain I would pass out.

"Raisa," I groaned, fighting the urge to grind against the lower half of her face. Pleading words stopped up my throat, and I couldn't quite let them out. Part of me still burned, too proud for begging. I wanted to come undone for her on my terms. "Make me come."

She gave a soft whimper that vibrated against me, almost as if she was disappointed I hadn't lasted longer, but she was nothing if not obedient. She sucked harder and the steady flicks of her tongue sped up. The subtle shift was more than enough on its own, but I looked down at her anyway. Our eyes locked, and I was lost. A sharp shudder raced through my body, and I used my hold to keep her in place as my climax finally tore through me.

Its power left me screaming. My inner walls pounded, and Raisa drew me even deeper. As soon as she did, the battering waves became a flood. Something inside me burst, and I watched in awe as a gush of wetness ran over her chin in glistening trails. She stopped sucking for a split second, obviously tempted to move down and taste me, but I stopped her by fisting her hair. I needed her lips around me and her tongue gliding over me until I couldn't stand it anymore.

She seemed to find renewed purpose, and she stayed fixed on the throbbing point of my clit until I had nothing left to give. My inner muscles continued clasping at nothing, but I was completely drained. I released the golden locks wound between my fingers, caressing the back of her head as gently as I could. She stopped and slid her tongue down, easing me through the last of my aftershocks.

By the time she pulled back, her face was as much of a mess as my hand had been. I pulled her up along my body and kissed her anyway, thrilled to taste myself on her mouth. We only parted when we absolutely had to breathe.

"Now what?" I asked, feeling a little more in control.

"We still have the rest of the night," Raisa said. "You can pack in the morning. Until then, I just want you."

My anger came flaring back, although this time, it didn't threaten to consume me. "We have more than the night. I'm not going."

"You need to go," she said, gripping my arm and staring at me, pleading. "I'm telling you to go."

I shook my head, tears welling in my eyes. "Then come with me. The rebellion doesn't need you as much as I do."

Raisa sighed, cupping the side of my cheek and tucking a few strands of hair behind my ear. "You know I can't. I'm too far along to go climbing mountains. Besides, I can help people here, at least in the healing tents. You aren't the only one who knows a thing or two about herbs."

"The healing tents? You're joking, aren't you? None of this would be possible without you. You figured out a plan to save us. You know the entire kingdom's history. You've earned your spot on the war council even more than I have." And that was when I realized the truth. Raisa was mine, but she wasn't just mine. The rebellion needed her, just like Princess Neva and my friends needed me. And Amendyr needed both of us.

I wept, releasing a flood of bitter tears, gutted by the knowledge that Larna had been right. "I'll come back," I sobbed, barely able to get the words out. "I promise I'll come back. I won't leave you again. I won't."

"I know," Raisa said, and I saw that she was crying, too. "I know, *Tuathe.* No matter what happens, you always come back to me."

Rae D. Magdon

Chapter Eight

Taken from the diary of Lady Eleanor Kingsclere

WE LEFT CAMP BEFORE the break of dawn, our moods as grey and colorless as the pale edge of the eastern horizon. The decision had been made, but none of us wanted to go. There was enough light for me to catch the haunted, resigned look in Cate's eyes and the tear-tracks on Ailynn's cheeks, but there was little time for goodbyes. Cate's hand slipped slowly from Larna's grasp, lingering at the fingertips, and Ailynn stopped hiding her face in Raisa's golden hair.

"I'm coming back this time," I heard her whisper as I passed them, heading for the bicorn saddled for me. "I swear, I'm coming back." Raisa drew her into a tender, heartbreaking kiss, and I politely averted my eyes. It was something I wasn't meant to witness.

While I swallowed around the lump in my throat, I felt a tug at my riding skirt. I looked down to see Jessith standing beside me, her tail sticking straight up in the air. "Do you really trust that thing to carry us?" she asked, eyeing the bicorn. "I know he only talks of racing and carrots, but I'd rather ride Brahms than this old nag."

My heart ached anew. The last thing I wanted to do was leave my beloved friends in someone else's care, but even the finest racehorses couldn't climb mountains. They were far too fragile to scale the Rengast's jagged peaks. "Raisa and Larna promised to watch over Brahms and Corynne," I said, although my voice wavered. "They'll be waiting for us when we come back." *If we come back.* "You don't have to come, you know." I scooped Jessith into my arms, letting her rest her front paws on my shoulder. "Raisa and Larna would take care of you, too."

Jessith whiskers twitched. "You're joking, Ellie. Raisa's sensible enough, but you can't honestly expect me to stay with Larna and her pack of wild dogs? I've come this far with you. I'm not staying behind now."

I was suddenly struck by how far from home Jessith and I were.

This tubby tortoiseshell cat had followed me halfway across the continent and straight into the middle of a brutal war without a moment's doubt although not without complaint. I hugged her tight until a rasping purr started beside my ear. "I love you, Jessith. People who say dogs are more loyal than cats have obviously never met one like you."

Jessith's purr grew deeper, and her wet nose tickled my ear. "At least you recognize it."

"Ellie?" At the sound of my name, I turned to see Neva standing beside me. I was pleased to see that her color looked normal. She had felt well enough to eat and move about yesterday, but her second encounter with Mogra had visibly shaken her. "What's Jessith saying?"

"I'd best not repeat it," I said, noticing Cate approach from the corner of my eye. Her feet were dragging, and her shoulders slumped. All in all, she looked only slightly better off than Ailynn. "It's a good thing you can't understand animals, Neva. They aren't often polite."

"I would rather understand animals than put the dead to rest," Neva said. "It seems like a lot more fun."

It was a statement I could not argue with. "Hopefully, there won't be any dead for you to put to rest where we're going," I said with false cheerfulness. "Come on. Help me put Jessith in my pack, and we'll get you on your bicorn."

Getting everyone settled didn't take long. I helped Neva onto her bicorn first, then prepared to mount my own. Before I could swing my leg up, a throat cleared behind me. I turned, expecting to see Belle, but Larna stood there instead. Her dark eyes were sad, but she smiled when I looked at her. She said something fluid in Amendyrri, and I was able to make out a few words. "Ride . . . help you?"

I gave her a grateful nod. I had learned a few things since crossing the border, although I was still far from fluent. "Yes. Please."

After a pause to make sure her touch was welcome, one of Larna's hands settled at my hip. The other took my arm, and she lifted me as if I weighed nothing at all. I was so surprised I almost forgot to swing my leg over the bicorn's back. Once I was seated, Larna let me go, giving the bicorn's flank an affectionate pat. He huffed, arching away from her in fear, and I stroked his neck to reassure him. "Don't worry. I know she smells like a wolf, but she isn't going to hurt you."

Like most animals, the bicorn wasn't surprised I could speak to him. He calmed down and snorted in acknowledgment, although he remained mostly silent.

"Ellie," Larna said, recapturing my attention. "Cate." She paused, as if searching for the simplest words. "Be watching her."

I tried to say I would, but realized my vocabulary was limited. "Yes," was the best I could do.

"Bad—" Larna used another word, but when I gave no sign of understanding, she struggled and came up with the Serian equivalent. "Dreams. Bad dreams."

At once, I understood. I had seen firsthand how Cate's visions haunted her. According to her journal entries, they had become a source of power for her instead of a constant fear, but I knew how terrifying they could be. "I know. I'll watch her," I said in Serian, hoping she would understand.

She seemed to accept my promise, because she smiled again before she left to speak with Cate one last time. I watched them whisper together, only turning away when another bicorn trotted up to stand beside mine. "Well, this is depressing," Belle sighed, glancing over at me from atop her mount. Her hair was pulled back into a sensible knot, although a few dark curls escaped and clung to her neck. "With Ailynn and Cate leaving their lovers behind, I feel almost guilty for coming."

"Please, don't. I need my valiant swordmaiden to defend me against the dragons."

Belle rolled her eyes, but I could tell she was secretly pleased. "Me? You're supposed to be our resident dragon expert. I'm just along for the fun of it."

"Right." I winced, shifting to find a more comfortable position. My blisters from the weeks of hard riding I'd done before arriving at camp had barely had time to heal. "Fun."

"It might seem fun once it's over. At the very least, it will make for a good story later. Just like when we met."

Belle and I hadn't been introduced under the best of circumstances, but I had to admit, thinking back made it easy to highlight the romantic parts and ignore the horrifying ones. "I hope you're right. I've no doubt it will fill another journal or two." I gave her my best cheerful look. "Perhaps it might even inspire Lord Erato to write a new collection of love poems?"

A slight blush tinged Belle's cheeks. "Perhaps it might at that."

By the time we started off across the plains, my heart was a little lighter. I was sad for Cate and Ailynn, but I selfishly allowed myself to take comfort in Belle's company. I couldn't help being grateful that we hadn't been separated, however unfair it was.

***

The next several days were a long, tiresome slog—worse than picking our way through the Forest had been. Amendyr's plains were empty, and every bit of landscape looked the same. If it hadn't been for the distant smudge of the mountains to the north, I would have gathered we were going in circles. But the red thread from Cate's hourglass led us onward, and we were always certain of our way, even if the paths seemed to repeat themselves.

Our party's mood improved a little after the first night away from Jett Bahari's camp, with one notable exception. Ailynn's sulking turned into a stubborn silence, and she hardly interacted with anyone, not even Cate. Getting a response from her was like squeezing water from a stone, and though I never saw her cry, her eyes were often ringed with red

It wasn't until the third morning that I managed to coax a single word from her at all. I came upon her sitting alone by the dying embers of last night's fire, slumped over with her elbows braced on her knees. Instead of gazing at her feet or off into the distance as I expected, I caught her stealing glances at the other side of camp, where Neva was admiring Belle's sword while Ulig supervised. The princess watched carefully, paying close attention as they demonstrated how to grip the hilt.

"You don't approve of her interest?" I asked Ailynn, taking the seat beside her. Although her solitary behavior didn't do much to inspire friendship, I knew Cate would want me to make an effort. If she said we would get along, I believed her.

"I do, actually," Ailynn said. A wistful look crossed her face as we both watched Neva stare up at Belle with a beaming smile. "I might not seem the type, but I'm fond of children, especially the curious ones."

"Neva is that." The princess regularly wrote a storm on the blank pages I had given her, and her journal had started to fill with random observations and silly anecdotes instead of only nightmares.

Ailynn sighed and turned toward me. "She just reminds me of Raisa. We grew up together. I was a few years older." She shook her head, as if chastising herself. "I'm sorry. You probably don't want to hear about this. I've been bad enough moping around camp in the middle of the night instead of sleeping."

I gave her a smile that I hoped conveyed reassurance. "So, I'm not the only one awake in the middle of the night. That explains a few of the noises I've heard. I thought I was being paranoid."

"You should be paranoid," Ailynn said, a waver of fear in her voice. "Mogra has eyes and ears everywhere."

"You sound more frightened of her than you do of the Queen."

There was a long pause, and I could tell Ailynn was considering something deeply. "I am. There is nothing more terrifying than seeing what you could become if you gave into your worst instincts. The Queen and Umbra are abstract evils to me, like villains in a legend. Mogra is my mother. It's different."

"I understand that better than you think."

One of Ailynn's auburn eyebrows arched. "Oh? Don't tell me your mother is an evil witch, too."

"Not exactly. My mother is dead." Ailynn's face fell, and she began to apologize, but I continued. "However, my stepsister tortured me for almost a year and tried to cheat me out of my inheritance. I'm not unfamiliar with dysfunctional families. When the Queen turned Luciana into whatever she is, this war became personal."

Ailynn folded her hands in her lap, fingers lacing together. "Cate has told me a little about what happened to you both. Not in great detail, but I know enough. If our plan succeeds, I suppose it's a race to see whether her pack of wyr or your flight of dragons will be the first to end her."

A shudder ran down my spine. I still remembered how horrible Luciana had looked riding after us on the back of the shadowkin as we fled Baxstresse. *Her face peeling apart at the seams, matted hair streaming behind her like a banner.* "Cate is more than welcome to her," I muttered, shaking myself free of the memory. "I'm no warrior, and she has more of a claim than I do. Honestly, she still terrifies me."

"But would you kill her, if you had the opportunity?" Ailynn's stare was more intense than I expected, and I knew she wasn't merely talking about Luciana. "Even if you didn't want to? Wouldn't you feel obligated, knowing the pain and destruction she's capable of causing?"

I did not have to think about my answer. Preventing Luciana from committing her evil acts was one thing, but killing out of obligation was quite another. "I don't feel an obligation to kill anyone. If she were about to strike Belle down, or Cate, or someone else I loved, I would risk my life to stop her. I have risked my life to stop her. But I don't feel any kind of responsibility for what she does. I don't think you should either."

Ailynn looked away, falling silent for a long time. Eventually she raised her head, and to my surprise, the expression she wore was a grateful one. "Thank you, Ellie. You've made a few things clearer for me."

Quiet descended again, but this time, it was comfortable. Both of us watched Belle, Neva, and Ulig for several more minutes, until Lok shut down their spur of the moment practice and enlisted their help gathering up the supplies. Ailynn and I left our seats to help, and our schedule resumed as usual.

The landscape was monotonous as ever, but I did notice a change in Ailynn as the day passed. She managed to share a few words with Cate in the afternoon, and as evening fell, she pulled her bicorn up next to ours. "Neva, are you fond of stories?"

Neva's eyes lit up, and she bounced excitedly in front of me. "Yes. Do you know any?"

"Do I know any?" Ailynn snorted, pretending to be offended. "Of course. Everyone who lives in Amendyr knows stories. Which one will you have?"

Neva thought for a moment. "What about dragons? Do you know any stories about them?"

I turned toward Ailynn, hopeful as well. A story would be a very pleasant distraction.

Ailynn smiled. "Amendyr is the kingdom of dragons. I could tell a hundred stories about them. But there is one that comes to mind."

"Please, don't tell her the one about Feradith," Belle called out from behind us. "Nothing too topical, or too gruesome."

"We'll save that for another night. The one I'm thinking of is about a princess named Saweya, a dragon named Reagan, an evil king, and a very tall tower."

Chapter Nine

Taken from the letters of Cathelin Raybrook, edited by Lady Eleanor Kingsclere

THE MIRROR HUNGERS AGAIN. Her fingers feather along its golden filigree. The hot metal hurts and soothes at the same time, but she wants more. Always more.

> Mirror, mirror, on the wall,
> Who in this land is fairest of all?

A ripple shudders across its surface. The biting scent of magic singes the air.

> You, my queen, are fair; it's true.
> But the princess beyond the mountains
> Is still a thousand times fairer than you.

She pounds her fist into the glass, screaming. "Useless witch! Why did you choose her? She knows nothing of your needs! I could—"

No.

The mirror grows, stretching tall until it towers over the entire room. Black flames burn within, devouring every scrap of light until only one source is left: overlapping rings of silver and gold in the shape of an eye.

You will feed me. That is your purpose. If the witch has failed, summon her here to build our army. Our pet will hunt the girl and bring her heart instead.

She raises her hand, palm open, and the fire retreats. The smell of burnt magic dissolves, and a rotting, sickly sweet smell takes its place, thick enough to clog her throat. Standing within the embers is the witch's abomination, lips peeled back over its pointed teeth. It is beautiful and ugly at the same time. She loathes it, this undead animal the mirror has commanded Mogra to shape, but there is no other choice. What has been ordered must be done. The girl's heart must be harvested.

She does not address the creature by name. She has some pride left. "You will surrender your army to Mogra and find the girl instead. Once you have captured her and killed her companions, you will bring her to me."

"Alive?" The creature's voice is far more human than her face. It is almost chillingly pleasant.

"Bring her or her heart. I don't care which. Now, go. I can't stand to look at you."

She turns away, but she can still feel cold, sightless, sealed-shut eyes burning into the back of her neck as the mirror retreats. She is relieved. Her master may hold this dog's leash, but it terrifies her.

My eyes snapped open. *Luciana.* I could still see her face in the darkness. The sound of her voice had wormed into my ears and burrowed beneath my skull. *Luciana is coming here.* It took me several moments to realize it was the middle of the night, and I was curled up on top of my bedroll. I reached out, groping for the reassuring warmth that was supposed to be beside me, but my hand passed through empty air. *Larna!* My heart throbbed against my ribs, and my throat closed, cutting off my breath. *I can't feel her. Can't smell her.*

"Cate? I heard you screaming from my tent. Are you all right?"

I flinched at the sound of my name, old protective instincts rising to the surface. My skin crawled, and my muscles knotted as I prepared to shift. Then, I finally made out a pale face hovering beside mine. It wasn't Luciana, or Larna, but it was familiar. "Ellie," my voice cracked. I wasn't sure what had prompted her to look in on me, but I was relieved. Aside from my mate, there was no one else I wanted to see.

Ellie opened her arms, and I crawled to my knees and leaned into them, burying my face in her shoulder like I used to years ago. She did not push me for an explanation, or seem to mind I was only wearing one of Larna's shirts. She simply held me and stroked my back until the worst of the shivering stopped. By then, tears streaked my face. *You don't have time to be afraid. We need to leave. Now.*

"She's coming," I said, clutching at the sleeve of her nightgown. "Luciana is coming here."

She understood my urgency at once. "How soon?"

"I'm not sure." A shiver coursed down my spine, chilling my blood. The vision I had seen was an old one, and I knew she was close, wherever she was. "But she's already on her way."

"Then we need to run. Now. Tonight." Ellie helped me to my feet, only clutching my elbow long enough to help me find my footing. While I dressed with shaking, stupid hands, she slipped from the tent to find the others.

She isn't here. I pulled on a pair of leggings. *You aren't in danger.* I checked my pack, making sure Kalwyn's hourglass was still tucked safely inside. *She doesn't have the power to hurt me anymore.* But I knew that they were lies. Luciana was coming. We were all in danger. And she very much had the power to hurt me. She had been terrifying before, when she was only a sadistic noblewoman with a penchant for raping and humiliating the help. Now, she was something worse.

The old Luciana hadn't been quite unhinged enough to kill, at least not before Ellie's arrival at Baxstresse. But the sorcerer's chain and Mogra and the Queen and the mirror had stripped away whatever humanity remained. The new Luciana would destroy anyone who stood between her and Princess Neva, and she would relish in it.

The princess. I have to warn Ellie. Luciana cannot be allowed to take her. I hurried outside, realizing I had not explained everything, but the second I stepped out into the night, a sense of dread crept over me. The smell of corrupted magic was everywhere. My senses screamed with raw, primal fear. I was the stag in my pack and I often hunted, and once more, my instincts begged me to shift.

I resisted the temptation and hurried to the small knot of people emerging from their tents. The dwellyn huddled protectively around their princess, muttering quietly to themselves while Belle stood a little apart.

"What's happening?" Belle's eyes widened in the darkness, and when her glance fell on the Forest trees, she lowered the blade of her sword. "Not another attack?"

"Your sister," I told her. I did not want to say Luciana's name anymore.

She gasped softly, and I noticed her flinch. Although Luciana had not physically abused her, Belle had suffered from Luciana's psychological torments far longer than me. "Whatever she's become now, she is not my sister."

"I don't think she's even human anymore," I said.

Belle's knuckles bunched around the hilt of her sword. "I know. I saw her face when..."

Before I could say anything, several more voices broke the short silence. Light shone in the blackness, and Ailynn raced toward us, black cloak swirling and her hand wreathed in flame. "Where is she?" she demanded, with such simmering anger I knew we could not be talking about the same person.

"Mogra is headed for Kalmarin, but—"

"Cate!" someone called, between a hissed whisper and shout. I whirled around and saw Ellie some yards away, her pale arm extended into the darkness. I followed it, and my heart dropped. Kerak. I knew them by smell, and I could see the shadows moving. Their mistress would not be far behind.

"We have to go," I said. "Take the bicorns as they are and leave everything."

But it was too late. The forward scouts were already converging, forming a circle around our clearing. Brush snapped, and the kerak's shrieks called through the trees on all sides. Soon, we would be surrounded.

I couldn't hold back my shift any longer. *Humans run. Wolves chase.* My bones broke and re-made themselves. My muscles burned and stretched. Claws sprouted from my fingers, and my clothes burst at the seams. My terror didn't leave as I came into my half-shape, but it was joined by a swell of courage and confidence. *Come find me, Luciana. Come see what I've become without you.*

The first kerak that leapt toward me met its death. Its black blood tasted foul flooding into my mouth, but I tore out its throat before its scythes could slice through the air. It had barely collapsed before another took its place. This time, I leapt first. Its sinewy chest ripped open like paper, peeling apart to reveal the slippery, grey-black sludge of its insides. A growl rumbled in my throat as it collapsed, and gore dripped from my muzzle. *I'm getting bored with your toys, Mogra. You and Luciana will have to work harder to frighten me.*

I turned to find the next cluster of enemies, but there were none near me. Instead, the coiling shadows converged on Princess Neva and the dwellyn. Lok's sword was a shining silver thread in starlight, but it severed everything it touched. The kerak before her had barely bent down to reach her before she thrust up into its gut, severing it in two.

Ulig was less subtle. He scrambled up another dwellyn's back and launched from their stocky shoulders, sailing through the air toward another kerak and bringing his blade down in a sideways swipe. Its head flew from its body, still screaming as it hit the ground.

Just as I began to feel confident, the earth beneath us quaked. The trees shuddered, and mighty trunks snapped like twigs. My fur bristled, and I dropped to all fours, bounding toward Ailynn and the hissing circle of ash around her boots. She was my best chance to fight the shadowkin without my mate at my flank.

When the first beast's bulk burst into the clearing, we were ready. She called up a bright beacon of flame, and I streaked between the shadowkin's forepaws, tearing at its tough underbelly with my teeth and claws. It roared, curling in on itself and swiping at me with a great paw. I feared I would be crushed. But fire began crawling along its pelt, devouring everything it touched. The creature hesitated just long enough for me to slip out from underneath its body. It howled, bleeding and burning until it was a giant twitching mountain.

Another broke into the clearing, then another, until five of them towered over us. They were as tall as houses, larger than any I had ever seen, and perched astride the largest of all was a slender figure. Even from such a height, I knew who it was. I could smell her even though her scent was wrong. *Luciana.*

Half of me wanted to cower, but the other half ached for blood. I crouched off to the side, preparing to lunge at her mount's enormous leg, but Luciana did not command it forward. She barely even seemed to notice me. Instead, she peered down at the defensive ring the dwellyn had made. When her sightless gaze landed on Princess Neva, who was huddled against Ellie's skirt, her face lit up—a fact made even more terrifying by the fact that she had no eyes.

"So, this is the heart I was sent to fetch? Funny. I thought you would be older."

Her voice gutted me. It was still the same, despite the horrible transformation she had undergone. My head swam with old terrors, and my heart raced at double-speed.

"I don't know why you're complaining, Luci." Out of the corner of my eye, I saw Belle step forward and break the circle. She looked incredibly small standing beneath the muzzle of Luciana's giant shadowkin, but her blade didn't waver. "You always liked your victims young."

Luciana's face twisted into a sneer. "Belle? This will be even more fun than I'd hoped. After I kill your wife for taking my eyes, I think I might leave you alive to miss her. Call it a sister's mercy."

I looked at Belle standing before the shadowkin. I looked at Ellie, shielding Princess Neva. I looked at Ailynn, her stern face glowing in the light of her flames. I couldn't let my friends face this thing alone.

"If you want the person who took your eyes, you've found her," I growled in my other-voice, stepping out of the shadows so Luciana could see me. "And if you're looking for the person who's going to end your miserable existence, you've found her as well."

At first, Luciana didn't seem to recognize me. Her brow, one of the clearest parts of her peeling face, furrowed. But I knew the moment she understood who I was. Her sneer spread, and she laughed—a low, self-satisfied sound I was intimately familiar with. "You? The serving girl? What on earth has that stupid witch done to you? Can you climb out of that body, or did she turn you into a monster permanently?"

"You are the only monster I see here."

"Really?" Luciana nodded, and more kerak started crawling out from behind the trunks of the shadowkins' legs. She seemed to have some hold over them, because they didn't rush at us right away. Instead, they waited, even more terrifying in their silence than they were when they screamed. "Count again, pet."

Rage flooded through me, and I jerked my muzzle toward Ailynn. "I'm ending this. Give me a boost."

It was one of the only times I saw her grin. One of her arms jerked, and the ground beneath me quaked. A slanting column of earth carried me upward, and when I launched for the shadowkin's back, a gust of wind helped carry me. My claws dug into its hide, and I held on tight as it reared and bucked beneath me.

Luciana snarled and her slender body began changing. Sharp spines sprouted from her back. Her arms and legs lengthened. Her jaw unhinged and grew, making space for her fangs. More cracks sprouted along her pale grey skin, as if she was about to slither out of it, and a strange light seemed to shine from beneath them. When she spoke again, her voice had many layers, all of them vibrating with anger. "Come on, puppy. Let's see how well you play."

I leapt, and the two of us crashed together in a tangle of claws. I was fast, but Luciana was faster. When we collided, I barely managed to raise my arm in time. Flecks of spit hit my face, and the sickly-sweet scent of rot clogged my mouth as I fought to keep back her gnashing teeth. I slammed into her despite my struggle to breathe, trying to shove her off balance.

Luciana started to sway, but she found another hold. She snapped, and pain pierced my shoulder, not just stabbing but burning as it split through my skin. I thrashed, trying to shake off the bite, but no matter how I twisted my spine, I couldn't dislodge her. We fell, rolling across the shadowkin's broad back, still tearing at each other as hot blood pulsed over our heaving chests.

I kicked with my back paws, but Luciana didn't even flinch when they caught her stomach. The bands of muscle sprouted along her body were like steel. My struggles barely registered. She released my shoulder with a sick sucking sound, jaws dripping with blood, staring down at me with her sightless, twisted eyes. "No surprise," she hissed. "You're right where you've always been. Flat on your—"

That gave me the surge of strength I needed to match her. This time, my lunge knocked her back. My teeth found her throat, and my jaws snapped shut, clenching tighter and tighter as hot blood gushed to fill my mouth. Luciana slashed at me with her claws, leaving several searing gashes along my pelt, but I didn't let go. Wyr called their holds death-bites for a reason. If she wanted to dislodge me, she would need to kill me.

More blood rushed over us, but I relished in the knowledge that the sour-black streams soaking my fur were mostly Luciana's. She wasn't going to win. Not this time. *Never again.* She made a gurgling sound, but I didn't hesitate. I bit deeper, preparing to rip with everything I had.

I didn't get the chance. Luciana's control had wavered, and the shadowkin beneath us realized it was not content to be a battlefield. It reared up on its hind legs and roared, a rumbling sound that shuddered through my bones, and the two of us went tumbling over its massive side, still locked together as we hurtled toward the ground.

We hit the dirt with a painful jolt, but it was worse for her than me. She landed first, and her body broke my fall. I heard something crack, but she continued writhing beneath me, trying to escape. An enormous paw towered over us, preparing to crash down. Luciana had realized she was losing, and instead of allowing me victory, she was going to kill us both.

"Stop!"

I couldn't see who was shouting, but the voice was high and clear. The shadowkin froze, its foot still hovering over us.

"Put your paw down."

The shadowkin's paw came back down.

"Stop them."

To my horror, I found myself being pulled away from Luciana by at least dozen slender grey arms. The kerak were pulling us apart, although they made no effort to harm me. Their shrieking was silent, and the gaping, spike-lined pits of their mouths remained closed. I sank my teeth further into Luciana's throat, unwilling to release my prey, but in such numbers, they were too strong for me. It took seven of them to pry me off, and they formed a circle around me, shielding Luciana from my line of sight.

"No!" I shouted, staggering to my feet and preparing to charge past them. But it was too late. Luciana sprinted for the trees. I only caught a brief glimpse of her before she vanished. Her monsters remained behind, motionless and eerily quiet. Without a master to command them, they were mere statues.

I prepared to give chase, inhaling to find Luciana's cloying scent, but a small figure approached from behind me. Princess Neva put a hand on my arm, stretching up to reach it. "It's all right, Cate. She's gone."

Gone. And I didn't kill her. I hadn't even realized how much I'd wanted to kill her until I'd come face to face with her again. But as the bloodlust wore off, I realized I should be grateful. The shadowkin would have crushed the two of us, and I had no desire to die for someone as disgusting as Luciana. I dropped to all fours, which brought my head more in line with Neva's face. "Thank you. How did you do that?"

Neva shrugged. Then, with a look of resignation, she turned away from me and toward the kerak and shadowkin. She looked surprisingly small standing before such giant creatures, swallowed up in a large shirt that hung down to her knees, but they drew back as she stepped forward. The shadowkin dipped their heads, and the kerak lowered their wicked scythes. One bent to its knees before her and she placed her hand in the middle of its forehead, above its gaping pit of a mouth. "Go to sleep. It's time for you to rest."

I hadn't even known kerak could have facial expressions, but the creature seemed almost relieved at Neva's words. It let out something like a sigh, and its body began to crumble. Soon, nothing remained but a small pile of ash.

"Maker, that's incredible," I heard Ailynn say from several yards away. "I sensed she was *Ariada*, but a *Kira'baas?*"

Neva turned toward her briefly, but didn't speak. Instead, she continued with her work. One by one, the kerak fell. They remained still, waiting their turn as she un-made them. Once they were gone, Neva turned her attention to the shadowkin. She un-made them too, and all of us watched in awe as their enormous bodies faded away to nothing.

In the end, only one remained: Luciana's mount, the one who had almost killed me. Neva approached it, but instead of placing her hand on its paw, she smiled. "I'm naming this one Stinky. What do you think, Ulig?"

Ulig seemed just as shocked as the rest of us, but the dwellyn quickly regained his composure. "Good name," he said, smiling hesitantly behind his beard.

"Are you sure you should name it?" Lok had sheathed her sword, but her face read concern. "This isn't the kind of pet we can take with us, Neva."

"This is exactly the kind of pet we should take with us." Belle stepped forward, craning her neck up to peer at the giant dog's face. "Did you save this one so we could ride it?"

Neva nodded. "He can move faster than the bicorns, and he's big enough to climb mountains. Besides, he won't hurt us. He follows the orders of whoever's controlling him. Now, that's me. Stinky, lie down." The shadowkin dropped onto its stomach, curling its great legs underneath its body. One of its forepaws remained stretched out, and Neva scurried up, using its leg as a ladder to scale its shoulder. "Come on. We shouldn't stay here."

One by one, we climbed the shadowkin's sloping limb: first the dwellyn, then Ailynn and Belle, and finally Ellie, whose pack had decided to start squirming. "Well, I'm sorry you're unhappy about it, Jessith, but we don't have much of a choice. You can just stay in there if you don't want to look at it."

A low, unhappy yowl followed, and even without the ability to understand her words, I had a fairly good idea of what Jessith was saying. Ellie ignored the noise and paused before going up, staring at me instead. "Cate, are you okay?"

I tried to take stock of my body. My fur was covered in matted blood, and my shoulder ached terribly, but aside from the plummeting exhaustion that came after fighting for my life, I felt whole enough. "I'm all right," I said. It was true, but my emotions were more mixed. Minutes ago, I had been about to die in the arms of my worst enemy. Now, she was gone, and I was alive. My chest held a strange emptiness.

Ellie touched my arm in a gesture of comfort. "Let's go up and join the others. I've got some bandages for your shoulder."

I had completely forgotten about my shoulder, but hearing her mention it brought the pain back. I winced, suddenly aware that my right arm was almost useless. My efforts to move it were pitiful at best. Wyr healed quickly, but I had a feeling this injury would last a while. "Maybe it's a good thing I didn't go after her. She was fast, Ellie. Fast and strong. I don't know if I could have fought her again this way."

"You will fight her again," Ellie said, offering a hand to help me up even though I was almost twice her size. "And next time, you'll win."

Chapter Ten

Taken from the verbal accounts of Ailynn Gothel, edited by Lady Eleanor Kingsclere

WITH THE HELP OF Neva's new pet, we reached the Rengast Mountains in record time. The shadowkin moved at a speed that horses could only dream of, and it carried us as if we weighed nothing. Although I was wary of using one of Mogra's creations at first, I couldn't help being impressed. She had obviously made some adaptations, because Stinky was much faster than the slow, lumbering beasts I remembered fighting. He reminded me more of the speedy mount Mogra had ridden while chasing Raisa, Hassa, and me to Ardu.

By the time dawn broke, the mountains stretched high into the pink sky, close enough to make us crane our necks. At mid-morning, we passed the timberline. In the early afternoon, the temperature dropped despite the brilliant light of the sun, and I began to notice the subtle signs of frost on the ground. Although the cold didn't bother me and Cate, Ellie and Belle had long since bundled up, and the dwellyn didn't look too thrilled with the temperature either.

"Too high," Ulig muttered, scowling back at the path we had taken up the mountainside. His bristling beard made him seem grumpy, but I could see a hint of nervousness in his beady black eyes.

"Don't look if you don't like it," Lok said, running an affectionate hand between his shoulder blades. "Common sense, pebble."

Ulig grumbled some more, but he followed her advice and pulled his hood further over his head.

The only one who wasn't bothered by the weather or our uncomfortable distance from the ground was Neva. The princess seemed positively bubbly, petting Stinky's enormous ears to guide him in the right direction. Since our mount was under her control, she had been given the important role of navigator. Cate had entrusted her with both the deadeye and the enchanted hourglass, and so far, she had handled them carefully.

Unfortunately, Cate was not so well off. She slept in restless fits, and when she opened her eyes, the pain in them was obvious. The cold wasn't bothering her, but I could tell that the deep bite in her shoulder did. It wasn't healing the way a wyr's wound was supposed to.

"Would you like me to take a look at that?" I asked, scooting closer to where she was huddling between Stinky's shoulder blades. "I can tell it's hurting you."

"I was just about to ask," Cate growled. She was still in her half-shape, but she changed as I approached, melting back into her human form. It was a fascinating process to watch, and I couldn't help staring as her bulky limbs shortened and the thick core of muscle around her waist melted back into curves. The change was so drastic I couldn't help wondering if it was painful, but Cate didn't seem to be in any distress as the last of her hair disappeared. Her long muzzle receded back into a human nose, and when she smiled, her teeth were blunt again.

"Amazing," I said, staring at her in awe. Then I realized that she was naked, and I blushed, averting my gaze. "I didn't mean…the shift."

"I know what you meant," Cate laughed, but the sound transitioned to a groan as she attempted to sit up.

"Hold still," I ordered, helping her settle back down. "It's just that you would make a fascinating subject for an in-depth study. Oh no, that sounds even worse."

Fortunately, Cate seemed amused by my embarrassment. "It's all right, Ailynn. You're a healer. I can see why we might interest you." She tried to find a relaxed position as I removed my pack. "Perhaps when this is all over, I'll volunteer to help you with that in-depth study. Learning more about wyr physiology could benefit injured humans."

"An intriguing idea," I told her, "but for another time. That shoulder looks even worse than it did under the fur."

"It doesn't smell right." Cate winced as she tilted her head out of the way to give me a clearer view. "The wound is rotten, somehow. I shouldn't be surprised. Luciana's always had a poisonous mouth." A snort of laughter came from behind us, and I realized Belladonna and Ellie were listening in.

"Thank you for making that joke," Belladonna said. "I wanted to, but I wasn't sure it would be appropriate coming from me."

"Please." Cate rolled her eyes. "By all means, insult Luciana as liberally as you like."

Ellie shook her head, and a bemused expression crossed her face.

"What?" Cate asked, brow furrowing.

"It just amazes me how much you've changed since we first met," Ellie said with a smile. "I like it."

Cate grinned back, although her forehead knotted with pain as I extended her arm. "I blame you entirely, Ellie."

"Hold still," I ordered, opening one of the pouches from my pack and dumping a few spear-shaped green leaves onto my lap. "Jokes aside, I think you were right. This wound shouldn't be so inflamed, especially at the rate you heal. Belle, how much water do you have left?"

"Enough to spare some." She passed over her canteen, but remained beside me afterward, watching with interest as I began tearing the leaves apart. "What are you doing?"

"Making a poultice," I said, laying out a strip of bandage and dumping the wetted leaves inside it. "Comfrey and lavender. Good for sucking infection out. I'm not sure how well it will work on magical poisons, but it's better than nothing."

"Where did you learn all this? Because I'm always looking for more books to add to my library."

"I didn't learn from a book, I'm afraid. Healing used to be the family business." I placed the poultice on Cate's arm, guiding her other hand on top of it to add some pressure. "Hold that in place for about half an hour. We'll need to do this four times a day until it shows improvement."

Cate let out a grateful sigh. "It already feels better. Thank you."

"That's the lavender working. It should prevent scarring too once the wound closes up."

Her expression fell in mock disappointment. "No scar? What's the point of narrowly escaping death if you don't have a scar to show for it?"

"I'll be happy to never see you narrowly escape death again," Ellie said.

Cate began to protest, but before she could respond, Neva clambered between Stinky's shoulders to join us. "Cate, your thread is ending," she said, her voice rising in excitement as she held out the hourglass. "Do you want to look?"

"Ending? Let me see." Cate took the deadeye from Neva's hand, peering through the hole in the middle. Her lips pulled into a frown, and she passed it over to me. "Here, Ailynn. Take a look."

I lifted the stone to my eye and looked through. The magical crimson thread stretched from the middle of the hourglass to a ledge slightly above our position before disappearing completely. I shielded my eyes with my hand, but the sun's glare made it difficult to pick up the trail. "Lok," I said, motioning the dwellyn over, "do you think there could be a cave over that ridge?"

"It wouldn't surprise me," Lok said. "It's rare to find caves at this elevation, but the Rengast Mountains are right on top of the largest fault in the continent. Between the earthquakes and the constant weather erosion, even solid rock like granite can give." She joined me in peering up at the ledge, and despite the brightness, she seemed satisfied with what she saw. "Besides, the make-up of the rock beneath us is interesting. I suggest we stop and follow the trail on foot."

"Foot," Ulig grunted, seeming relieved. "Good."

"He doesn't say much in Amendyrri, does he?" Cate said.

Lok shrugged. "He doesn't say much in general, but his Serian's even worse. At least when he does have something to say, it's usually important. Come on then, Cate. Let's see if we can get you down without jostling that poultice and ruining Ailynn's hard work."

With Lok and Ellie's help, and my supervision, Cate managed to slide down Stinky's arm. Belle went to help Neva, but Neva climbed down on her own like a squirrel, and her feet hit the ground first. Ulig wasn't far behind. He nearly sagged over when he landed, and I thought he might actually kiss the ground. Once we were all together again, I passed the hourglass over to Ellie and opened my pack again. "Here, Cate. Take my spare shirt. You can't go exploring caves naked."

"We aren't even sure there is a cave yet," Belle pointed out. She squinted up at the ridge.

Ulig seemed to understand her, because he nodded. "Cave." He stomped his boot, as if that explained everything. "Tunnels under."

"How can there be tunnels under us?" Belle asked, alight with curiosity. "Did your people build them?"

"Oh no," Lok said. "Dwellyn prefer flatland caves. What Ulig is trying to say is that we aren't standing on a mountain at all. It's hard to tell from a distance, because it's so old and the clouds shroud its peak, but this particular mountain used to be a volcano."

"A volcano?" Ellie and Belle repeated at the same time, nervous and excited respectively.

"Used to be?" Cate added, popping her head through my white shirt.

"I couldn't say from here, but the hollow spaces beneath us are probably lava tubes. During an eruption, magma can harden and form—

"

Ulig shook his head and tapped Lok's shoulder to silence her, and his gruff face dimpled with uncharacteristic affection. "Don't tell. Show."

"I'm not sure I want someone to show me the inside of a volcano," Ellie muttered, but still, she was the first one to begin climbing up to the ledge. There was an unhappy squalling from her pack, and I heard her huff in annoyance. "Jessith, we can't stay out here. At least inside the mountain, you'll be away from the shadowkin."

"The cat's got a point for once," Belle said. "Neva, what are you going to do with Stinky?"

Neva didn't seem worried. "Oh, he'll wait for us. I told him to." She took Belle's hand, practically bouncing. "Come on, I want to see inside!"

"I'm not sure that's a good idea," Belle said, and I caught her sharing a skeptical look with Ellie and Ulig. "Besides, someone needs to stay out here with Jessith and Stinky." She opened Ellie's pack and withdrew what had to be the unhappiest feline I had ever seen. Jessith huffed but seemed relieved to be placed in Neva's arms.

Neva wasn't thrilled but being put in charge of Jessith seemed to mollify her. After only a bit of arguing, she agreed to stay outside with the animals. "Don't get lost," she called out to us as we started our climb. "And if there's a dragon inside, bring it out to meet me!"

I was not nearly so enthusiastic as I followed the others up to the ledge, but there was little choice. We had to go where the thread led us.

After just a few yards of climbing, the mouth of the cave came into view. I gasped. The tunnel burrowed straight into the mountain, just as Lok and Ulig had said. Its entrance was tall enough that we didn't need to duck our heads, and though it descended into darkness, the stone had an eerie, orange-gold glow around the edges. For the first time since our separation, I was glad Raisa wasn't with me. My *Tuathe* had seen enough narrow, endless passageways for one lifetime, and so had I.

"Well," Ellie said as everyone else stared in awe. "This looks like an appropriate place for an ancient being of fire and magic to live, doesn't it?"

"You're already writing about it in your head, aren't you?" Belle quipped, but her joke was somewhat lost in the awe we all felt.

"It's beautiful." Cate tilted her head back to stare at the ceiling, hypnotized. "Look at how it shines in the dark."

I saw what she meant. The walls were threaded through with glittering mineral veins and pockets, almost like living tissue. It reminded me of someone's throat, and although I knew it was only my imagination, I was half-convinced I could hear the cave breathing around me as I stepped inside.

"Well?" Lok asked, interrupting my trance. "What does the magic thread say?"

I lifted the deadeye again and examined the hourglass. The thread spooled straight into the depths of the cave. "It wants us to go forward," I said, although I would have known anyway. The entire cave reeked of old, powerful magic, enough to make my nose tingle and my skin hum.

"We first," Ulig said, peering up at me. "Dark eyes. You behind, have light."

I nodded at him and passed the hourglass back to Cate. "I'll light the way if you'll guide us."

Cate draped the deadeye back around her neck and held the hourglass up. My heart raced faster when I noticed there were only a few stubborn grains of sand left clinging to the top. "All right," she said, giving Ellie a smile of reassurance. "Let's go find you a dragon."

We followed the tunnel in pairs—Lok and Ulig, then Cate and me, with Belle and Ellie taking up the rear. After only a few yards, the sunlight began to fade before vanishing completely. I reached within myself, feeding from the energy that always lived there and setting my hands alight. The scent of magic grew stronger, and I was surprised at how easy it was to summon my flames. It was almost as if something other than air and my own flesh fed them.

"I don't like this," Cate whispered, stepping closer to my shoulder. "It feels hungry."

It was a strange word to describe the sensation, but I couldn't deny that it was accurate. "Like we're about to be eaten," I whispered back. Then, we fell silent. Both of us were too afraid to talk.

Gradually, the quiet sounds of our footsteps and the echo of our shallow breaths were overtaken by something else—a deep, rhythmic rumbling sound. It was low enough to make my bones vibrate, and I tensed. Cate's eyes met mine in the dark, as wide and terrified as my own. She didn't speak, but the question in them was clear. *What was that?*

I shrugged. Whatever it was, it made me want to turn around and run. But Lok continued on, and Ellie and Belle were still behind me. I forced my stiff legs to keep moving.

The deeper we went, the louder the noise grew. Soon, it was all I could hear. It filled my head, and with sudden clarity, I realized what it was. *Snoring. Oh, Maker, how big is this thing?*

A few steps more, and the narrow passage opened into a wide, sloping cavern. It was large enough to hold an entire lake in its belly, but instead of water, it was filled with large glowing orbs. They seemed to pulse, and my fire only lit a fraction of them. An enormous shadow rested on top of them, a ship on the ocean of gold.

Slowly, the shadow stirred. The low noise stopped. A humming sound swelled through the cavern instead, and a wall of raw power washed over me. This was the source of the magic and the clawing hunger. It was overwhelming, and I knew it knew we were here. A roar split my ears, loud enough to make the stone beneath me quake. The cave flashed brighter than the sun and sweltering heat threatened to swallow us whole.

Rae D. Magdon

Part Three

Taken from the accounts of Lady Eleanor Sandleford, Cathelin Raybrook, and Ailynn Gothel. Edited and summarized by Princess Rowena, Keeper of the Royal Library.

Chapter One

Taken from the diary of Lady Eleanor Kingsclere

"SECUTEM!"

A SHIELD OF rock and wind curved in front of us, arching over our heads before a brilliant column of fire swallowed us whole. It heated the stone beneath our feet and crackled through the air, sending heat through every inch of my body. My tears dissolved before they could fall, and steam rose from my skin. I groped for Belle, but I could scarcely stand to touch her. Grasping her arm burned. *Saints, we're going to die. We're all going to—*

As suddenly as they had appeared, the flames vanished. The room plunged back into darkness. We were still alive. Ailynn had shielded us. I waited for someone to do something, to confront the great monster I had glimpsed, or at least run away. But no one moved, and no one spoke. All at once, I understood everyone else was waiting for me. This was the entire reason they had brought me here, to convince the dragon not to kill us.

But what am I supposed to do? Just ask it politely to stop? It was the only semblance of a plan I had. I heard a deep inhale, and the knowledge that the fire would return spurred me into shouting. "Wait! We only want to talk to you."

The second blast never came. Instead, the cavern began to flicker, and I made out a great reptilian face hovering above me. It had three twisted horns on top of its head, and a latticework of golden scales covered its leathery hide. The dim light allowing us to see came from its giant slitted nostrils and its huge reflective eyes. Eyes fixed directly on me.

"You," it said, washing me in a wave of hot breath. "You do not speak as humans do. You use our language. Why have you disturbed Feradith, Eggmother of Caer-Naloth?"

Feradith? My mind raced. *Surely this cannot be the same dragon. Those who thought she was real at all told of her living hundreds of years ago!*

"Speak, or be eaten. Feradith hungers."

I gathered the few thoughts in my head that weren't swirling with fear. *She's referring to herself in the third person. So formal.* "Feradith." *Her title. What was her title?* "Eggmother of Caer-Naloth, we have come to request your aid."

Feradith opened her mouth, and the sound she made set the cave trembling. It took me a moment of blind panic to realize she was laughing. "Aid? The Great Flight does not involve itself in the affairs of humans. You may have a dragon's tongue, but you speak only foolishness. That is reason enough to devour you." Her jaws opened wider, revealing rows of pointed teeth almost as large as I was.

"No! We need you to help us stop Umbra!"

Feradith paused. Her mouth closed, although her lips remained peeled back over her fangs. "Umbra," she repeated, in a much more thoughtful voice. "That name is familiar. He is the one who escaped. The one Feradith did not eat." Her glowing eyes narrowed over me. "You say he has returned?"

"Yes." Smoke poured from Feradith's nose as more of her coiling bulk emerged. I scrambled to soothe her impatience. "He's using the Queen to build an army."

"Humans always build armies. Your kind enjoy slaughtering each other. How do you know Umbra commands this one?"

"Our shaman has seen visions of his presence in a giant mirror," I explained, trying to mask my fear and awe. I still hadn't quite processed the fact that an enormous dragon of legend stood before me, actually speaking to me. "He uses magical objects to control his servants. They corrupt whoever they touch."

"Impossible," Feradith declared. "No human *Ariada's* magic is powerful enough to cheat death for centuries and possess other bodies."

No human magic. Pieces of the puzzle came together in my head; the way the sorcerer's chain had burned me with the sheer force of its power, the sketches Cate had uncovered, the tale of Feradith's bloody revenge. Suddenly, I knew what to say. "But dragon magic is." I looked up at her, unflinching and unafraid. "He's using your hatchling's magic. I've felt it myself. It's kept some part of him alive all these years and—"

"*What?*" Feradith let out a mighty roar, and the cavern rumbled around us. It was loud enough to hurt my ears, and bits of dust and shale rained down over our heads. We all crouched, and I felt Belle's

The Mirror's Gaze

arm come up and around my shoulder to shield me. "The audacity! He is not only a murderer, but a thief as well. The Great Flight's flames will consume his army, and when whatever sniveling form he has taken is found, Feradith will devour it herself!"

"Ellie, what's happening?" Belle muttered in my ear, still clutching my arm. "What did you say to make her do that?"

"She isn't angry at us," I whispered back. "I think she wants to help."

"Help?" Ailynn gasped. "She looks like she's about to eat us!"

Ulig let out a low wail of fright.

"You need to calm her down," Lok said, an edge of urgency in her voice. "If she keeps thrashing like that, the entire tunnel could collapse."

I slid out of Belle's arms. She reached for me, but I stepped forward, standing on the edge of the precipice. "Eggmother Feradith!" The dragon's head reared high above me. Smoke poured from her mouth, and an angry fire blazed in her eyes. I spoke before I could lose my nerve. "We want to see Umbra destroyed, too. Let us take you to him. After that, he is yours. A sacrifice for the death of your hatchling."

"Not a sacrifice," Feradith growled. "Justice. His life will be payment for the life he stole. Does this shaman you spoke of know Umbra's hiding place?"

I turned back to glance over my shoulder. Cate cowered beside Ailynn, and she looked about ready to bolt. I couldn't blame her. Feradith's roaring was probably even more terrifying without words attached. "Cate? She wants to talk to you."

Cate looked at me in disbelief, then at Feradith. "Me?" she mouthed.

When Feradith spoke again, it was in a grating, accented version of Amendyrri, one I struggled to understand with my limited knowledge of the language. "The human with the dragon-tongue says you have seen Umbra within a mirror. Is this true? Where is it?"

Cate stood, trembling. Her voice wavered, but her speech was a little clearer. "The mirror is in Kalmarin. He's using it to control the Queen and his army. I think he's living inside it."

"The white cliffs. I know Kalmarin." She turned back to me, speaking once more in her own language. "He has clung to life in the place where he slaughtered Feradith's hatchling. You will take Feradith to him. Vengeance will be delivered, and the power he stole will be obliterated." She rose from the sea of glowing orbs beneath her, placing her enormous front feet on the ledge where we stood. More rock crumbled, and we all scurried backwards to avoid falling as she hauled herself out.

"We accept your terms," I said once I had my balance. "We will show you to Umbra, and you can destroy him."

"Terms?" Feradith chuckled, smoke pouring out of her blunt nose and from between her teeth. Her wicked, mirrored eyes seemed almost amused. "This is not an alliance. It is a demand. You will take The Great Flight to Umbra." The "or you will perish" did not need to be added. It was already implied.

I swallowed. "I'm sorry, but what is The Great Flight?"

Feradith's stare intensified, and it took me a moment to place her expression as one of disbelief. "It has only been three hundred years since the last mating flight. Surely even humans can remember?" She paused, then growled, obviously unsatisfied with our stupefied expressions. "Dragons have no kingdoms or borders. We are not divided. We are The Great Flight, and The Great Flight is us."

My jaw dropped. "So, you mean...every dragon is going to come to Kalmarin? All of you at once?"

Feradith made nothing of my astonishment. "The Great Flight serves all Eggmothers. It will satisfy Feradith's vengeance." Her brief answer left me bursting with more questions, but before I could ask them, Feradith noticed Belle. "Is this one of your drones?" she asked, leaning in closer. "Why is it staring?"

Belle was indeed staring, eyes wide and neck craned back. Apparently, awe had won out over fear. I nudged her side, and she startled.

"A drone?" I stammered. "No, this is my, um." I hesitated, unsure whether dragons had any concept of marriage or the word "wife." "My mate."

"Yes. Your drone. Tell it to stop peering at Feradith with its tiny eyes, and command the rest of your Flight out of my hive."

That, at least, was a request I could understand. "She wants us to leave," I told the others. "I think she's going to follow us out."

"You don't have to convince me." Cate loped off down the passageway as soon as I said the words, clearly relieved to escape the cavern. Ulig wasn't far behind her, and Ailynn and Lok didn't linger either. Only Belle seemed reluctant to leave.

"I can't help wondering what's down there," Belle whispered, squinting over at the ocean of glowing orbs beneath Feradith's huge back legs. "There must be hundreds of them. Do you think they're eggs?

If I could get a closer look—"

"Don't you dare," I hissed, dragging her out by her sleeve. "She wants to devour Umbra for hurting her hatchling. We're leaving her eggs alone." It didn't surprise me at all that Belle's curiosity had taken hold, but she had already annoyed Feradith once. I didn't want to think about what would happen to us if she got it into her head to snoop through a dragon's clutch. I hauled her back the way we had come, hurrying to catch up with the light of Ailynn's flame. A loud shifting sound followed behind, and I knew without turning that Feradith had emerged from her pit. She slithered after us, and the tunnel vibrated with her motions.

It didn't take long to leave the mountain and re-emerge into the sunlight. Neva, Jessith, and Stinky were still there waiting for us, and the princess brightened when she saw me. "Ellie! Did you find the dragon? Am I going to—" Her jaw dropped, and she stared over my shoulder in awe, much the same way Belle had. "You did! Maker, it's huge!"

I circled in time to watch Feradith emerge from the mouth of the tunnel. She took up almost the entire space, and in the afternoon sunlight, she was even more impressive. Her scales glittered a brilliant gold, and her horns twisted high above her head, one on either side of her narrow face with a third straight down the middle of her skull. She unfurled her wings, and the shimmering, translucent layers looked almost like smoked glass. She dipped her head, regarding Neva with some interest.

"You have a hatchling," she said, addressing me with an increased amount of respect. "What is your title, Eggmother?"

I didn't correct her misconception. Something with that many teeth could think Neva was my daughter if she wanted to, even if we looked nothing alike. "Eleanor Sandleford of Baxstresse."

She gazed around at my companions. "And this is all of your Flight? It is small. Humans usually live in bigger hives."

"No," I told her. "There is a much larger Flight waiting for us at Kalmarin. We only came to ask for your assistance."

"And you shall have it, Eggmother Eleanor," Feradith said, raising her head once more. Her great jaws fell open, and a mighty roar ripped from her throat. All around us, the mountain shook, almost as if it had come alive to roar with her. Sheets of rock tumbled, and my companions dropped to the ground, tucking their arms over their heads. Belle grabbed for me, shielding me as best she could, and I pulled Neva close to my chest, preparing to drag her down with us.

Before we could dive for safety, a deep shadow fell over us. It swallowed the entire mountainside, stretching further and further. The air seemed to hum, and I looked up, inhaling a sharp breath of surprise and amazement. The sky above us was no longer blue. Instead, it was filled with moving black shapes. They erupted from within the mountain, swarming overhead and blotting out the sun. *There have to be dozens. No, a hundred. No.* I was too astonished to speak, but Neva gripped my sleeve with one hand and pointed up with the other.

"Look, Ellie, dragons! A whole flock of them!"

Feradith bowed her head once more. "No, hatchling," she said, in the same grating version of Amendyrri. "Flocks are for birds. This is only Feradith's portion of The Great Flight." She fixed her blazing eyes on me, showing all of her pointed teeth. "Feradith's drones will summon the other Eggmothers, and Feradith's workers will accompany us to Kalmarin. The Great Flight will blacken the sky and rain fire down on the murderer's army. He will not escape our justice again."

Chapter Two

Taken from the letters of Cathelin Raybrook, edited by Lady Eleanor Kingsclere

"ARE YOU ALL RIGHT, Cate?"

Ailynn's mouth was right beside my ear, but I could barely hear her voice. The wind whipping across my face swallowed most of the noise, even when I crouched low over the dragon's back. Feradith had ordered her workers to carry us—smaller, skinnier dragons of a burnished bronze shade rather than their leader's brilliant gold—but despite Ellie's reassurances that they could handle passengers, I was terrified of falling. My injured shoulder made it difficult to get a good grip on its spines, and the added security of Ailynn's arms around my waist didn't help much.

"Not really," I shouted back. "You?"

Ailynn shifted uncomfortably behind me. "Would be better if your hair wasn't blowing into my mouth." I was sorry I hadn't put it up, but nothing in the world could have convinced me to fix it. Ailynn would just have to manage. "What's down there? Can you see anything?"

"Don't ask me that," I muttered, but I doubted she heard me. The wind had picked up again, buffeting the dragon's gossamer wings and making it tilt to compensate. We veered slightly, and my stomach lurched. *Maker, why did I agree to this? I should have stayed behind and taken Stinky back down the mountain.*

"I said, can you see?"

"Fine. I'll look."

It took me several moments to screw up my courage, but eventually, I stole a peek at the ground. Or, more precisely, where the ground should have been. I could see nothing but thin wisps of cloud below me, and somehow, that was far more terrifying than making out the world below at a distance. I had no idea how far up we were, but it was much higher than any human or wyr had a right to go.

"I can't see anything," I called. "Just sky." Ailynn leaned over to confirm what I had said, but I tore my eyes away from the vast expanse of emptiness, huddling close to the dragon. Its warm, leathery body and Ailynn's provided some warmth, but not much. The air around me was still biting cold. "If you were going to look yourself, why ask me?"

"Because you're sitting in front."

I didn't argue. Instead, I prayed for mercy. The dragons had to land soon. We were moving at an incredible pace, and we had already been flying for hours. It couldn't possibly be too much longer.

The dragon tilted downward in a graceful dive, and for one brief, terrifying second, my body felt weightless. I closed my eyes, trying not to be sick. "I take it back," I groaned. "We can stay up here. There's no reason to—"

"Cate, look!"

Against my better judgment, I looked. All around us, other dragons were doing the same, hurtling back toward the earth. They circled like gulls, but somehow, their movements were all timed to perfection. The Great Flight moved as a single unit, spiraling down and down, and all I could manage to do was scrabble for a better hold on my dragon's hide.

Suddenly, the clouds around us broke, and the ground hurtled into view. Glaring sunlight shone across a jagged, rocky coastline, and I could make out the glittering blue of the sea off in the distance. I gasped, forgetting my fear of flying as I stared in awe. From this high up, the sparkling water of the ocean looked as smooth as glass.

"Cate, look!" Ailynn called, tugging at my sleeve.

"I am. The ocean."

"No, down."

I turned to look straight down past my shoulder, and the sight beneath the shadow of The Great Flight's wings was much less beautiful. A large black mass was crawling across the plains. It seemed like a swarm of ants at first, but as we swooped lower, I caught a clearer picture. An army of kerak and shadowkin marched for the coast, moving at a sluggish pace. I could make out their target, rushing closer and closer by the moment—Kalmarin, white stone walls standing tall and proud above the cliffs.

That must be Mogra's army. It looks like we got here just in time. But where is the rebellion? Our dragon dove again, and for the first time, I began to hear something other than the screaming rush of air and Ailynn's voice. The city was wrapped in a second mass of black, roiling and twisting. A battle stretched out below us, and I could smell the burning stench of magic drifting up along with the thick pillars of smoke.

My heart clenched. *Larna. Larna is down there somewhere, fighting with our pack.*

"There it is," Ailynn shouted, pointing past my head. "We need to get down."

I didn't know if the dragon could understand her, but it tucked its wings close to its body, streaking down. For a moment, I felt like I was floating. Then the force of the dive kicked in, and everything around me became a blur. The ground hurtled closer and closer. I clutched tight to the dragon's spines, certain we were about to crash.

The collision never came. We veered up at the last possible second, and light blossomed everywhere as a whirling column of fire blasted from the dragon's mouth. Its whole body vibrated, and heat washed over me in a thick wave. All around us, other dragons were doing the same, flying close to the battlefield and burning everything. Whole swathes of kerak crumbled to dust, and even the shadowkin were no match. Those that weren't devoured in the flames were torn to pieces by The Great Flight's claws and teeth.

A loud roar echoed over the din, drowning out the shrieks and the clang of metal. Soaring high above the chaos was Feradith, wings outstretched, twice the size of the other dragons and gleaming golden against the sky. Her enormous head turned straight toward us, and her huge jaws opened, breathing out plumes of hot-blue fire. Thankfully, our dragon dipped off to the side. It came in for a landing, settling down gently on the patch Feradith had just cleared.

Even with a war raging around me, I had never been so happy to set my feet on solid earth. I slid off the dragon's back, catching myself on my good limbs as my body stretched and shifted. The last of my dizzying vertigo left as I settled into my half-shape, and I was off before the transformation finished, bounding toward the worst of the fray.

The wall of kerak I encountered were no match for me. They had numbers, but I was determined. Until I found my mate, they were merely obstacles. I continued onward, nose pointed to the wind. I couldn't make out Larna's scent over the smell of magic and blood, but I did see a few large, bristling wyr bodies writhing amidst Mogra's creatures.

Another shattering roar came from overhead, and a large shadow stretched past me, blotting out the sun. Feradith was flying straight above me, but this time, I could see the passenger on her back as well. Ellie was perched astride the beast's great golden shoulders, and with the light at her back, I could see one of her arms extended. She was pointing me in the opposite direction, away from where I had been headed. I turned tail and sprinted, sucking in air to fill my stabbing lungs.

At last, I caught the scent I was looking for, buried amidst the smoke and tinged with fear. Larna filled my nose, and her name swam through my head with every breath, giving me the surge of speed I needed. More kerak fell before me, and I avoided the lumbering shadowkin, streaking past them before they even saw me. I dropped to all fours, sprinting until the trail ended. A dark, hulking shape was thrashing beneath a mass of twisted grey bodies, baying as it tried to shake free.

I knew that call in my bones. I leapt, diving past the mass of tearing limbs with all my strength. Scythes slashed into my pelt, but I ignored the pain, tearing with my teeth. Kerak fell to pieces around me, spilling rivers of foul black blood through my fur. I fought my way through to the middle of the pile. Larna was there, snarling and snapping as she tried to rip her way out. With my help, she burst free, staggering on all fours for several paces and swaying from side to side. She was soaked in blood as well, but some of it was hers, streaming from an open wound on her side.

I positioned myself in front of her, lips peeled back over my fangs, but the rest of the queen's horde gave us a wide berth. Nothing dared come close. Once the enemy thinned, I ducked my shoulder beneath hers, helping her to stand on two legs.

"*Tuathe*," she rasped, her voice thick with pain. "What was keeping you?"

I laughed, blinking back human tears. "You don't tell a dragon how fast to fly."

"Dragons." Larna pointed her muzzle at the sky, and her eyes widened when she saw The Great Flight swarming over us. "You and Ellie were really bringing them. And just in time."

That was when I noticed the other corpses that littered the ground. Most were human, but two were wyr still in their half-shape, and one was recognizable. *Kera*. Her body was pointing toward the place where Larna had struggled, and I knew what had taken place. I had gotten through. She hadn't. Dead piled high around us.

"Larna, what happened here?" I asked, gazing around in horror. I had been expecting casualties, but not this much destruction.

"We were expected," she growled, lowering her head. She stared at Kera too, teeth clenched. "The Queen's army waited on all sides.

When we were approaching the walls, they closed in, surrounding us like prey."

Anger boiled within me. Before, both armies had been marching across the kingdom in search of us. It was not mere coincidence both of them were converging on Kalmarin at the exact same moment the rebellion had arrived. "Could it be Mogra? She has eyes everywhere. Maybe she discovered our plan."

"Perhaps," Larna said, but she did not appear convinced. "But how was she finding our camp in the wilderness? How was she knowing about Neva?"

"The mirror," I said, fists clenching in frustration. "The Queen and Umbra are watching us through it. They're always going to be one step ahead of us until we destroy it."

Larna nodded but didn't speak. She glanced once more at Kera before pulling away from me, and I was relieved to notice the flow of blood along her side had lessened. The wound was already healing.

I was not so lucky. With the fear of death rapidly wearing off, my shoulder stabbed with pain once more. I swallowed, trying to shake it off, but Larna noticed. "Cate, you be hurt," she murmured, touching my arm lightly with her paw. It was nowhere near the injury, but I winced at the slight motion my arm made. Larna inhaled, and I saw a shadow cross her face. "This wound is smelling wrong. Rotten inside."

"Luciana," I said in a shaking voice. I didn't want to talk about her, didn't even want to think about the terrifying creature Mogra had made her, but I knew better than to conceal what had happened from my mate. "She found us in the forest. Her new form is more dangerous than I thought."

Larna bristled, and I could sense her spike of anger. "She willna touch you again. I will tear out her throat before she is even getting close."

"You'll have your chance. We flew over the Queen's second army on the way here, and I'm certain she's rejoined them. At the rate they were moving, I would expect them just after nightfall."

"Then we should be hurrying." With one last regretful look at Kera's body, Larna turned away from the carnage and started off toward the nearest group of rebellion soldiers, several hundred yards away. They were not engaged in any fighting, and instead, most of them appeared to be staring up at the sky, watching the dragons soaring overhead. "This is the calm before the storm," Larna said. "The dragons saved us, but we dinna have the numbers to be fighting a second army out in the open, and not at close quarters, unless we are wanting to be burned as well."

I took in my surroundings more closely. Up close, Kalmarin's high white walls seemed even taller than I had thought. "Then we need a way into the city itself. If we kill the Queen and her guards, we can use the fortress to defend ourselves."

Larna gave me a small smile. "Aye. But first, we find Jett Bahari, and you will be having your shoulder looked at."

"And your side."

"And my side, but while we go, tell me, was that really your friend Ellie I was seeing on the biggest dragon's back? How did she talk such a beast into carrying her?"

I drew in a long breath. I was grateful for the sound of Larna's voice, and a subject to distract me from the corpses and piles of burnt ash. "I'm not sure you would believe me if I told you."

Chapter Three

Taken from the verbal accounts of Ailynn Gothel, edited by Lady Eleanor Kingsclere

"RAISA!" MY LOVER'S NAME burst from my lips as soon as my feet hit the ground. Cate was off like a flash, diving into the thick of the fray, but I ran in the opposite direction, toward the pillars of smoke on the other side of the field. Where there was smoke, there were sure to be humans. I knew I would find Raisa tending to the wounded.

Raisa. Tuathe. The word summoned heat within me, and I lashed out with spitting tongues of flame. I was a storm of fire and air, tearing apart everything in my way. Unholy shrieks pierced my ears, and twisting grey bodies crumbled around me, but I didn't stop or even slow down. I had a promise to keep, a family to find and protect.

Even the shadowkin couldn't stand before me. Their giant steps shook the ground, but in my desperation, I could move the earth. I didn't even need my Words of Power to split the ground and send jagged faults racing toward their feet. The beasts came thundering down, and I continued blazing a trail forward.

I fought for what felt like an eternity. I fought until my hands were a raw mess and my entire body dripped with sweat and clouds of dust and smog followed me wherever I went. I stumbled, choking, blinking back hissing tears, burning everything in my path. Eventually, I didn't even have to summon the fire myself. The dragons above me swooped down, breathing over the battlefield, and I fed their flames, building them higher and higher. My entire world was fire and ash. I was unstoppable.

At last, I saw a smudge in the distance. A cluster of tents came into view a bit further on, just past a ragged line of warriors. They had no formation, and as I drew closer, I saw that they weren't one band, but three. Tall liarre archers fired volley after volley into the oncoming horde, standing over the fallen bodies of their comrades. The dwellyn cleaved out a safe space for them, blades dripping with black blood. Human warriors fought with everything they had, wielding torches and spears and sometimes their bare hands. But the horde was falling back, scattering like flies.

As Mogra's creatures fell and flames cleansed the trembling earth, a chanting cry went up, and they began fighting even harder. "*Fel'rionsa! Sha, Fel'rionsa!*"

Fire...what? At first I thought they were talking about the dragons soaring overhead, but as I drew closer, the cheering grew louder. The beleaguered army was shouting for me. When I arrived, I was almost swallowed up by those left standing. My light died out, and I might have been swept away if a familiar figure hadn't curled around me.

"I see you've picked up a new nickname," Hassa said, dropping to his knees amidst the carnage. "Get on, Fire Princess. I'll take you to Raisa."

The sound of Raisa's name shook me out of my stupor. I hopped onto his back, allowing him to carry me through the crowd. "Where is she, Hassa? Is she all right?"

"Thanks to you and those dragons. Mogra's forces were waiting for us. Our line was about to fall before you arrived. The pocket of kerak you just wiped out have been keeping us pinned down here for hours."

My eyes caught a familiar flash of golden hair, and my friend's words faded out. I swung my leg over his side and hopped to the ground before he could stop, falling into a sprint despite my exhaustion. Raisa's face was covered in dirt and what looked like smears of someone else's blood, but she smiled when she saw me, and my heart cracked right down the middle.

"Ailynn!"

I didn't call her name back. Instead, I rushed into her arms, tears of relief streaming down my cheeks. I held her close, letting my blistered hands roaming across her back despite the pain, but I could find no injuries. She was alive, breathing and laughing in my arms, and the heavy weight I had carried with me ever since leaving the rebel camp suddenly lifted. "*Tuathe.* Are you all right? The twins? Did you—"

"I'm fine," she panted, cupping my face in her palms and forcing me to gaze into her eyes. "We're fine. I might not know as much about healing as you, but I've been making myself useful. What about you?"

"I...I'm fine," I stammered. "I'm sorry we didn't get here sooner. I tried—"

"You and your friend Ellie's dragons got here just in time," another voice said. I glanced left to see Jinale approaching, her quiver nearly empty, sucking on the last of her arrows.

"Jinale!" I said, sighing with relief. "I'm so glad to see you. But I wasn't trying to—"

"It doesn't matter what you were trying to do." Rufas stood beside her, his face and fur streaked with war paint and his axe dripping with black gore. He wore a nasty gash on his side, and it was still bleeding freely. "Another few minutes, and we would have been wiped out. You've done our people a service, *Fel'Rionsa.* One we won't forget." To my complete and utter shock, he dropped to his knees. "When you go to slay the witch, it would be my honor to carry you."

I gaped. Aside from riding Hassa, who had become my close friend, and the times Jinale had carried Raisa because of her pregnancy, I had never seen another liarre offer to carry a human. I had been told that it was considered an incredibly demeaning act among their people, and the fact that Rufas was offering, a liarre who seemed to care little for Amendyr and its people, was almost impossible to believe.

I stammered, groping for some kind of grateful response, but thankfully, I was saved from embarrassment by a loud whoosh coming from overhead. All of us looked to the sky, and a great shape descended through the clouded air, wings extended and long neck arched toward the sun. As it drew closer, I recognized Feradith. Her golden scales gleamed, and everyone began to shout and point as she came in for a landing.

"Maker," Raisa gasped, staring just as eagerly as everyone else. "It's enormous! Are all the other dragons as large as this one?" She peered up, craning her neck even further. "And is that Ellie riding it?"

I nodded. "It's Eggmother Eleanor now. Apparently, Feredith thinks she's our leader."

Raisa shook her head, her face still transformed with awe. "If that's what the giant dragon thinks, I'm not going to argue."

Both of us watched as Feradith gave a graceful dip, allowing Ellie to climb down from her neck. Ellie's eyes landed on us almost immediately, and she waved, hurrying over with her skirts in her hands. "Ailynn, Raisa, I'm so glad I found you. Most of the first army is gone, and the survivors have retreated back inside the gates. None of our people could get through in time, but we're safe for the moment."

"No, we aren't," I insisted. "You saw that second army. It's twice as big as the one we fought here, and Luciana's probably marching right at the front. We need to find Jett Bahari and warn him."

"Agreed," Jinale said. "Hassa, take over here. Rufas and I need to find Rachari and convene for a war meeting." She gazed at the high white walls of Kalmarin, gleaming past the fading smoke. "If we don't get past those walls, that second army will wipe us out, dragons or no dragons."

***

"Actually," Raisa said, gazing around Jett Bahari's tent, "I have an idea about that, too."

As one, the members of the war council turned toward her. Jett Bahari and Jett Markku gave her identical attentive looks, the latter bearing a fresh slash across one side of his cheek. Obviously, he had run afoul of a kerak sometime during the slaughter. Cate and Larna remained side by side, listening quietly, arms linked. Ellie stood nearby, distant enough to give them space, but close enough for Cate to translate if she had trouble understanding the discussion. Lok and Ulig had been joined by a third dwellyn, a female I had never met before with jewel-twined tusks and a blade strapped across her back. Next to them were the three liarre, and to my delight, even Rufas was gazing at Raisa with an expression of grudging respect.

"Your idea to bring the dragons seems to be working well enough, Raisa," he said, addressing her by name and with more civility than I had ever heard him use before. Apparently, the liarre Raisa had healed and my display on the battlefield had finally won him over. "What do you have for us this time?"

Raisa's chin tilted up with well-deserved pride. I squeezed her fingers a little tighter, running my thumb over her knuckles. Since our reunion, we hadn't been out of each other's sight, and rarely were we out of each other's touch.

"We already know what we have to do," she said, addressing the rest of the group. "We need to breach the walls of Kalmarin and storm the palace before the Queen's second army arrives. Getting into the city should be easy now that the dragons are here, but breaking into the palace won't be so simple. It's built straight into the cliff, and it's bound to be heavily guarded, not just by the undead, but by the Queen's human forces."

"Why not use the dragons for that as well?" Rachari asked, tail lashing back and forth. "Surely they're big enough to break down some walls."

"Feradith and her Great Flight can try," Raisa said, "but just in case, I have a back-up plan. One that will keep the palace standing."

I braced myself. Raisa's plans were always brilliant, but they had often proved to be dangerous as well over the past several months. I doubted I would entirely approve of whatever she had in mind.

"Several of Amendyr's old stories describe a series of catacombs beneath the palace, including the original legend of Umbra and Feradith. If we do manage to break in, I guarantee that's where the Queen will go. Those cliffs have to be full of limestone caves and tunnels. Why shouldn't we use them first?"

I breathed a sigh of relief. That didn't sound quite so crazy as setting off in search of dragons. In fact, I couldn't help smiling with pride at her cleverness. Ulig's bushy beard spread as he smiled too, and Lok's eyes lit up. "I like the way you think, Raisa. Inda, can you find us a way in?"

The unfamiliar dwellyn's velvet grey cheeks dimpled with a confident smile. "I can't believe you're even asking. If the dragons can get us past those walls, my people will have us inside the palace by nightfall."

"It has to be before nightfall," I said, remembering what I had seen on our flight from the Rengast Mountains. "The second army is coming, and it's enormous. If they catch us before we get in, with the losses we've taken, we're done for."

"Then we need to get in fast and hole up," Rufas said. "The first army already wiped out over half our forces, and every soldier we lose is another body Mogra can use to make more of her abominations."

"Has anyone seen the witch?" Jett Bahari scanned our faces for an answer. "According to the reports Jett Markku collected from the survivors, she didn't even show her face."

"She wouldn't," I muttered, mostly to myself. Mogra was dangerous, clever, but not particularly brave. She preferred to create things to do her killing for her instead of handling the job herself. "But, believe me I'm going to find her. And when I do, she won't be able to use any more of our dead."

"There's another reason we need to go in through the catacombs," Cate said, speaking up before an awkward pause could settle over us. "In my visions of Umbra's mirror, the Queen was always surrounded by darkness and stone walls. I suspect she's keeping it underground, below the palace itself, perhaps even in the place where Umbra drained Feradith's hatchling. If we can find it and destroy it, we would be destroying the source of her power."

"Then it's decided," Jett Bahari said, folding his arms. "The bulk of our army will breach the city walls with the help of Eleanor's dragons.

Hopefully, we can fortify ourselves inside before the second army arrives. Meanwhile, a smaller group will gain entry to the palace itself through the cliff tunnels."

"Very well," Inda agreed. "My people won't let you down."

"Aye, and nor will mine," Larna said. "You'll be needing trained warriors, ones with good noses who are after seeing in the dark."

"If you and our people are going, I'm going with you," Cate said. For a moment, she and Larna shared a silent look. "If we meet Mogra inside, so be it. I'm not afraid of her, or anyone else."

She turned toward me, and my heart clenched in my chest. I knew what Cate was waiting for, and this time, I did not throw a tantrum or protest. There was no fight left in me. I would simply have to trust Raisa and I would be lucky enough to escape this battle with our lives one last time. "I'm with you, too. Mogra is my responsibility. I need to end this, once and for all."

"You won't be alone, Fire Princess," Jinale said. "Rufas and I will oversee this expedition personally."

"Will you?" Rachari gazed at Rufas, whiskers twitching with what I realized was her version of a smile. "That is a welcome surprise. I'll make sure our army meets you both on the other side."

The others continued talking for a few moments longer, but my attention wavered. Instead, I stared down at Raisa's hand, still clasped in mine. "Promise me something," I whispered, after a quick check to make sure we weren't the center of attention.

"Anything," Raisa mouthed back, gazing into my eyes.

"Go with Ellie and Eggmother Feradith. She'll protect you. Apparently, dragons have a soft spot for expectant mothers."

Raisa sighed, squeezing my hand. "I suppose I can't turn down the chance to speak with a dragon. She does speak to us mere mortals, doesn't she? Not just druids?"

"Oh, she speaks extensively. And in the third person."

Raisa snorted, but I saw a hint of a smile creep onto her face. "Ailynn, promise me something, too?"

"Anything."

"Come back alive."

I took a deep, steadying breath. "I will. I always do."

Chapter Four

Taken from the diary of Lady Eleanor Kingsclere

"YOUR PLAN IS A good one, Eggmother Eleanor," Feradith said, her large horned head looming high over mine. She lay twisted into a great golden coil just beyond the tents, and the tip of her tail lashed restlessly from side to side, almost like a cat's. Her translucent wings remained tucked close against her body, but her scales still reflected the low sunlight, radiating warmth. "It is clever to hide within the walls of the city before Umbra's army comes. The Great Flight will burn them to ash while they are trapped outside, without the fear of devouring your army as well."

I bit my tongue, deciding it was best not to tell her that it hadn't precisely been my plan. If we were going to succeed, we needed her full cooperation, and for reasons I still didn't fully understand, Feradith seemed to respect me far more than Jett Bahari or any of the liarre representatives. The dwellyn kept an even greater distance, and rightfully so, if my memory served me. Serian translations of Amendyrri fairytales weren't always accurate, but I supposed the parts about dwarves disliking dragons were true.

"How long do you think it will take for your workers to carry us over the walls?" I asked instead. "Could they do it by nightfall? We only have a few more hours."

"Well before," Feradith said. "Feradith has sent scouts to fly over the city. It has been abandoned. If any of Umbra's creatures remain inside, they have retreated into the palace to protect him and the humans he controls. This is merely a matter of transportation."

"Then we should get started." My voice trailed off when I realized that Feradith was no longer looking at me.

Her shining, reflective eyes had fixed on a point slightly further on, and I turned to see a small figure hurrying toward us. Neva was making her way over, a familiar furry bundle bouncing in her arms. When she noticed I had spotted her, she shifted Jessith over to one arm and started waving.

"Go to your young one," Feradith said, in a kinder voice than I had ever heard her use. "I will see that my Flight begins preparations. We have some time left."

"Thank you," I told her, surprised by her informal speech, but grateful for the reprieve. The entire day had been a whirlwind, and a moment to check on Neva was exactly what I needed. I started back toward the tents, meeting her halfway. She seemed surprisingly cheerful despite our grim surroundings, and I hoped she hadn't seen too much of the battle from high in the air.

"Here," she said, holding out Jessith and offering her to me. "Take her. She missed you."

"How do you know?" I asked, scooping the cat into my arms. Jessith's whiskers twitched, but I could tell she was pleased, and the raspy purr didn't escape my notice.

Neva shrugged. "Because I missed you."

"You saw me less than an hour ago. That's hardly enough time to miss me."

Neva cast her eyes to the ground. "Well, I guess I mean I'm going to miss you, after all this."

My stomach gave a slight lurch. Neva was only a child, but she had seen far more horrible things than most girls her age could even dream of. She knew death, and not only because she was *Kira'baas*. I hated to think that she had been imagining her own death, let alone mine or anyone else's.

"You and I will be perfectly fine," I said, crouching down to meet her eyes. "The dragons are going to help us get inside the city where we'll be safe, and—"

"I meant once the fighting is over. If we lose, I'll be dead, and I won't miss you. But if we win, that means I have to be the new Queen. And it means you and Belle will go home to Seria and leave me here."

Although she spoke casually about the possibility that she might not survive, a tremor broke through in her voice when she spoke of becoming the new Queen. I set Jessith down—a decision she seemed to understand and did not protest—and squeezed Neva's shoulder. "I understand why you might not want to be Queen. I'm not sure I would be up for the job either, and I'm grown up."

Neva's expression melted into one of relief. "Really?" she asked, brightening noticeably. "I thought you were going to tell me I had to. No one's even asked me whether I wanted to be Queen or not. They all think...I don't know what they think. Jett Bahari would be a much better ruler than me. Or anyone else, really."

I laughed despite the weariness weighing on my shoulders. "You're right. Jett Bahari would make a wonderful ruler. But you shouldn't be worrying about this right now. No matter what happens, I promise I won't leave you alone. Belle and I aren't going back home to Seria the second the war is over."

"Do you think Lok and Ulig will stay, too?" Neva asked, unable to disguise her hope.

"For a little while, maybe."

Neva leaned in closer, as if she was whispering something secret. "Gurn says he and the others are going to stay with me. He said Belle wanted to go into the caves with Cate and Larna and Ailynn, but Lok told her to stay behind with us."

That piece of information was new to me, but with some effort, I managed to keep my expression neutral. Though the thought of sending her off into danger with only a few weeks of sword training under her belt terrified me, there would be a time and a place to confront her about it, and that time and place was far away from Neva.

Neva didn't seem to notice my pause, but Jessith gave me a knowing feline smirk. "I suppose you and Belle are going to have words later, aren't you?"

I aimed a subtle glare in her direction before returning my attention to Neva. The girl bit her lip, and a shadow of fear returned to her face. "I know why they don't want to go with the rest of the dwellyn. They think the Queen is going to try and take me. And if she does, we won't be able to stop her."

"The Queen isn't going to take you. And Gurn is right. You're going to stay right here with me and Belle. If anything, we need you to protect us, like you did in the Forest. Feradith can only burn so many of those creatures, you know."

"It isn't their fault," Neva said with a sigh. "They don't know what they're doing. Someone has to put them to sleep."

"You will." With a short embrace, I stood and scooped Jessith back into my arms, handing her over again. "Go find Raisa. I'm sure she could use your help," I said, shepherding her away. "And I need to find my wife before we go over the walls," I added under my breath.

"And you complain about my claws," Jessith drawled, peeking at me from over Neva's shoulder. "You might check your new tent. I believe she's still there, polishing her sword."

She isn't going to need it. I made my way back into the remains of camp. *And I think she'll find that my tongue is much sharper.*

***

Belle wasn't polishing her sword when I entered the spare tent that had been hastily set up for us, but the clothes she was wearing were enough to make my stomach lurch all the same. As much as I had grown to appreciate the sight of my wife in pants and more practical Amendyrri clothes, the pads across her shoulders and the light leather breastplate she was currently sporting were far from reassuring. Bent over to pull on her sturdiest set of boots, she looked like she was in the middle of dressing for battle. Even though I knew it was necessary, the thought was deeply unsettling.

"Ellie," she said, smiling, "I see you've found me. Did Jessith tell you where I was, or is this a pleasant coincidence?"

"Oh, she told me," I said, closing the flap behind me. I doubted anyone outside would hear us, but I still felt an instinctive desire for privacy. "And Neva informed me that you volunteered to accompany Cate, Larna, and Ailynn into the palace. Please tell me she was mistaken."

Belle's smile vanished. She sighed, abandoning the laces she had been fiddling with and straightening up. "I did offer to go with them, but you'll be happy to know they didn't want my help. They think it would be better for me to stay with you and Neva."

Despite the disappointment on Belle's face, I couldn't hide my relief. "Thank the Saints," I murmured, suddenly feeling like I could breathe again as the large knot in my chest loosened. "Belle, I know you want to help, and I'm amazed at how much you've transformed in just a few weeks, but the thought of losing you terrifies me. It's bad enough I have to see Cate off. Don't make me say goodbye to you too."

"It wouldn't be goodbye," Belle protested, taking a few hesitant steps toward me. "For someone who claims to be amazed at how much I've transformed. You have remarkably little faith in me."

"I do have faith," I insisted, but I couldn't quite meet her eyes. My own started to sting, and I cast my gaze at the floor instead. "Can you blame me for being afraid? You saw all the corpses out there. You saw the army that's coming for us. How can you look at all that and tell me you aren't scared?"

Warm hands cupped my shoulders, and I looked up at last. "Oh, Ellie. Of course I'm scared." Belle's voice had lowered to a whisper, and her lips trembled ever so slightly. "Who wouldn't be? But I haven't given up hope, either. I think we can win. No, I'm certain we can win. A notion you don't seem willing to consider, even when it would do you some good."

At first, I was angry. I wanted to argue, to pound my fists into that stupid breastplate, to bury my face in something and scream. Instead, I made a cracked noise of pain and frustration, swiping at my eyes with my sleeve. "How can you be so certain?" I asked, my voice slightly muffled by the edge of my arm. "How can you make yourself believe in something so tenuous? When we might not even live out the night?"

"It isn't easy." Belle continued holding my arms, gently, but refusing to let me shy away from her embrace. "I find it comforting to imagine what our lives will be like after all this. You know, when the two of us go home to our quiet, boring lives, and our biggest worry is the gossip about us at Prince Brendan's palace."

The palace recently overrun with the undead. "It won't be the same as before," I muttered, still sniffing even though I hadn't really let myself cry in the first place. "Even if we survive this war, it's going to stay with us."

"So did what happened with Luciana two years ago. That doesn't mean we didn't get our happy ending. Don't be so quick to give up hope."

"My hope has been in short supply lately."

"Then let's pretend." Belle began toying with a lock of my hair, and I shuddered as she twirled the strands through her fingers. "Let's pretend it's several months from now. We're back home with all our friends, and everything is normal again. No more dragons, no more Luciana, no more Queen, no more Mogra, and no more undead armies."

"That's your suggestion?" I asked, half exasperated and half impressed. "Just pretend none of this is happening?"

"Why not?" Belle's hand curled behind my neck to draw me closer, lighting up the sensitive skin there with the edges of her nails. "We both have vivid imaginations, and this isn't so far off from reality."

"Sometimes I think it's bad luck to believe in a happy ending. I'm afraid if I imagine this mess turning out well, it won't." I sighed, lowering my eyes again, but she didn't let go of me. "That sounds foolish, doesn't it?"

"No, it isn't foolish, but I'm not convinced it's healthy." Belle began kneading my stiff shoulder muscles, and a groan slipped from my lips. Everything about her touch tempted me to let go of all the tension I was carrying. "You've already spent months considering the worst possible outcomes. Why won't you let yourself imagine the best?"

I couldn't see the flaws in her argument. I leaned forward, resting my forehead against her shoulder and inhaling her scent. The leather was different, but underneath, her smell was the same, warm and sweet. "You're so optimistic these days," I murmured. "What happened to the gloomy, woe-is-me Belle who was content to mope and brood while her sister ruined her life?"

Belle stroked up and down my back, soothing the tightness there as well. "She fell in love, of course. With a beautiful woman who never let her doubts keep her from reaching for the happiness she knew she deserved."

A flush heated up the points of my cheeks, and I placed a kiss against her throat, pulling back enough to gaze up into her eyes. "Thank you for reminding me," I said, giving her a genuine smile. "So, it's a few months from now. We've returned to Baxstresse."

"With all our friends."

"And the animals."

Belle laughed. "And the animals, of course. And Neva."

I knew that was unlikely, but I didn't correct her. If this was supposed to be our ideal future, I wanted it to be a good one. "And I come up to the library after helping Mam and Sarah with dinner. You've started a fire, and you're curled up in your favorite chair, reading a book."

"What sort of book?" Belle began undoing the laces on the back of my traveling dress, something she could accomplish without even looking.

"A treatise on Amendyr's people," I suggested, remembering the many nights I had observed her with her nose buried in a book. "Your brow would furrow, and you would complain about how inaccurate the information was."

Belle peeled open the top half of my dress, sliding the sleeves down from my shoulders. She took her time stroking the newly exposed skin, and I shivered at the contrast between the cool air and the warmth of her hands. "Actually, I think I would be reading a romance novel. Something completely inappropriate, so I start to put it away before I realize it's only you."

"Then what?" I lean closer. Soon, her lips hovered less than an inch above mine.

"Then you pluck the book out of my grasp and drop it on the floor beside the armchair," she whispered. "And you tell me that you think you can show me something far more entertaining."

"Think?" I slid my hands up from her waist, letting them wander beneath the hem of her shirt in search of more bare skin. "I know I would be able to show you something far more entertaining."

Belle's eyes flashed, and the need in them stole my breath. "Show me now?"

I kissed her with all the passion I could. Even in darkness, Belle could always awaken a brilliant light inside of me. Her lips were warm and welcoming, and at last, I let myself believe in a happy ending. The two of us had made one before. There was no reason we couldn't do it again.

We clung to each other as our mouths tasted and took, stumbling back toward the pallet on instinct. As we sank to the ground, stripping out of our outer clothes as best we could without breaking our string of kisses, I imagined we really were in the library, tumbling in a tangle onto the armchair instead. The library was the place where Belle and I had first declared our love for each other, and it was the place I wanted to be more than anywhere else.

Eventually, we had to part for breath. I took the opportunity to finish shoving down Belle's pants and strip her breastplate and shirt over her head, groaning a little as I realized her chest was directly in front of my face. "Then what happens?" I slid my mouth along her collarbone, teasing before I reached my goal. "What do I do after I throw your book away?"

"You mean after we kiss each other breathless and tear off our clothes?" Belle ignored my wandering mouth in favor of shoving the top half of my underdress down to my waist, although she trembled as I drew closer to the tight point of her nipple. "The chair can't hold both of us for long, so we sink to the rug beside the fire."

I took her mouth in another kiss, angling one of my knees up to press between her legs. Heat glided along my thigh, and I gasped. Without her smallclothes, I could feel how eager she already was. Her hips bucked, and I braced my heel on the ground, giving her a steady surface. "And?" I whispered, trapping her lower lip between my teeth for a soft tug. Her pelvis jerked again, and more wetness painted my skin. "Which one of us was on top?"

That was a difficult question. Imagining myself straddling Belle's waist was an appealing picture, but feeling her solid weight on top of me in the present sent a rush of warmth straight to my core. "You for now, my beautiful swordmaiden," I murmured into her mouth, unwilling to give up our current position. "But after that," I ran my hand down her back, brushing her long hair aside, feeling coiled muscles bunch beneath smooth skin, "I can't make promises."

Belle only tolerated my slow pace for a few moments. She snatched my wrists in a steel grip and dragged them above my head, pinning them beneath her forearm. This time, she was the one nipping at my lips and trailing a chain of bite marks down the column of my throat. I closed my eyes, focusing on the heat of her mouth and the blunt edges of her teeth. With her help, I was transported to someplace safe, someplace where only she and I existed.

While her arm continued pressing down on my wrists, her other hand slid lower, following the curve of my side to cup my hip. She pushed into my thigh, sending more slickness spilling beneath my knee.

"So beautiful," she muttered, mouth lingering near my pulse point. "What did I do to deserve you?"

I often asked myself the same question, but in that moment, I didn't care. I was simply grateful. Then, I forgot everything else as her fingers moved purposefully between my legs. As soon as they found me, my eyes fluttered shut. Belle knew just how to touch me, the perfect stroke and speed to use. When she began circling the stiff bud of my clit, I had to bite the inside of my cheek to stifle a scream. I pulled in swift, heavy gasps of air, but it wasn't enough to stop my head from swimming. The taut muscles of my thighs twitched each time she trapped me beneath her fingertips, and I couldn't keep from squirming.

"Belle, please," I breathed

Belle stopped in the middle of marking my shoulder. Her tongue dragged back up along my throat until her mouth was close enough to whisper in my ear. "Please, what? Belle, please, faster?" She sped up her fingers, and my eyes snapped open again just in time to see stars. Before the brightness could overwhelm me, she eased up, leaving me pulsing and unsatisfied. "Or Belle, please, harder?" She increased the pressure of her fingers, and my hips snapped up. "Or." Her lips wandered closer to mine, covering them in a series of short pecks. "Maybe." Kiss. "You want me." Another kiss. The soft slide of her tongue. "Inside?"

I couldn't remember how to say "yes." Her hands and mouth had the power to make me forget everything else. I locked one of my knees around her hip and rocked forward to encourage her. Thankfully, she didn't tease. She slid deep inside of me with one smooth thrust, first with one finger, then two. I whimpered at the sudden stretch, but she hardly gave me time to adjust. Her fingers formed a hook, dragging over the sensitive place she always found so easily.

The blissful fullness helped me reclaim my voice. I cried out, completely forgetting about the other tents surrounding ours. In my mind, we were still in the library. The flickering flames painted moving shapes over our bodies, and the rug rubbed along my back as Belle began to move on top of me. She used her whole arm to increase the force of her thrusts, curling at the end of each one. I tried to reach down, desperate for something to grip, but she kept my wrists pinned high above my head. A bolt of need shot through me. I was trapped, unable to do anything but submit.

I had felt nothing but helpless for the past few months, but somehow, choosing it came as a relief. I quivered, but my entire body relaxed at the same time, and warmth spread through every inch of me. Pressure began pounding along my front wall, straining each time Belle's fingers found it. I looked up into her eyes, and I was lost. She was staring down at me with such passion, such hunger, and such love I couldn't hold back. Heat raced through me, and I clutched tight at her fingers as my muscles shuddered with heavy pulses.

A beaming look of pride broke across Belle's face as she felt my release spill out around her fingers. She buried them one last time and kept curling up, offering me the heel of her hand to grind against. It pushed exactly where I needed, and my clit throbbed against the welcome pressure. I filled her hand all over again, arching beneath her as the fullness inside me continued spilling out in thick bursts. Just when I thought I couldn't stand anymore, her lips seized mine in one last scorching kiss. I shattered to pieces, shaking as I surrendered everything I had.

At last, the powerful waves became soft ripples. I blinked to clear the light, hazy layer of tears from my eyes, and my cheeks hurt from smiling. Even with everything else falling apart, being with Belle was always perfect.

"Your turn," I rasped when I finally recovered enough to speak. "I never promised you could be on top the entire time."

Belle's eyebrows arched, but she removed her forearm from over my hands and allowed me to sit up. "So, what happens in this story after I ravish you by the fire?" Her voice was tight with need, and I could tell she wouldn't last long once I started.

"After that, my mouth relearns every inch of you."

I launched myself into her arms, and we fell over in the opposite direction, trading short kisses back and forth. She laughed as my fingers skimmed her sides, and I couldn't resist digging in a little more to make her squirm. After a brief "scuffle" and another fit of giggles, I succeeded in straddling her hips.

"Not fair," she gasped. The points of her cheeks were flushed, and her chest heaved as she tried to catch her breath. "You know I'm ticklish."

"Oh? I had no idea." I lowered myself onto my elbows, letting the edges of my hair skim her chest as I began kissing down from her collarbone. "Does this tickle?"

"A little." Her muscles stiffened, and I could tell she was trying to stay still as I settled into the cradle of her legs.

"What about this?" A shiver coursed through her body as my lips sealed around the hard point of her nipple, and I lashed my tongue over the tip in feather-light flicks. Her hips bucked up, and she groaned as she found purchase against my stomach. If my mouth hadn't been busy, I would have smiled.

"Yes. I mean, no." Her fingers threaded through my hair, guiding me across to her other breast. I conceded, but only after trapping the tight bud between the edges of my teeth for a swift tug.

"Well, which is it?" I scattered kisses across her chest. "Yes or no?"

Belle struggled to answer as I dragged my tongue along the flat plane of her abdomen. She forgot her efforts to hold still when I drew close to her navel, and her grip on my head flexed, as if she wasn't sure whether she wanted to push me further down or pull me back up. "No," she groaned. "Saints, Ellie, where did you learn to be such a tease?"

"From you," I whispered in between touching up a faint, blushing mark a few inches in from her hipbone. "Or have you forgotten who taught me how to do this?"

Belle seemed to make up her mind. She pushed harder on my hair, trying to direct me between her spread legs, but I took my time getting there. I lathered layers of kisses across her abdomen as I draped one of her knees over my shoulder, exposing her even further. Her outer lips were already swollen and parted, revealing the soft pink folds between and the straining bundle of her clit.

I bent forward, coaxing a sharp cry from above me the moment my lips made contact. More warmth ran over my chin, but I was completely focused on my goal—making Belle shudder to pieces just as she had done for me. I savored her reactions, tailoring my efforts to get the ones I wanted. Her knee pulled tighter over my shoulder whenever I moved my tongue in circles, and her stomach tightened every time I pulled her further in. When I did both at once, her hips levitated off the pallet, and she whispered my name. "Ellie, please. Oh Ellie, just like that."

I released her with a soft pop before she could tip too far over the edge. She cast a pleading look down at me, but I ignored it, dragging my tongue lower to press against the tight ring of muscle at her entrance. This time, I had full access to the flood I had only felt before. I hummed in satisfaction, gathering as much as I could and raking my nails along her tense thigh to keep her still. She made even sweeter sounds as I pushed inside of her, and the honey that filled my mouth almost made my eyes roll back in my head.

Causing my strong, beautiful lover to break down before me was just as satisfying as surrendering to her. I craved her pleasure as much as my own. *This,* I thought as she began to tremble and sigh, *is all I need for the rest of my life. Just this. Just her.* When I couldn't stand to wait anymore and her entire body was quivering with need, I finally took her back into my mouth. Belle stiffened then shook, twisting her fingers tightly through my hair in her desperation.

She came a few seconds later. More wetness and heat burst against my chin, and the stiff bud of her clit twitched in the seal of my lips. Her hips gave a few unsteady jerks, but mostly, she held still and shuddered, as if my mouth was almost too much to endure. When I cast my eyes up along her quivering body, I noticed that her soft blue eyes were locked on me. They were filled with such love I could not put it into words, but it didn't matter. She understood I felt the same. I eased her through the harshest ripples, only backing away when her waves became eddies. She breathed a sigh of relief and collapsed back onto the pallet, staring at the top of the tent with a glazed expression on her face.

"Well, that's certainly something to fight for," she mumbled. "How can I fail when I have a lifetime of that to look forward to?"

I smiled. Before, joking about our own mortality might have upset me, but now, I felt more confident. I believed in the picture my wife had painted of our future together. I believed we could make it back to Baxstresse and resume our lives. I believed the two of us and all our friends could survive this war, and I wasn't going to let fear take that dream away anymore. "I love you," I said, grinning as I climbed up along her exhausted body. "And I'm happy to give you all the incentive you need to stay alive."

Belle's hand left my hair and slid down my back, teasing the base of my spine. "Likewise. Now, why don't we rest for a minute before we get cleaned up and save the kingdom? I'm not ready to let you go yet."

Chapter Five

Taken from the letters of Cathelin Raybrook, edited by Lady Eleanor Kingsclere

BY THE TIME THE dragons finished flying the bulk of Jett Bahari's army over the city walls, the sun had dipped dangerously low in the sky. Its light had begun to curve over the horizon, and the chill of night was swiftly descending. With each glowing orange ray that slipped away into blue and each faint star that winked above us, the tension grew. Anyone left outside of Kalmarin wouldn't live to see the morning.

Larna and I remained with our pack, helping our injured onto the dragons, making sure everyone was fed, and waiting by the cliffs for the signal to proceed. The dwellyn had secured sturdy rope ladders to the crags near the top, and when I had nothing more pressing to do, I watched them scurry up and down. Inda had already located an entrance large enough for the liarre to pass through and once the walls were breached, we would make our way down into the tunnels.

"Catie?"

The soft touch of a hand on my good shoulder startled me, but I relaxed as Larna's scent wrapped around me. "*Tuathe.* Do you need me?"

Larna offered me a slight smile, although her eyes remained worried. "Aye. Always."

I leaned into her side, resting my cheek briefly against her shoulder. If we only had a few moments left before the battle, that was where I wanted to be. "I love you," I told her, tucking beneath her chin and folding an arm around her waist. Her heartbeat thumped steadily beneath my ear, and my own slowed down to match.

"I love you, too."

"Cate?"

Reluctantly, I drew away to answer the second call of my name, leaving my fingers on Larna's hip until the last possible moment. When I saw a familiar messy bun of golden hair and bright green eyes, my annoyance faded a little. "Ellie. What are you doing here? You're supposed to be with Feradith, flying over the walls."

"I will be, in another minute. I came to say good luck."

She means goodbye, I realized, with a sharp pang in my chest. None of us had any idea what we would find in the tunnels, and some of us might not come out of them. "It's past time for luck, I'm afraid," I said as I left Larna's embrace and approached her. "We're going to need one of those divine miracles you Serians are always preaching about."

"Don't talk like that. Cate, you've done so many incredible things since you left Baxstresse. If only one person destroys that mirror and makes it to the palace gates alive, I know it will be you."

On impulse, I reached over to rub my shoulder. "I wouldn't take that bet," I told her, glancing over at Ailynn. She was several yards away, standing with Jinale and Rufas and their band of soldiers. "I'll put my coins on our fire princess."

Ellie huffed. "Then Saints, stay next to her and duck a lot. You aren't going to die."

"She won't," Larna said, to my mild surprise. Although I had been teaching her, her Serian wasn't the best, and I was impressed she had been able to follow the conversation. She draped a strong arm around me, pulling me against her. "I won't let her."

Ellie nodded stiffly, and I caught the glistening in her eyes. "You'd better not," she said, before pulling us both into a big hug. My eyes began to water as well, and when she kissed my cheek, its surface was tracked with tears. "Come back, Cate. I need my best friend."

"All right. I will."

Ellie finally pulled away and made her way back to the abandoned tents in the distance. Larna laughed softly. "You'll be after marrying that woman someday, *Tuathe*," she said, tucking a lock of my hair back behind my ear.

"When we're both dotty old widows and you and Belle have died of old age, maybe," I teased. "But I don't have any intention of losing you before then. I'm not leaving through the palace gates without you, Larna. I can't."

"You willna have to." Her gentle hand crept around the back of my neck, and when her lips descended over mine, I found a moment of peace. This was the woman who had mended my heart, and I would fight to protect it—to protect her—with every bit of strength I had.

***

The steady drip of water echoed as we made our way deeper and deeper into the cliffside caves. The light from outside had long since faded into darkness, and the damp, coppery smell of limestone stung inside my nose every time I breathed. Mixed with the biting scent of magic, it was difficult to bear. The rock seemed to throb with it, almost like Feradith's cave, and its pulse thudded deep in my bones.

Inda and the other dwellyn moved at the front of the group, so swift and silent I scarcely would have known they were there if the flicker of Ailynn's fire hadn't illuminated their small bodies. Their shadows twisted along the walls, far taller than they were as they walked in single file. The Farseer pack followed along behind, tense and anxious, fur bristling and noses twitching. Most of us had already taken our half-shape, although a few glided by as wolves, muzzles held aloft.

"How much farther?" Larna growled beside my ear. She prowled along beside me, breathing lightly, almost as quiet as the dwellyn. The only sound that gave her away was the slight splash of her paws in the shallow pools of cave water.

I closed my eyes and focused. Kalwyn had taught me how to pull on the threads around me and sense where the knots gathered, but the raw stink of magic was so strong I had difficulty pinpointing the source. After some hesitation, I glanced back toward Ailynn. She was a few yards back with the liarre forces, perched on Rufas' back, hands glowing faintly with flame. I nodded left, chin raised in question, and she dipped her head in agreement.

"This way," I whispered up to Inda, repeating the motion. "We have to be getting close."

She nodded, and the dwellyn veered left, navigating down another tunnel. The caves inside the cliffs were like a tangled spider web, radiating in all directions and doubling back on each other. Without their guidance, I was sure we would have been lost a few turns in.

Then, suddenly, twin lights flashed in the distance. They were round, floating in midair, and my nose picked up something musky beneath the other smells. I sniffed, letting the stale air wash into my mouth, and beside me, Larna did the same. The two of us looked at each other, and Larna barked out a command.

"Wyr! Be ready."

Her shout broke the tension, and the darkness exploded with growls and snarls. Heavy, bristling bodies hurtled along the passageway, heading straight toward us, and in Ailynn's faint light, I could see we had been right. Mogra had left some of her pets beneath the palace to wait for us, and they were not as mindless as the kerak. They were swift, savage, and deadly cunning, and if their jaws closed in a death-bite, they would not let go.

There wasn't time to be afraid. The baying of wolves echoed in the darkness, and our forces met in a savage tear of teeth. I lunged, snapping at the nearest target I could find. My jaws closed on a stout foreleg, and I crunched down to the bone, ignoring the way my opponent thrashed. Fangs flashed above me, sinking into the scruff of my neck, but the wyr didn't find a hold. A huge black body leapt toward us, knocking into its side and sending it crashing to the ground.

Larna. The two of us tore free together, twisting in the cramped quarters. The brawl around us had turned to chaos. Mogra's wyr were everywhere, and in the shadows, with the stench of magic and blood and fear saturating everything, it was almost impossible to tell friend from foe. The dwellyn at the front of our group had drawn their blades, defending themselves against creatures three times their size, but the liarre were more hesitant. They couldn't release their arrows well at such short range, and they couldn't tell us apart either.

"Ailynn," I roared, whirling to meet another set of swiping claws. I saw a flash of a face near mine—twisted, hungry, muzzle dripping with spit at the jowls. Teeth clicked near my throat, and I had to kick and writhe to avoid them. "Light the tunnel."

Suddenly, the world exploded in a flash of white. My eyes burned, and howls of agony bounced from the walls. "Run, now," Ailynn called, shouting to be heard. "Find somewhere open!"

The battle became a chase. As one, our forces moved, crawling and clambering and cleaving our way out of the writhing mass of bodies. We had to climb over several dead corpses to do it—theirs and ours—but after a few frantic moments, the first of us found freedom in a tunnel to our left. I started to run, but at the sound of screams, I had to look back. The sight struck me like a blow. More wyr poured out of the nearby tunnel branches, more than I could have possibly imagined, tearing apart everything they touched.

Liarre fell, shredded to pieces. Dwellyn were crushed beneath their feet. Still, they kept coming—an unstoppable tide, too numerous to count. I tensed, preparing to leap back anyway, but another shout stopped me.

"Go, Cate." Jinale towered tall and proud beside me, bow drawn, poison arrows ready. "Take Ailynn. Find the mirror and destroy it."

"My pack," I protested, pleading, but Rufas and Larna were already boxing me in, urging me to continue.

"Cate," Larna barked, shoving into me and forcing me to move. "Move! The pack will follow."

But I knew they wouldn't. They wouldn't, and neither would Rufas and Jinale's warriors, and neither would Inda's dwellyn.

Rufas seemed to understand. He dipped his head, passing her the rest of his own quiver, and then turned away. There wasn't time. I ran, fleeing down the tunnel with Larna and Rufas sprinting beside me.

I looked back only once, and wished I hadn't. Jinale was still standing at the mouth of the passageway, firing arrows into the darkness as the shadows swallowed her up.

***

I couldn't tell how long we spent weaving through the tunnels by the light of Ailynn's glowing flames. Distant shouts and the howling of wolves made tracking time difficult, and the constant hum of magic was worse. It became our guide, but as we followed the thrumming strands through the catacombs, the intense energy seemed to sense us as well. It coiled around me, licking at my skin, boring into my head and throbbing there like an awful heartbeat

Ailynn wasn't much better off. She swayed on Rufas' back, and her breaths were shallow. The caniarre remained stalwart and silent, and with what little light there was, I could see tense lines on his face. Only Larna remained unaffected. With no magical abilities, she didn't seem to sense the vibrations, smell the singe of burning air, or jerk along to the lurching pull. She brought up the rear, ears pricked up, constantly listening.

I knew what she was thinking. She had hope that some of our friends, some of our pack, had managed to escape. Perhaps they had found shelter somewhere in the network of caves, but I doubted it. Mogra's wyr hadn't been a pack, but an army and they had been waiting for us. Waiting to stop us from finding the mirror.

Just when I thought my skull would split open and I couldn't stand another second of the swelling magic and the echoing screams, the tunnel branched out into a large, dark cave. *No, not a cave.* Ailynn's fire flickered brighter. *A room.* We entered a large cavern that judging from the smooth walls and level floor had been made by humans. As we stepped forward, I noticed that Ailynn's magic was not the only thing lighting our way. A high, cold beam of light fell down from the ceiling, illuminating a large stone platform.

At first, I was furious. The mirror we had fought so hard to find was nowhere in sight as it had been in my visions. Then, I noticed that the platform was not empty. Pale white bones, strangely delicate, but much too large to belong to a person, lay scattered across its surface. When I saw the shape of the hollow skull and looked into its missing eyes, I knew—and I also Knew. This was no ordinary skeleton. It had once belonged to a dragon.

"Feradith's hatchling," said a voice, carrying through the room despite its softness. "Still here, after all these hundreds of years."

I turned toward Ailynn, thinking she had spoken, but the line of her jaw was tense and unmoving. She was staring straight ahead, not at the bones, but beyond them into the darkness. A cloaked figure stepped into the beam of light, and I saw a spill of auburn hair beneath the hood. Instantly, I shook off my surprise and dropped into a crouch. I could guess who she was, even though I had never seen her take this shape before.

"The others are gone, of course," the figure said. She did not seem to be frightened of us, or even distressed. Instead, she spoke as if from far away, in a dreamlike trance. "The magic they unleashed was too powerful for them to hold. It disintegrated them in an instant. All except for one—the strongest. The one who drew on the power of his focus object to save himself and became part of it."

"Where is it, mother?" Ailynn asked, fire flaring to life around her fists.

"The mirror?" Mogra pushed her hood back, and her resemblance to Ailynn was striking. "She's taken it."

"Where?" Ailynn demanded, louder this time. "If there's anything of you left that isn't his, tell me."

Mogra gazed up at the swirling column of light, letting it wash over her face. It started to shift and change, and wrinkles flickered in and out along its surface. "To the girl, of course. How better to claw his way free of death than with the body of a *Kira'baas?*"

Chapter Six

Taken from the verbal accounts of Ailynn Gothel, edited by Lady Eleanor Kingsclere

MY MOTHER'S WORDS SHOULDN'T have surprised me. This wasn't the first time she had seen a child as an object she could use, merely a means to an end. But as I stared at her face, hauntingly familiar and yet so different from the person I remembered, my chest clenched. Despite everything Mogra had done, part of me had still clung to faint hope—hope that somewhere beneath everything, some piece of the woman who had raised me still existed.

Now, I knew. This was the woman who had raised me. There was no telling when Umbra had begun to infect her, or how, but it didn't matter. The last of my sympathy snuffed out like the dying flame of a candle.

"I won't let you do this," I told her. Fire blossomed around my hands, blazing hot and raw. "You only saw me as one of your treasures, and you gave Raisa to me like some kind of pet. Neva's a person, not a body to be possessed!"

Mogra's expression faltered. Her eyes softened, and the lines carved into her face faded. But then her lip peeled back, and her gaze narrowed to a thin, sharp line. "*Ruach!*"

Rufas, Cate, and Larna charged, but we were already too slow. The cavern around us trembled, shaken by a blustering gale of wind, and Mogra began rising into the air. Her auburn hair whipped about her head in a storm, her cape fluttering behind her like the ragged wings of a raven. She rose toward the hole of light high above us, but I refused to let her reach it. She was my mother, my responsibility.

"*Erets!*"

The Word seared my tongue and the earth beneath the four of us moved. It shuddered, groaning and grating as it cracked, and we shot toward the cavern ceiling on a pillar of stone. Mogra broke through the roof of the catacombs, soaring away into the sky. Cate and Larna landed a short distance away, but I clung to the fur of Rufas' back, shouting into his shoulder. "Don't let her get away!"

"I won't. Hold on tight."

He bristled, muscles tensing in preparation, and when we exploded into the world above, he leapt. His paws hit the ground hard, and he ran, following the flashing black shadow above us. The darkness made Mogra difficult to see, but the corrupted call of her magic shone like a beacon. I would have been able to follow it for miles.

We raced through what seemed to be a courtyard, heading toward a giant gate several times our height. It towered above us, but as Mogra sailed over the wall, Rufas didn't slow. He continued barreling forward, picking up speed.

"Bring it down," he barked, and I summoned everything I had, letting the force of my rage surge through my arms. Stone rumbled. Fire blazed. Metal melted and wood splintered. The gate burst wide open, giving beneath the force.

Rufas jumped over the smoldering wreckage and sprinted out into an open space lit from one end to the other with torches. Suddenly, we were flying through the wide streets of a city. Figures swarmed all around us—human, liarre, and dwellyn; wyr, kerak, and shadowkin. Dragons roared and veered above us, setting the world ablaze. Smoke and ash clogged my throat, and I gagged on the biting stench of magic.

While I choked and sputtered, Rufas ran. He was locked onto Mogra like a hunting dog, every point in his body quivering. I bent low over his back, trusting him to carry me. A coward like Mogra wouldn't stay in this chaos. She had to be making her way toward clearer ground. At last, we found it, a patch of green amidst the burning buildings. It had once been an open square, but a full third of it had been devoured by flame, leaving scorched tracks across the torn ground. I saw Mogra's dark shape trying to rise higher, but the flashing sky was just as dangerous.

As the beating of wings and spinning columns of dragonfire forced her down, I saw our chance. "Rufas, go!"

He rushed forward. I summoned my flames. Mogra met them with a jutting slab of earth, and the two of us vaulted over, buoyed by a gust of air. Rufas raised his club high above his head, but he never got to bring it crashing down. A heavy blast of wind buffeted us backwards, and I toppled from his shoulders. I hit the ground hard, rolling several feet before coming to rest against the newly made wall.

Or what had once been a wall. With a sickening crack, Mogra

brought it crashing down. I covered my face with my arms, acting on instinct. "*Secutem*!"

My shield sprang to life just in time. Loose rock crumbled everywhere, beating against the barrier, but somehow, it held. I fed it with all my strength, gritting my teeth and sealing the weak spots until the shower of stone had stopped. As the dust settled, I climbed to my knees, ignoring the ache in my bones. I whipped my head around and saw Rufas had not joined me. He lay on his side, most of his body trapped beneath a mountain of rubble.

I crawled over, preparing to shift it, but when I saw the glazed look in his eyes, I knew it wouldn't do any good. My shield had saved me, but it hadn't been big enough for him. "Rufas, I—"

"Don't," he rasped. His voice was half breath, and a ribbon of dark, crimson blood leaked from his mouth onto the ground, forming a sticky pool. "End her." He jerked his head slightly, and I saw Mogra's shadow approaching. She had finally decided to stop running from this fight. I squared my shoulders, preparing to struggle to my feet and face her.

"It was an honor...to carry you...Ailynn."

When Rufas said my name, I froze. First, I had been "human" or "witch." After I had helped bring the dragons and saved his warriors, he had addressed me as fire princess. Now, at last, he had finally called me Ailynn like an equal.

I swallowed and nodded, my face a mess of smudged dirt and tears. When his eyes closed, I forced myself up, teeth gritted in anger. "It's over, Mother." Threads of heat crackled around my clenched fists. I released a brilliant stream of fire, not at Mogra, but high into the air, hoping someone would see it amidst the flashing flames of the dragons. I had watched Mogra kill more people than I could bear to think about, but Rufas would be the last. Even if I fell while fighting her, surely someone would see the flames and come. I couldn't allow her to escape and continue her destruction.

My display didn't seem to unsettle Mogra. She pulled back her hood again, and I gazed into a copy of my face, watching it twist with smug hatred. "Are you calling for help because you don't think you can kill me on your own, Ailynn?" She summoned her own fire, flashing her teeth. "You've always been weak. I should have taught you better."

"The only thing you've taught me is the price of greed and selfishness."

Mogra's face contorted. The earth beneath me quaked, rumbling as it split open, and my footing slipped. I staggered, struggling to regain my balance, only to see Mogra extend her arm. A whirling column of fire and wind whipped toward me, ripping through the air.

I reached into the ground beneath me, tugging hard. A slab of solid stone shot up, shielding me from the blast. My wall cracked and warped under the intense heat, melting into slag, but it held long enough for me to recover. When it came down, I was ready with a sharp gust of air.

Mogra redirected it with a wave of her hand, as if she was banishing a gnat. "Your shields won't help you, Ailynn." Flames wreathed her entire body, and she almost didn't look human anymore. "You can't hold them forever."

But I didn't have to hold them forever, just long enough to take her down. Rapid jabs of fire flew toward me, one after another, but I was better prepared. I wove across the courtyard, sweeping them aside. She had made a mistake in using fire. Mogra seemed to realize it, too, because she changed tactics. The shattered remnants of my wall quivered, rising into the air and shooting straight toward me.

I leapt, catching a few sharp stones across my cheek before I made it clear of the avalanche. The blows stung, and something wet ran down one side of my face, but I raced for the other side of the courtyard, feet barely even skimming the ground.

Mogra was after me in an instant. Streams of air propelled her forward, and it was everything I could do to stay one step ahead of her. Gusts of air and clods of earth kept hurling toward me, cutting off every avenue of escape. There was only one place left to go—the sky. I jumped, letting a surge of flame and air carry me upwards.

It was a mistake. I only made it about five feet off the ground before a sound like thunder tore through the sky. A sharp gust of wind hit me head on, throwing me off course. I tried to shout, but all the breath had left my lungs. I sailed backwards, slamming into something.

The collision sent me lurching. I shook myself, trying to clamber back to my feet, but my limbs trembled, refusing to obey. I slipped several times, clambering over the rubble of what had once been a building. Mogra's attacks were tearing the city apart piece by piece.

"Foolish girl," Mogra screeched, and I whirled to see her closing in from above. She touched the ground gracefully, her cloak fluttering around her. "You can't fly away from me, either."

I braced myself, planting my feet and squaring my shoulders. "I'm not running. That's your game."

Mogra sent another beam of fire racing toward me, but desperation lent me speed. I matched it with my own, pouring out all the heat and anger I had within me. Our flames met, spitting and crackling, feeding from each other and swelling high above our heads. I felt the push of her magic, a wave of boiling fury, and I met it with every ounce of defiance I possessed. *I won't let her fire eat mine. I won't let her hatred consume me.*

But Mogra was stronger than I expected. She pushed again, an overwhelming surge of raw strength, and I faltered. The writhing mass of flame slipped from my grasp. Mine melted into hers, doubling its size, and the courtyard blazed bright as day. Mogra held the towering inferno high over her head, preparing to unleash all its power.

There wasn't even time for a Word of Power. Mogra sent her flames hurtling toward me, and I threw up my arms, shielding myself with everything I had left. A cushion of air surrounded my body, whirling around me in a small storm and sealing me in. Broken bits of rock whipped toward me, caught up in the spiral. Strands of fire wove in between, and I tightened the laces of the net. Mogra's flames hit with a shuddering explosion. I couldn't hear it, but I shook with the force of the blast. Still, my shield held in the eerie, brilliant silence. Sweat rolled down my face and heat scoured my skin, but the cocoon I had made didn't crack.

When the flames finally dissipated, I was in the middle of a deep, charred pit. All that remained was scorched earth, Mogra, and me. The broken building and courtyard had disintegrated. When she saw that I had survived, she screeched with rage, hurling angry, unpredictable bursts of fire and rock in my direction. None of them made it through. She couldn't touch me, and she knew it. The two of us were at a stalemate.

"Witch!" A great shout carried across the battlefield, rising above Mogra's howl and the throbbing hum of magic.

Through the blurry edges of my shield, I saw a figure approach, enormous even from a distance. He jumped down into the pit, approaching with giant, determined strides, and I saw the gleam of metal against his shoulder.

Jethro! I realized at once. *He must have seen my signal.*

Mogra turned away from me, whirling on him with a snarl. "Who are you?" She spat in disgust. "How do you dare—"

"It doesn't matter who I am." Jethro hefted his axe, and his barrel chest swelled. "You're finished. I'm going to put you down like the rabid dog you are."

Mogra rolled her eyes at the threat. She waved her arm with an almost disgusted motion, summoning more fire around her hand. Jethro didn't wait for her to unleash it. He charged, axe raised high, and Mogra drew back her flames.

While she was distracted, I took my chance. I unleashed all the power in my shield, sending it straight toward her. By the time she saw my magic, it was too late. She raised her arms, trying to block. A shower of rock, air, and fire sent her flying backward, crashing into the side of the pit. I hit the ground running, prepared to attack again, but she didn't get up.

Jethro and I reached Mogra at the same time. She wasn't dead, but clearly injured, trying to claw up the side of the pit. Her face read pain and desperation, and the look made my stomach lurch. She looked like an old woman once more, ancient and exhausted. I steeled myself, burning hands clenched. *My mother. My responsibility.* I looked at Jethro. He was waiting expectantly, a look of fury still on his face. I closed my eyes then opened them again slowly.

"You do it," I told him. "For your wife." *And because Raisa and all of my friends were right. I shouldn't have to live with this.*

He nodded once, almost in gratitude, and I turned my back. Moments later, the wet thud of an axe fell. I brought my sleeve up to my face, wiping away blood and tears. I had expected Mogra's death to bring me some kind of closure, but instead, I felt only emptiness. My eyes went to the other side of the pit, where Rufas' body had lain. Mogra's great fire had devoured nearly everything, and I wasn't sure where the remains of his corpse were, but I would find them. He deserved that and more.

I'm so sorry, Rufas, I thought, hanging my head. *And I'm sorry, Mother.*

Chapter Seven

Taken from the letters of Cathelin Raybrook, edited by Lady Eleanor Kingsclere

LARNA AND I LOPED out through the gate, stumbling onto a raging battlefield. Torches blazed everywhere, and dragons spiraled high overhead. Humans, liarre, and dwellyn battled Mogra's forces, but in the chaos, it was difficult to tell who had the upper hand. Corpses littered the ground, and smoke thickened the air.

"This way," Larna barked, jerking her head left. We ran as one, weaving through the mass of bodies, tearing down any kerak that stood in our way. A shadowkin loomed over us, teeth bared, but to my shock, it didn't attack. Instead, its tongue lolled out of its giant mouth, and its tail began wagging in greeting.

"Stinky?" I asked, not quite believing it. "How did you find your way back here from the mountains?"

Stinky tilted his head, ears perking up.

"Do you know where Neva is?"

At the sound of Neva's name, Stinky let out a booming bark before turning and plowing his way through the mass of bodies. Kerak and wyr scattered beneath his enormous paws, leaving a clear path ahead. We took off behind him, following the trail of destruction. It led straight through the heart of what looked like a large city, although several of the buildings were on fire. Enemies and allies alike had thinned out, and we only came across a few stragglers.

With Stinky leading the way, we made swift progress, and the giant white walls grew taller and taller as we approached the edge of the city. He lifted his head halfway down an empty street, seeming to catch a scent, and sped up, baying in excitement.

Try as we could, Larna and I couldn't match his pace. We lagged behind, slowing to a trot and trying to catch our breath. "Where is he going?" Larna huffed beside me.

"Not sure," I panted. "The walls? That's where Ellie and Neva were going to wait."

Larna didn't answer. She came to an abrupt stop, nose pointed up. She sniffed, and a low rumble started in her throat. "Catie," she growled, "what do you smell?"

I inhaled, and my blood turned to ice. A rotting, sickly-sweet smell crept in from all sides, filling the air and clogging my throat. I choked, whipping around to try and find the source, but I saw no signs of Luciana among the burning wreckage of the buildings. "She's here," I whispered, heart hammering inside my chest. "Larna, I know she's here."

Movement came from off to one side, and I whipped my head around. I couldn't see her, but I could feel her presence, and every instinct screamed at me to run. Larna seemed to agree. She turned, looking toward the nearby walls. "Cate, go find Ellie. Be telling her—"

A large black shape exploded out of the darkness, crashing into Larna's side and sending her skidding across the ground. The two of them tangled together, snarling and writhing, slashing at each other. I lunged toward them, trying to tear them apart, but I couldn't tell where Larna began and the hulking form on top of her ended. They were a mass of claws and teeth, fur and leathery hide.

They finally did break away from each other, one of Larna's sides streamed with blood, and I got my first look at her opponent. Luciana stood before us, in her monstrous other-shape, fangs bared and spines quivering. Her rotting grey flesh was cracked in some places, sloughing in others, and the stench of death made my eyes water. The twisted snarls of her eyes fixed on Larna, and her lips peeled in a horrifying version of a smile. "I see you have a guard dog this time," she laughed, in a rasping voice.

Larna bristled beside me, muscles bunching. She took a step in front of me, shielding me with her body. "Go find Ellie."

Fear crawled through every inch of my body, but I didn't budge. "No, *Tuathe*." Larna was my mate, and Luciana was my fight. I would not turn my back on either of them.

"Ellie?" Luciana said, head tilted in a kind of terrifying curiosity. "And I suppose my sister is here with her. Perfect."

I circled Larna to stand by her side. "I won't let you hurt them, and I won't let you hurt my mate."

Luciana's sightless gaze fixed on Larna again. "Oh? Try and stop me."

She leapt for me, and Larna met her halfway in the air, putting herself between us again. They came together, bodies thrashing, fighting to find a hold. Once more, I tried to intervene, but it happened too quickly. Larna ended up flat on her back, kicking up with her back paws and clawing at Luciana's belly. Luciana recoiled, but she responded with a darting snap. Her teeth dug deep into Larna's shoulder, and Larna let out a piercing yelp. Her kicking stopped, and instead, she began to jerk. After a moment, she went limp. Blood pooled beneath her, and her muscles twitched.

I charged, trying to reach her, but Luciana blocked my path, coiling around Larna's body almost like a serpent. "She won't last long," she said, sneering. "If the bleeding doesn't kill her, the poison will."

I refused to listen. I would not let that happen. I crouched, haunches bunching as I prepared to spring.

Luciana didn't seem to take the threat seriously. "You think you can do better?" Her laughter was mocking, high and cold, amplified but otherwise every bit the same as it had always been. "That, I want to see."

The two of us crashed together in a clash of fangs and claws. Luciana's first blow swiped just above my head. I ducked, ramming my shoulder into her stomach. Pain jolted up through my arm like a spike of lightning, but it worked. She staggered, grunting in surprise, and I followed after her, jaws snapping in search of a hold.

I wasn't quite fast enough. She threw me off and knocked me aside again with an inhuman surge of strength. My teeth clicked through empty air.

Separated once more, we circled each other warily. "You shouldn't play games you can't win, puppy," she hissed, flecks of saliva flying from her mouth. Even through her horrible transformation, there was something familiar in her face—an expression of cruelty her rotting flesh and snarled-shut eyes couldn't conceal. "I think it's time for you to roll over and play dead."

She lunged. I dodged. Anger blazed within me, but instead of a distraction, it only heightened my concentration. I was the edge of a blade, sharp and ready to slice into her at every angle. "I hope your ears work better than your eyes," I growled, dropping to all fours and crouching low, "because I think I hear birdsong."

The taunting worked. Undead Luciana was just as easily enraged as the human Luciana had been. She surged toward me, and this time, I met her charge. Fire raked down my side as her claws caught the edge of my belly, but I didn't let her escape. I sank my teeth into her shoulder, dragging her down onto the ground. We twisted—her in search of escape, me in search of an opening. My muzzle was already slick and matted with foul spurts of her blood, but my bite wasn't high enough. I needed her throat.

I tried to sink my teeth into her neck. When I loosened my hold, she took advantage, using her weight to flip me onto my back. I snarled, bringing up my back paws to protect my belly and baring my fangs, but hers were always there to counter them. Our teeth clashed together until our lips were cut and bleeding, but I couldn't break past her guard. When she sliced into my already-wounded shoulder, driving a spike of pain through my chest, I faltered. My head spun, and my vision blurred.

I slipped, weakening, as though I was treading through cloudy water. My lungs wouldn't take in air, and my limp muscles refused to respond. Somewhere in my swimming panic, I realized what was happening—Luciana's toxic bite was starting to take hold. Her sweet, rotting smell clogged my throat, and my heart pumped frantically.

No. Not like this. I'm not dying on my back underneath her. Larna needs me. A fresh surge of energy flooded through me, hot and desperate, clearing my foggy head. I refused to let Luciana end me this way. I refused to let her end me at all. She had destroyed my life once before, but I had more to lose now and more to live for. I would not let her break me.

I didn't go for her throat. Instead, I fastened my teeth onto her right arm, shaking my head with a swift jerk and snap. My jaws crunched to the bone, and Luciana's wounded howl vibrated through me. I kicked with my back paws, throwing her onto her back and diving in for her left side. These were the hands that slapped me, pulled my hair, the arms that caged me against walls and bookcases. I wanted to break them, to rip them off. My second bite caused another howl and more broken bones.

Without the use of her arms, Luciana had to rely on her teeth. She fought, shrieking and spitting, but injured as she was, it wasn't a fair fight. I didn't care. Now, she was the one with nowhere to run. Dark spots started floating around the edges of my eyes, but I shook them off, struggling to focus for a few more seconds. Her ridged throat throbbed, pulsing with the false heartbeat Mogra had given her, and I didn't hesitate. I dug in, piercing and ripping with all my might.

It was over after a few beating twitches. Her life poured into my mouth in bitter streams of black blood. When she no longer moved, I let go and spat, staring down at my kill. Part of me expected her to rise again, to lunge at me, but there was only an eerie stillness. The front of her throat was gone, ripped open, and a still, dark pool had gathered under the upper half of her body.

I rolled off of her corpse, shivering too hard to walk even on all fours, and dragged myself away, toward the place where Larna had collapsed. Somewhere through the haze of pain and receding fear, I could see her side rising and falling, although her pelt streamed with blood. *She'll live,* I told myself as I continued crawling toward her. *She has to. I have to. Tuathe.*

The world continued to swirl and tilt, and as I reached her, I could feel a blanket of darkness sliding over me. In the end, I had to surrender. I rested my chin on one of her haunches, breathing in her scent beneath the stench of death and gore and burning torches. My eyes closed, and the last thing I heard before nothingness swallowed me whole was the ragged, shallow sound of her breathing and the slowing thud of our hearts.

Rae D. Magdon

Chapter Eight

Taken from the diary of Lady Eleanor Kingsclere

I GAZED OUT OVER Kalmarin, taking in the city from atop the battlements in flashes of brilliant fire. Dragons soared overhead, scorching the ground with whirling columns of flame, and countless creatures scurried below, crawling amidst a sea of torches. Smoke filled the air, and I had to hold my own torch further away to breathe. I suspected that when it cleared, there wouldn't be much of a city left for the survivors to claim.

Sadly, I glanced at Neva. She stood a foot away, with Belle's arm around her shoulder and one of the dwellyn holding her hand. They watched Kalmarin burn with her, and my heart ached. Whatever fear and grief I was feeling—for my friends fighting for their lives below, for the destruction of a city I had never known, it must have been even worse for her. Kalmarin was her home. I couldn't even imagine what it would have been like to watch Sandleford burn to the ground, especially as a child.

"How are you doing?" I asked, tucking myself beneath Belle's other arm.

"This is because of me," Neva murmured, staring at me with brimming eyes. "If Umbra didn't need me, she wouldn't have taken over. And if she hadn't taken over, this war wouldn't even be happening."

"This isn't because of you at all." Belle gave Neva a reassuring squeeze. "You can't blame yourself."

"But people are going to die. I can feel them dying. And even though I want to, I can't bring them back. Then I wouldn't be any better than them."

My heart sank like a stone. I could hear the heaviness in her words, the responsibility—a burden no child should have to carry. "They aren't dying for you," I told her. "They're fighting. They're fighting because they want to keep Amendyr safe. That's why we're all here."

"What about you?" Neva said. "You don't live here. You could have gone back to Seria once we found the dwellyn or once you brought me to Jett Bahari's camp. Why did you stay?"

"Because people we cared about needed us," I told her. "Cate and Larna,

Ailynn and Raisa, and you, too."

For a moment, Neva's face brightened. Her cheeks dimpled, and she looked her age again as she smiled. "Me?"

Belle nodded. "Of course. You didn't think you could get rid of us, did you?"

Neva opened her mouth to speak, but a sharp, baying howl covered her words. We peered down over the edge of the wall in surprise. "What was that?" Lok asked, hurrying over from where she had been conversing with the other dwellyn. "It sounded close."

Belle pulled away, drawing her sword, but Neva shook her head. "No, it's all right. He's not going to hurt us."

I held my torch high, and I was able to make out the hulking form of a shadowkin sitting at the base of the wall. He peered up at us, his muzzle pointed into the air. "Stinky?" I said, shaking my head. "How did he get here?"

He gave an urgent bark of warning, placing his paws against the wall, but he was too large to climb. A strange feeling crept over me, a shuddering, burning sensation that crawled over my skin and ate into my flesh. It was familiar at once, and I gasped in surprise and pain. The same blistering sensation had come over me before, whenever I had been in the presence of Luciana and the sorcerer's chain. "Belle," I said, touching her arm. "Something's wrong. I think—"

The dwellyn surrounded us, forming a circle and drawing their blades. Something approached out of the darkness, stalking across the wall, and as the flames spiraling overhead swelled, I saw the figure clearly. She was tall and blonde, with a strange black glow pulsing from her pale skin. A crown of gold was perched atop her head, and just looking at her made my eyes ache. Magic gathered and billowed around her in a cloud, and she clutched a mid-sized mirror in her hands, thin fingers curled around its filigreed edges. The glass was turned toward us, rippling like the surface of a deep, bottomless pond, and it seemed to shine with its own black light.

Beside me, Neva gasped. She stiffened, trembling in fear, and I placed myself in front of her. She didn't need to explain who this woman was.

"It took me long enough to find you," the Queen said, ignoring us. Her entire focus was on Neva, and her voice sounded like an arching phrase of music. "But I suppose if you need something done right, it's best to do it yourself."

"Get away from her!" Lok brandished her sword, tusks jutting out in anger. "You've tortured this poor girl enough."

"Torture? No. I simply need her. My master hungers."

The hiss of those words was too much for Ulig. He growled, swinging his arm forward, and the dwellyn changed formation. They broke their circle and charged forward across the battlements, blades bared, forming an arrow with him at their head. The Queen, however, cared little for their display of courage. The dwellyn only made it a few steps before she waved her hand carelessly in their direction. The mirror glowed, her palm glowing along with it, and the bored gesture froze the dwellyn in place. In the eerie light, I could see Ulig's eyes rolling in his head, but despite his fear, he and the others couldn't move.

"You see the power my master bestows" the Queen said, not speaking to the dwellyn, but to Neva. "I am his hand, and his power flows through me." She extended an arm, slender fingers curling, beckoning. "Come to me, child. If you do, I have no reason to hurt your friends."

I wrapped my arm around Neva, shielding her from the Queen's gaze. Without the dwellyn, only Belle and I stood between her and the ravenous light of the mirror. "And what does your master want with her?" I asked, stalling for time. "What possible use could he have for a child? If he's as powerful as you say, why does he need her?"

For a moment, the Queen's beautiful mouth pulled into an angry snarl. It was obvious I had touched upon a sore spot. Instead of answering me, she glared at her own ghostly reflection in the black mirror. "Master, why do you need her? You know that I could—"

The mirror flashed, cutting off her question, and a look of intense pain transformed her face. Her mouth fell open in a silent scream, and her skin tightened around her high cheekbones and the sockets of her eyes, making her look more like a skull than a beautiful woman. A deep, many-layered voice boomed from the mirror, sending lances of pain through my very bones.

"*You do not question. You serve.*"

I froze, blood turning cold with recognition. The voice had come not from the Queen, but from within the mirror itself. I had heard the same voice speak to me in my dreams, coming from within a blazing golden eye. There was no doubt in my mind this was Umbra—or whatever remained of him. This was the wizard who had murdered Feradith's hatchling and drained its magic. This was the *Ariada* who had reached out through the ages to possess Luciana and Mogra and the Queen.

As quickly as it had begun, the torture ended. The Queen seemed to come back to herself, although her white face was covered in a fresh sheen of dripping sweat. "Come," she said to Neva again, this time in a voice that did not sound quite so thick with honey, but sharp-edged with fear. "It will be worse for you if you don't."

I tried to pull Neva further away from the Queen and the mirror, but she slipped from my grasp and stepped forward, away from our protection. Belle and I both began to rush after her at once, but the Queen waved her hand again. My feet clung to the ground, and a rush of magic enveloped my limbs, blazing hot and ice cold at the same time. My skin screamed, and when I tried to jerk, I found that my joints were locked into place. Tears of helpless fury stung in my eyes, and beside me, I heard the crash of Belle's sword clattering to the ground.

Neva glanced at us, fear painted clearly on her face. She turned back to the Queen. "Will you really leave them alone?" she asked, chin held high despite her shaking. "Do you promise to let them all live if I come with you?"

The Queen's ruby lips curled into a smile. She was her confident self again, once more under the mirror's sway. "Yes. Just come and look into the mirror. Your companions will not be harmed."

"Neva, no," Ulig grunted in a choked voice. He hadn't moved an inch, but apparently he could still speak. "Run."

"He's right," Belladonna said through gritted teeth. "She's alone. Run down to Stinky."

"She isn't alone," Neva said, staring past the Queen into the darkness beyond. Other shapes emerged from the shadows, stalking across the battlements toward us—kerak and wyr, more than we could count. Their eyes flashed with the mirror's light, and their jaws dripped as they waited. "I can only protect you from the undead. The wyr won't listen to me."

"Don't do this," I pleaded. "Go while you can. We'll be—"

I didn't get the chance to lie and say "all right." Neva shook her head. "No. I won't let her hurt my family again. I can't." She looked back over her shoulder, and I saw her lower lip tremble. "You're all I have left."

"A wise choice," the mirror said. Each word was a hot poker in my ears, but I couldn't scream. *"Step forward and gaze into the mirror. Look into my eyes."*

Neva stepped forward, but she halted again as the Queen let loose a shriek of rage. "Master!" she cried, turning the mirror and staring down into it herself. "You promised me the girl's body! You said I would live forever, that I could—"

"Your service was appreciated, but it is no longer needed. I have found my host."

The mirror floated free of the Queen's hands, hovering under its own power. She stumbled back in horror, wearing a twisted mask of betrayal, but even that soon cracked around the edges. The magical light shining from her became unbearably bright, and her skin split. She brought her hands to her once beautiful face, screaming, but it was too late. She fell to her knees, and then lower still as her body began to disintegrate. Pieces of her crumbled away, turning to dust and ash and floating toward the mirror. They disappeared into its surface and the glow within flared stronger.

Once nothing remained of the Queen but her crumpled clothes, the mirror tilted, fixing on Neva once more. *"Look at me, Kira'baas. With your body and your power, I will return to flesh and raise an army of the dead even greater than the one that useless witch shaped for me."*

The Mirror's Gaze

Neva gasped, stepping back. "No. That wasn't part of the deal. She said—"
"She is dead. You are mine."

The mirror rippled, and a beam of its light fixed on Neva's face. She froze, and her skin crawled with the same unearthly light that had pulsed from the Queen before. Neva's body jerked in sick spasms, and she floated off the ground, moving closer and closer to the mirror.

All at once, the pulsing power around us seemed to snap. The burning ice vanished, and I could move again. The dwellyn regained the use of their bodies as well, and Belle dove for the ground in an attempt to retrieve her sword.

"No!" Ulig charged forward again, and the rest of the dwellyn followed. Their blades sliced through the night, but Umbra's creatures stopped them. Kerak and wyr flooded over the battlements, surrounding us. Neva remained a few feet away as they fought, painfully close, but impossibly far away

"Ellie, move!" I shook out of my stupor when I felt Belle tug at my arm. "Help me get to Neva."

A screech sounded beside us, and she whirled around, plunging her sword through a kerak's chest. Its jaws snapped, inches away from her face, and I swung my torch, setting its skin ablaze. It hissed, disintegrating to ash, and the two of us ran. Together, we slashed and burned our way through the horde. I whipped my torch around wildly, not even sure what I was doing, but I didn't care. My eyes remained fixed on Neva.

Something snarled beside me, and I saw a hulking, fanged beast lunge from my left, but Lok was there, her blade glinting. The wyr fell, leaving a little more of the path clear, and she gestured forward. "Go! Ellie, grab Neva. Belle, your sword—"

Another kerak lunged, and Lok turned to face it. We ran, drawing closer. Four steps, three, two. I grabbed Neva, dragging her back to the ground and out of the mirror's light, but as soon as my fingers circled her wrist, searing magic crawled along my arm. My hand began to burn, and I screamed, but I didn't let go. I let the magic eat at me, holding her tight. Images flashed before me—spinning columns of dragonfire and searching golden eyes and a smoking field of bodies stretched as far as I could see. My head pounded.

"Let the girl go," the voice said, driving through my skull like a spike. *"She belongs to me now."*

I didn't let go.

"Let the girl go, or I will show you pain beyond imagining."

I didn't let go.

"Let the girl go. You cannot save her. You cannot even save yourself."

I didn't let go. Tears streamed down my face. Fire ate into my skin. My mind fogged with pain, but I didn't let go.

"Ellie!"

I blinked my stinging eyes, turning toward her voice, and somewhere through the haze, I saw Belle. She stood before the mirror, brandishing her sword.

"Break it," I shouted, the words slicing up through my throat.

Belle drew her arm back, and she drove her blade into the mirror. A loud crack echoed around us, splitting the air, followed by a rumbling roar. The wall beneath us trembled, and more black beams of light poured from the mirror's surface, lighting the sky above. I turned away, dropping my torch and folding Neva into the safety of my arms. I held her tight, shielding her with my body until the great shuddering stopped.

When I opened my eyes again, the light had disappeared, and the air was filled with ash. The kerak were gone, dissolved into nothing. The wyr standing atop the wall seemed stunned, gazing around in confusion. Once they seemed to realize where they were, they ran, scattering in what seemed like fear. The dwellyn no longer had to defend themselves, and Belle stood before the shattered remains of the mirror, sword hanging loosely from her hand. She turned toward me, her expression both fearful and relieved.

"Is it over?" she asked, with uncertain hope.

I blinked, head still swimming. The mirror truly seemed broken, and I could no longer feel Umbra's presence. "I think so," I said, shaking my head. "Neva? Are you all right?"

Neva didn't respond. She remained limp in my arms, still and unmoving.

"Neva!" I stretched her body out across the ground, but her eyes didn't even flutter. Belle and the dwellyn hurried over to her, crouching down beside me.

"She isn't...she isn't dead, is she?" Belle asked, struggling to even form the words.

Lok checked her pulse, placing two fingers under her chin. "No. I feel a heartbeat, and she's still breathing." Neva's chest rose and fell, although only barely. Her face seemed almost peaceful, as if she was fast asleep.

I scanned her body, checking for any injuries, but I found none. "I don't see any blood," I said, with increasing hope. "Maybe she's just unconscious?"

A frown crossed Lok's face. "No, I feel something. Maybe an enchantment? It's very faint." She looked at Ulig, who nodded. He glanced over at the mirror, and I understood what he was thinking.

"But the mirror is broken," I said. "Belle destroyed it, didn't she?"

Lok shrugged. "It seems so, but this is beyond my knowledge. She doesn't seem to be in immediate danger, but I'll need a second opinion, and we should get her proper medical attention."

"Ailynn," Belle said at once. "If anyone can help Neva, it's her."

"I'll get her," I said, already rising to my feet. "She has to be somewhere down there." I peered over the edge of the battlements, and thankfully, the swarming creatures below seemed to be gone. The only figures I saw within the city were humans, and they didn't appear to be fighting. "It looks safe. I'm going to find her."

"I'll come with you," Belle said, but I shook my head.

"No. Stay with Neva, in case she wakes up." Both of us shared a look, somehow knowing Neva wouldn't wake, but Belle didn't protest any longer.

"Be careful," she whispered.

"I will." With one last embrace, I left the battlements to go in search of Ailynn, grateful to see that the first pale rays of the sun were following me. Day had broken at last.

I reached the bottom of the wall and Stinky was there waiting for me. He wagged his tail and thumped his giant front paws on the ground, letting out a hopeful, booming bark. Once he realized his mistress was not with me, however, the noise turned into a low whine. He hung his enormous head, and if I had been able to reach, I might have tried to scratch his ears.

"Don't worry," I told him, gazing back up over my shoulder. "She's still in one piece, and so are you." I decided to take it as a good sign. Since Stinky hadn't disappeared with the rest of the undead, that meant Neva's powers were still strong enough to keep him alive. Hopefully, it wouldn't be too difficult for Ailynn to bring her out of the magical sleep. "Can you help me find Ailynn?" It probably wouldn't be wise to travel through the wreckage of the city alone anyway.

Stinky tilted his head, as if he had understood, but then something else caught his attention. He raised his nose to the air, sniffing the wind. I looked up as well, just in time to see a dark shadow pass overhead. The weak shimmer of dull grey sunlight that had begun to peek over the walls seemed to brighten, and I caught a flash of brilliant gold as Feradith circled high above us. She swooped low, preparing to come in for a landing. Stinky and I skidded back to get out of her way. The ground shuddered slightly as she touched down, and her long tail lashed behind her like a gleaming whip as her translucent wings glittered.

"The aura of this place has changed, Eggmother Eleanor," Feradith said, peering down at me with wide, burnished eyes. Something in me interpreted the look on her reptilian face as one of immense satisfaction. "Feradith can no longer feel Umbra's presence, and his creatures are gone. Has justice been served?"

I bowed my head. "Yes, Eggmother Feradith. Umbra is gone. Your hatchling has been avenged."

"And what of yours?" Feradith asked. "Will she take her place as ruler of this kingdom now?"

My heart sank. I had some hope, more than before, but I needed to find Ailynn quickly. "She's injured. Asleep. I need to find a healer."

Feradith did not question me further. "Come up," she said, lowering her bulk closer to the ground. "Feradith will help you find your healer and save your hatchling."

She did not need to coax me. I climbed onto her back, sitting behind the joints of her great wings and holding on tight. Once I was settled, she launched into the air, flying low over the smoldering wreckage of the battlefield. Many of the buildings had been burned, but in the new light of day, I saw that not all had fallen. In the distance, the castle was still standing. "Head further into the city," I called to Feradith, pointing to where I saw smoke and a mass of figures and tents. I suspected that I would find Ailynn there, working in the middle of the mess.

Chapter Nine

Taken from the verbal accounts of Ailynn Gothel, edited by Lady Eleanor Kingsclere

BY THE TIME JETHRO and I clambered out of the charred pit, the streets above were quiet. Corpses and piles of ash littered the ground, and I saw no signs of movement amidst the smoldering ruins. I surveyed the damage, but most of the fallen appeared to be Mogra's creatures. The dragons had done their work well.

"Seems like most of the fighting's stopped," Jethro said, hefting his axe onto his shoulder. "Do you think it's over?"

"It's over in this part of the city." I gazed back sadly at the giant crater Mogra had left behind. "Did killing her bring you some peace, Jethro?"

"Yes, but perhaps I should have asked you that question. Would it have brought you peace?"

"I kept telling myself over and over that killing her was my responsibility, but if murder is a responsibility, I don't want it. Maybe that sounds foolish in the middle of a war."

Jethro shook his head. "You did what needed to be done, Ailynn. No one could have asked more of you."

With a long sigh, I turned, staring down the street. I had hoped Mogra's death would bring me some kind of closure, but instead, there was a strange hollowness in my chest. I didn't feel as though I had accomplished anything particularly brave, or heroic, or righteous. I had, as Jethro said, done what needed to be done, and my anger rapidly faded into grief.

"I miss her," I whispered, blinking away tears. "Even with all the horrible things she did."

Jethro nodded, placing one of his giant hands on my shoulder. "I miss my wife."

It wasn't a statement meant to make me feel guilty, but one of empathy. He had lost someone important to him, too. He had watched a member of his family transform into something savage and horrible. I suspected he understood all too well how I felt.

"I guess we should leave," I said after a long time. "There's nothing more for us here."

Jethro removed his hand. "No, there isn't."

We took to the street together, making our way toward the front gate. As we moved through the city, we saw more clusters of people—several were injured, but to my relief, they didn't appear to be fighting. Healers had already started helping the wounded, and there didn't appear to be any remaining enemies. I reached inside myself, trying to summon what little remained of my strength. *I can be of use here. We're going to need all the healers possible.*

"Ailynn!"

A familiar voice called my name, and for the first time, something other than fury and sadness rushed in to fill the empty place inside me. I lifted my head, turning in time to see Raisa running toward me. Her golden braid streamed behind her, and her arms were already outstretched. I rushed to meet her, falling into them and holding her tight. "*Tuathe,*" I gasped, burying my face in her shoulder. "Are you—"

"All right?" Raisa interrupted. "Your clothes are half burned off!"

I hadn't even noticed. Come to think of it, my arms had felt a little cold. My sleeves had probably caught fire sometime during the struggle. "I'm fine," I told her, swaying her lightly back and forth without letting go. "What about you? What happened?"

"I think it's over." She seemed to shake herself, sliding out of my arms despite my attempts to keep her close. "Ailynn, you need to come with me. We found Cate and Larna near the walls, and neither of them are doing well."

My happiness faded in an instant. "Show me."

Raisa took my hand, guiding me to a small cluster of tents and stretchers. "We don't have many supplies," she said with worry in her voice.

"Then I'll have to make do with what we've got."

She stopped beside one of the stretchers, and I helped her to her knees before sinking onto my own. Cate lay flat on her back, in her wyr form instead of her human one, fur matted with black blood and eyes glazed over. Her shoulder was a raw, bloody mess, and her breathing sounded shallow and strained.

"Ailynn," she said, blinking when she saw me. "Is—"

"Don't talk," I told her. "Mogra is gone."

The edges of her muzzle twitched in what could have been the canine version of a smile. "So is Luciana."

I suddenly understood. Cate's body was fighting against more of the poison that had prevented her shoulder from healing. "Then relax. Your fight is over." I turned toward Raisa. "Hand me some comfrey and lavender. I need to make her another poultice."

Cate lifted her head. "Larna," she said, gazing at me with a sense of urgency. "Larna first. She saved me."

It was then that I noticed a second stretcher beside hers. Larna's black fur made her harder to see in the darkness, but as I crawled to the foot of the pallets, I saw she was even worse off. Her eyes were closed, and when I laid my hands on her body, I could feel heat radiating from her fur. "All right," I said, partially to keep Cate from moving. "Larna first. Has she been unconscious this whole time?"

"Yes."

"Here," Raisa said, passing over a basket. "Show me what to do, and I'll help Cate."

For the next several minutes, the two of us worked in tandem. I offered instructions, and Raisa copied me. "Mogra should have given you lessons too when we were growing up," I told her as I finished with Larna's second poultice. "You have some talent for this."

"I've had to pick up a few things. How does that feel, Cate?"

Cate let out a low sigh. "Better. Larna?"

I looked down at my patient. She still hadn't stirred, but her breathing was a little easier. "I don't know, Cate. She's a little cooler, but we'll have to wait."

"Don't let her die, Ailynn," Cate said, gazing at me with tortured eyes. She reached out into the empty space beside her, groping weakly until she found Larna's hand with hers. "I need her."

I nodded. I couldn't give Cate the promise she wanted, but I would do everything I could. I understood her agony all too well.

***

The remainder of the night passed quickly, and what little was left faded into an early grey morning faster than I expected. I worked through my weariness, desperate to keep Larna and Cate alive. Through it all, Raisa stayed close by my side. She was my strength, and her mere presence was enough to keep me going. I had just let out a jaw-cracking yawn as I finished changing Larna's poultice yet again when someone set a light hand on top of my shoulder. I blinked and turned, expecting Raisa, but instead, I saw another familiar face.

"Ellie?" I asked, surprised she had found us at all. Only a short time had passed since the end of the battle, and everything around us was still mostly in chaos. "It's good to see you. Are Belladonna and the princess all right?"

Ellie gave me a weak, tired smile. "It's good to see you alive and well too, Ailynn. Feradith had a hard time finding you."

"Feradith?"

She pointed up, and I glanced up in time to see a large, glittering golden shape soaring away toward the main gates. The thought that I had been working too long crossed my mind. If I had missed something as large as a dragon, I probably needed some water and a bite to eat at least.

"Belle is fine and I don't think Neva is in immediate danger. I'll explain in a moment." Ellie dropped to her knees beside me, peering over the pallets. "How are they? Please tell me they're only resting."

"They're still fighting off the poison, but they're both better than before," I told her. "Cate was awake when I first saw her. If it gives you any comfort, she told me she gave Luciana a painful end."

Ellie sighed, shoulders sagging in relief. "I knew she would. She made a prediction about it years ago." She ran her hand over Cate's forehead, stroking her short fur, gazing down at her and Larna's joined hands. "I'm sorry to pull you away from them, but we need someone with magical abilities to look at Neva."

I was on my feet in an instant, grabbing for my basket. "Show me."

"She isn't injured, but she's fallen in some kind of magical coma," Ellie said as she led the way. "Umbra tried to possess her through the Queen's mirror, but the spell was interrupted. She fainted, and since then, we haven't been able to wake her up."

My heart sank. It seemed that while I had been busy fighting Mogra, the Queen's evil plan had come to pass after all. "I'm sorry. If I had known sooner."

"You might still be able to help," Ellie said, gesturing for me to climb a set of stairs. We had arrived at the walls, and I could see distant figures waiting for us atop the battlements.

I wasn't so certain. Whatever had happened to Neva sounded like the product of necromancy, and that area of magic was well outside my area of expertise. "What about the magic mirror?" I asked as we ascended the stairs. "What became of it?"

For a brief moment, a look of satisfaction crossed Ellie's face. "Belle happened to it. Dwellyn swords are excellent for breaking enchantments." I sensed there was more to the story, but I didn't ask. It was enough to know that she and Belladonna had stopped the evil Queen from releasing Umbra's spirit.

At last, we reached top of the battlements. A small crowd waited for us; Lok and Ulig and their seven followers, Jett Bahari, Doran, Rachari, and last of all, Belladonna. She knelt on the ground beside the princess, hovering closely over her.

"News travels fast," Ellie said, glancing at them in surprise. "I guess it took me longer to find you than I thought."

"Ailynn," Rachari said, taking notice of me first. "Thank goodness you're here. Can you tell us what happened inside the palace? We haven't heard from any other survivors."

Weight descended over my shoulders once more. If they hadn't heard from survivors that meant almost everyone in the cave had been slaughtered to provide us with an escape. Jinale, the Farseer pack, the dwellyn.

"Ailynn can explain later," Jett Bahari said. "Let her look at Princess Neva first."

"It's all right," I said, bracing myself for the guilt to flare up again. "I'm sorry, Rachari. Jinale and most of your warriors didn't make it out of the cave. An army of Mogra's wyr found us in the caverns. Rufas, he carried me all the way out of the palace. When we caught up with Mogra, I'm afraid I couldn't protect him."

Rachari gave a slow blink of her slitted eyes. "Then he died as brave as he lived. For all our disagreements, I never doubted him. Tell me you killed the witch, Ailynn. He deserves that and more."

I nodded. "Mogra is finished. Your people didn't sacrifice themselves for nothing."

Doran stepped forward, placing one of his hands on my arm in a gesture of comfort. "It's time for the dead to rest, *Acha*. You should see to the princess. She might not need to join them."

As I looked into his eyes, my own welled with tears. I wanted to tell him that I had allowed Jethro to strike the final blow, but I knew it could wait. He was right—Neva needed to take precedence over my confusing grief. After gripping his hand back, I knelt beside Belladonna and Lok, joining the dwellyn in their protective circle.

"How long has she been like this?" I stared down at Neva's face. She didn't seem to be feverish, or in any pain. Her expression was almost peaceful, although her eyes were closed.

"Since just before sunrise," Lok said. "I've done what I can for her, but I'm afraid this is beyond my knowledge, even after examining the mirror." She gestured a small distance away, where several broken shards of glass lay inside a warped golden frame.

I focused, but I couldn't sense the hum of magic coming from the remains of the mirror. Whatever monster had lived inside it was gone. I pressed my fingers to Neva's neck instead, checking her pulse. It beat steadily beneath my touch, and her chest rose and fell in an even rhythm.

"You can see this isn't a natural sleep," Lok insisted. "Please, tell me what you feel."

I concentrated again, this time on the princess. A faint pulse of magic swirled around her, but it seemed old and distant, like a spell that had weakened and faded long ago. "It's strange," I said, brow furrowing. "There are traces of an enchantment, but something else, too."

"You sense it, too," Lok said, giving me a nod. "That's why I wanted a second professional opinion."

"What does that mean, Ailynn?" Belladonna asked, fear crossing her face. "Please, tell me you can do something to help her." She gazed down at the sleeping girl, stroking the side of her face. Ellie came to stand beside her, resting both hands on the back of her shoulders.

"I'm sorry," she said as Belladonna struggled. "We've both come to care for her a great deal."

They hadn't needed to tell me. I could see the devastation in their faces, and I understood what it meant. I ached to tell them that I could help, but in all honesty, I had no idea how. Neva's sickness was magical, not physical, and there was no sign of its source. "I promise to try," I said, with all the determination I had left. "She seems stable, so it should be safe to move her. I suggest we bring her down to camp and set her up somewhere more comfortable."

"Right. Of course." Belladonna seemed relieved to be given a helpful task. She slid one of her arms beneath Neva's shoulders and the other beneath her knees, cradling the girl in her arms. Belladonna was a tall woman, and her sword training had broadened her shoulders slightly, and Neva looked incredibly small against her chest. "Where should I take her?"

"Perhaps to Larna and Cate," Ellie suggested. "We can see to all three of them at once."

I nodded, granting my permission.

"We come," Ulig said when he saw the gesture. "Our princess."

"Very well. As long as everyone promises to stay out of my way."

Together, our small party made our way back down from the battlements. Ellie and Belle went first, carrying the princess, with the dwellyn escorting them on either side. Rachari and Jett Bahari followed, with solemn looks on their faces. Doran and I went last, taking the stairs together. He didn't speak, but I sensed that he was waiting for me to say something.

"I can't believe it's over," I murmured, soft enough so the others couldn't hear. "She's dead, and I don't feel anything."

"What were you expecting to feel, *Acha*?" Doran asked.

I hadn't considered that question. "I don't know. Relief? Sadness? Not this numbness." I hung my head. "In the end, I couldn't even do it. I had her, but I let Jethro make the final blow. I was too much of a coward."

"You are no coward, Ailynn." He wrapped an arm around my shoulders, squeezing lightly. "Choosing not to kill someone you loved is the furthest thing from cowardice I can imagine. That guilt was not yours to take on. You defeated her. That is enough."

I breathed in slowly. Hopefully, someday I would be able to believe those words. Until then, I would be grateful. Grateful for Raisa, for my children, and grateful that some of my friends had made it through the night alive. If I had made that possible in some small way, then perhaps I had done enough.

We arrived back at Cate and Larna's pallets a few minutes later. Raisa looked up as we approached, but she wasn't the only one. To my surprise, Cate sat up on her pallet, in her human form once more. A blanket had been draped over her bare shoulders, and she was gazing down at Larna with tears streaming down her face. It wasn't until I hurried closer that I realized they were tears of relief. Larna's eyes were open, and there was a slight smile on her face.

"It took you long enough," Cate said, her voice breaking on a sob. "I thought you were never going to wake up."

Larna gave a soft, hoarse laugh. "Aye, little bird. You may be faster, but I will always be catching you."

I averted my eyes as the two of them embraced, turning to Raisa instead. "I love you," I told her, stroking loose strands of golden hair that had escaped her braid out of her face.

Raisa smiled, embracing me and tucking her chin over my shoulder as I rested my hands gently against her stomach. "We love you, too."

Chapter Ten

Taken from the diary of Lady Eleanor Kingsclere

"ELLIE? ELLIE, WAKE UP."

I lifted my head from the cushion of my folded arms at the sound of my name, blinking the sleep from my eyes. Although I couldn't remember falling asleep, the fact I had done so at one of the kitchen counters did not surprise me. I had lapsed into unconsciousness in several odd places over the past two weeks, mostly because I rarely slept through the night anymore.

It took me a few moments to focus on the face hovering near mine, but I smiled in recognition when I saw Cate's red curls bobbing about her face. "Cate," I murmured, straightening up and stretching out the cricks in my spine. "I wasn't asleep for too long, was I?"

"Only about a quarter-hour," Jessith said, "although that wasn't the first time Cate said your name." She was curled up by the palace's kitchen fireplace—a passably acceptable substitute for Baxtresse's, or so she told me. Since its stone walls hadn't been too badly damaged by the dragon's fire, we had taken shelter in Kalmarin's palace following the end of the war.

"I wasn't asking you," I told her, fighting back a yawn.

Cate smiled, shaking her head. "Is Jessith being difficult again?" she asked, folding her arms across her chest.

"No more than usual." I sighed, losing myself in the bowl of cold stew I had been attempting to eat. "I don't suppose you've come to tell me that Neva's woken up?"

Cate shook her head. "I'm sorry. Belladonna's sitting with her now, but she hasn't opened her eyes. I'm just glad you're trying to eat without my pestering you, even if it is in the middle of the night."

I felt a stab of guilt. Although she had been preoccupied with Larna for the past few weeks, Cate had always taken time to make sure I was fed while I sat at Neva's bedside. Belle and I took it in shifts to watch her along with the dwellyn. There was always someone with her, even in the small hours of the morning.

"How is Larna? Better today?"

"Well enough to bark orders and assert her dominance," Cate said, in a tone that suggested she was not entirely pleased. "I wish she wouldn't push herself so soon, but she thinks it's necessary. All the wyr who were freed from Umbra's influence need someone to lead them, and she seems determined to make sure that someone is her."

"I think it should be her. She's a good leader. It gives her a sense of purpose. "I wanted to say more, but decided not to. Cate probably didn't need to be reminded of her loss.

"Perhaps, but she's not a very good patient," Cate muttered. "Just ask Ailynn. It's a wonder she hasn't strangled Larna yet."

I pulled out the chair beside me, urging Cate to sit. "What about you?" I asked, turning toward her so we could speak. "These past few weeks have been…" 'Difficult' did not seem a strong enough adjective, and I struggled for a suitable word. So many had died, and even more had been injured.

"I know." Grief flashed in Cate's eyes, an echo of my own. The war had left its mark on both of us. "Sometimes, I still can't believe I killed her. My nightmares are gone, but when I realize that over half of my pack died in those tunnels to make sure Larna and I got through, I'm not sure if it's worth it."

"It was," I said, reaching out to take her hand. "This wasn't about any one person. Not you, or me, or Neva."

She closed her eyes for a moment, gathering herself again. "You're right. They followed us willingly, and I suppose I should be grateful Larna didn't die with them. I worry."

"Of course you do, but she needs you now more than ever." I gave her fingers a brief squeeze before letting them go. "And your new pack is going to need you, too. Maybe helping them will give you a new sense of purpose."

"Maybe." She rested one elbow against the table, drumming her fingertips over its surface. "At least my kill isn't haunting me. Some moments, when she isn't treating her patients, Ailynn acts more like a ghost than a person."

I had noticed it, too. Although Raisa was always guaranteed to bring a smile to her face, and Belle had coaxed her into the parts of the royal library that hadn't been destroyed, Ailynn carried a constant shadow with her wherever she went. Mogra's death haunted her, even if she didn't say so.

"Give her time," I told her. "Losing my mother was difficult, and she didn't turn evil first. That has to make things even more confusing."

"Oh, that reminds me." Cate reached into the folds of her shirt, withdrawing a crisp sheet of paper. "Raisa asked me to give you this."

She passed it over, and I unfolded it, my eyes widening. It wasn't a message, but a sketch, done in a delicate but precise hand. Three figures peered back at me, and I recognized them at once: Belle and I were pressed close with our arms around each other, and Neva stood between us, smiling broadly. The likeness was astounding, and I sucked in a shaking, unsteady breath. "How did she do this without a reference?" I asked, unable to conceal the wavering note of emotion in my voice.

"She's quite talented, isn't she?" Cate said. "I think she hoped it would make you feel better."

A thick, burning lump formed in my throat, and I had to clear it several times before I could speak again. "I will have to tell her thank you. This is, it's beautiful."

"Don't think of it as a keepsake," Cate warned with a knowing look. "Think of it as something to hope for. She could wake up. Larna did."

"I know," I said, although my faint stirring of hope was tempered with doubt. Neva's enchanted sleep still hadn't ended, despite Ailynn's best efforts. "I don't want to leave her," I confessed, hanging my head. "Even though I know Belle and I should go back to Seria."

"Then don't leave her," Cate said, with a small smirk. "You've always had a habit of taking in strays."

"She isn't a stray," I insisted. "She's a princess."

"A princess without a family. And I'm sure she could use one, especially right now."

I nodded, unable to find anything about the statement to argue with.

***

The halls were still and empty when Jessith and I returned to Neva's room. Kalmarin's royal palace was large, but I had learned its layout. I knew the fastest path from the kitchen to the second floor, and it was no trouble for me to find one of the servants' staircases by candlelight. Halfway up, Jessith seemed to lose her energy. She flopped onto her side, gazing at me imploringly, and I bent to scoop her into my arms.

"At this rate, you're going to get fat again."

Jessith rested her forepaws on my shoulder, tail lashing up to tickle my nose. "Since you feel the need to comment on my physical appearance, I can always comment on yours. If you don't start eating, you're going to look like a kerak."

"I just ate," I protested. Food hadn't been one of my priorities lately. There was always so much to do, and with Neva constantly on my mind, I had little appetite.

"Half a bowl of stew hardly counts. If Belle and Cate didn't force you to visit the kitchens, you would have wasted away by now."

I decided it was best to ignore her. Experience had taught me that cats could rarely be argued with. I reached the top of the stairs and turned left, pulling Jessith closer to my body to ward off the draft and heading along a wide corridor that led to a series of private rooms. When I reached the door I needed, I opened it softly. Belle had taken to sleeping upright in the chair beside Neva's bed, and if she had dozed off, I didn't want to wake her.

I found her with her nose buried in a book instead, reading by candlelight. "Welcome back," she murmured, marking her place and setting the volume aside. "Are you feeling any better?"

I shrugged. "As well as I can feel, I suppose." I set Jessith down on the foot of the bed and perched on the arm of Belle's chair. "What are you reading?"

"A volume about the names and history of dwellyn swords. The tradition for titling famous blades is much more complicated than I expected."

"I suppose your sword has earned its name," I said, leaning in closer. "Do you have any ideas?"

Belle gave me a small smile. "I was considering Starshatter. It sounds appropriately alliterative."

"Starshatter," I repeated, testing the name. "That would look nice printed in a volume about Amendyr's history, don't you think? *'And then Belladonna lifted Starshatter and drove the blade through the enchanted mirror.'*"

"Don't be ridiculous," Belle snorted.

"I'm not being ridiculous. You do realize we're heroes again, don't you?"

She heaved a sigh of resignation, slumping further back in her chair. "I think I preferred it when no one except for Prince Brendan knew we were heroes." Her eyes shifted over to Neva, and I saw the smile drop from her face. "It doesn't feel as satisfying as the books always say, does it?"

I understood. Neva looked so small swallowed up in the covers, especially with Jessith curled on her chest. "It's been two weeks," I whispered, leaving the chair and walking over to the bed. "I'm starting to wonder if she'll ever wake up."

"Ailynn says she might," Belle said, but she didn't sound particularly hopeful. "Perhaps it was foolish, but before all this happened, I wished we could take her back to Baxstresse with us. I think she would have...I think she would like it there."

I reached down, taking one of Neva's hands in mine, still warm to the touch. "I wished for the same thing. She told me she didn't want to stay and become queen of Amendyr, and honestly, she shouldn't have to. She's already done more than enough for her kingdom."

"It would be a shame to separate her from Jessith," Belle agreed, "but where would we keep that enormous dog of hers?"

Jessith cracked open one eye, whiskers twitching. "That thing isn't coming with us. I've only just gotten used to Larna. Besides, it wouldn't even fit in the stables."

"Well then, we'll just have to find space for him inside the manor," I told her. She huffed, but I continued holding Neva's hand, running my thumb over her knuckles. "We do have plenty of space, you know, if you want to come with us when you wake up. You're welcome to stay at Baxstresse for as long as you like." I sat on the edge of the mattress, letting her arm rest in my lap. "But you need to wake up first. You need to open your eyes."

Of course, Neva didn't respond.

I swallowed hard. The passing days should have given me time to adjust to this new reality, but my grief still welled up, gathering painfully in my chest. "Please," I whispered, even though I knew she couldn't hear me. "We need you to wake up. We love you."

Nothing. She continued breathing softly, but her lashes remained heavy against her cheeks.

Fighting back tears, I lifted Neva's hand, pressing a kiss to the center of her palm. To my surprise, my lips met something other than skin. I drew back, studying it more closely. It was hard to see in the dark, but I thought I caught a glint of something glittering. "Belle, bring your candle over here."

She gave me a look of confusion, but she left her chair and carried her candle over. As she held the flickering light near Neva's hand, I gasped. A tiny sliver of glass, no bigger than the edge of my thumbnail, was embedded in her skin. At once, I knew what had happened. "Go get a pair of tweezers, and hurry!"

Belle left without asking for an explanation. I continued holding Neva's hand in mine, still stunned. It seemed ridiculous that such a tiny thing could have caused her enchanted sleep, or that none of us could have noticed it, but Ailynn had instructed us to disturb her as little as possible. Against my better judgment, hope began stirring within me. Perhaps if we removed it, she would wake.

"Let me look," Jessith said, crawling across Neva's stomach to peer at her hand. Her ears flattened against her head, and she hissed. "This reminds me of that enchanted comb. It smells the same."

A moment later, Belle rushed back into the room, brandishing the pair of tweezers. "Here," she said, passing them over. "See if you can get it out."

While she took up her candle again, I dug out the shard of glass. It didn't come loose easily, but finally, I managed to pluck it free. It pulsed with light, and a single drop of crimson blood welled up from the tiny prick in the middle of Neva's palm. Her eyes fluttered, and for the first time in two long weeks, she opened her mouth. "Ellie? Belle? Jessith!" She sat up, wrapping her arms tight around Jessith's neck.

"I see who gets the most enthusiastic greeting," Belle said, but her grin gave her away.

Neva let go of Jessith and latched onto both of us, tucking her face into my shoulder. "You're still here. I'm so glad."

Belle laughed, squeezing the two of us tighter. "How could we think of going anywhere without you?"

"I told you we weren't going to leave," I said, blinking back my tears. They streamed down my face anyway despite my attempts to stifle them. "Didn't I promise?"

Neva looked up at me, her eyes brimming as well. "You did. And I love you both, too."

Afterword

ACCORDING TO THE SOURCES used throughout this manuscript, it took several months for things to return to normal in the kingdom of Amendyr, but return to normal they did. With Feradith's need for justice met, the dragons departed and returned to the Rengast Mountains.

Under Jett Bahari's leadership, Kalmarin was rebuilt to its former glory, although not quite the same as before. The courtyard where Ailynn's battle with Mogra remained, transformed into a monument for those who gave their lives.

As for Ailynn herself, she and Raisa stayed in Kalmarin for some time afterward, making a study of its library and assisting with the restoration efforts until the birth of their children—twin boys who gave Ailynn the sense of peace she had struggled for so long to find. With Raisa's permission, she named them Rufas and Hassa, after the two liarre who had carried her. Despite her considerable efforts, she was never fully able to shake her title, and *Fel'Rionsa,* the fire princess, was remembered as the most powerful witch of her generation.

Cathelin Raybrook and Larna returned to their home in the forest in order to rebuild the Farseer pack together. Their numbers swelled with the addition of the wyr Mogra had enslaved, and though there was a considerable amount of mistrust between the survivors and the new recruits, Larna managed to merge them together successfully. Cate took over the use of Kalwyn's hut, and many wyr with magical abilities were honored to call her their teacher. To this day, the Farseer pack is still led by their descendants, and the villages near the border no longer fear the Forest's dangers.

Lady Eleanor and Lady Belladonna returned to Seria with several extra additions to their party. After much argument, it was agreed that Neva should accompany them. Mostly because she refused to attend her coronation, and no one felt like challenging a ten-year-old girl who could converse with the dead. She and her new guardians arrived to find Baxstresse recovered from the traumatic night of their escape.

Most of their friends were unharmed, and to Belladonna's immense relief, the library was still intact.

The Serian court was, of course, scandalized when Princess Neva was first presented, or rather, re-presented there, especially since she was accompanied by a giant undead dog and several dwellyn. But after Mogra's attack on the palace, Prince Brendan had no patience for their shock. He married the Lady Sarah, despite numerous protests, and at his firm insistence, Seria became much more friendly with its neighbors to the west. Though it took time, the stigma against those with magical abilities gradually began to decrease. After several decades, Ronin did indeed become a place of learning almost as fine as Kalmarin, just as Cieran and Cassandra had always hoped.

All six of our heroines kept in close correspondence until the end of their days, and they lived happily ever after.

Your servant,

Rowena
Princess of Seria, Keeper of the Royal Library

About Rae D. Magdon

Rae D. Magdon lives and works in the state of Alaska. Over the past few years, she has written many lesbian-themed novels, including *Dark Horizons, the Amendyr series, Death Wears Yellow Garters,* and her first published work written with Michelle Magly, *All The Pretty Things.* A two-time nominee of both the Rainbow Awards and the Golden Crown Literary Awards, she enjoys writing fantasy and science fiction, in addition to modern-day romances. When she is not writing original fiction, she ~~wastes~~ spends her time dabbling in ~~unapologetically smutty~~ romantic lesbian fanfiction. Her favorite fandoms are Mass Effect, The Legend of Korra, and The 100 Fandom. In her free moments, which are few and far between, she enjoys spending time with Tory, her wonderful spouse, and their two cats.

Connect with Rae online

Website: http://raedmagdon.com/
Facebook: https://www.facebook.com/RaeDMagdon
Tumblr: http://raedmagdon.tumblr.com/
Email: raedmagdon@gmail.com

Other Books by Rae D. Magdon

Amendyr Series

The Second Sister
ISBN: 9781311262042
ELEANOR OF SANDLEFORD'S entire world is shaken when her father marries the mysterious, reclusive Lady Kingsclere to gain her noble title. Ripped away from the only home she has ever known, Ellie is forced to live at Baxstresse Manor with her two new stepsisters, Luciana and Belladonna. Luciana is sadistic, but Belladonna is the woman who truly haunts her. When her father dies and her new stepmother goes suddenly mad, Ellie is cheated out of her inheritance and forced to become a servant. With the help of a shy maid, a friendly cook, a talking cat, and her mysterious second stepsister, Ellie must stop Luciana from using an ancient sorcerer's chain to bewitch the handsome Prince Brendan and take over the entire kingdom of Seria.

Wolf's Eyes
ISBN: 9781311755872
CATHELIN RAYBROOK has always been different. She Knows things without being told and Sees things before they happen. When her visions urge her to leave her friends in Seria and return to Amendyr, the magical kingdom of her birth, she travels across the border in search of her grandmother to learn more about her visions. But before she can find her family, she is captured by a witch, rescued by a handsome stranger, and forced to join a strange group of forest-dwellers with even stranger magical abilities. With the help of her new lover, her new family, and her eccentric new teacher, she must learn to gain control of her powers and do some rescuing of her own before they take control of her instead.

The Witch's Daughter
ISBN: 978131672643
Ailynn Gothel has always been the perfect daughter. Thanks to her mother's teachings, she knows how to heal the sick, conjure the elements, and take care of Raisa, her closest and dearest friend. But when Ailynn's feelings for Raisa grow deeper, her simple life falls apart.

Her mother hides Raisa deep in a cave to shield her from the world, and Ailynn must leave home in search of a spell to free her. While the kingdom beyond the forest is full of dangers, Ailynn's greatest fear is that Raisa will no longer want her when she returns. She is a witch's daughter, after all—and witches never get their happily ever after.

Desert Palm Press

Death Wears Yellow Garters
ISBN: 9781942976011
Jay Venkatesan's life was going pretty great. She had Nicole—her perfect new girlfriend—and her anxiety was mostly under control. But when Nicole's grandfather dies under mysterious circumstances at his 70th birthday party, Jay is thrown into a tailspin. Her eccentric Aunt Mimi is determined to solve the mystery no matter what she thinks about it, and the police are eyeing Nicole as one of their prime suspects. No matter how often Jay insists that real life isn't like one of her aunt's crime novels, she finds herself dragged along for the ride as the mystery unravels and the shocking truth comes to light.

Written with Michelle Magly

Dark Horizons Series

Dark Horizons
ISBN: 9781310892646
Lieutenant Taylor Morgan has never met an ikthian that wasn't trying to kill her, but when she accidentally takes one of the aliens hostage, she finds herself with an entirely new set of responsibilities. Her captive, Maia Kalanis, is no normal ikthian, and the encroaching Dominion is willing to do just about anything to get her back. Her superiors want to use Maia as a bargaining chip, but the more time Taylor spends alone with her, the more conflicted she becomes. Torn between Maia and her duty to her home-world, Taylor must decide where her loyalties lie.

Starless Nights
ISBN: 9781310317736

In this sequel to Dark Horizons Taylor and Maia did not know where they would go when they fled Earth. They trusted Akton to take them somewhere safe. Leaving behind a wake of chaos and disorder, Coalition soldier Rachel is left to deal with the backlash of Taylor's actions, and soon finds herself chasing after the runaways. Rachel quickly learns the final frontier is not a forgiving place for humans, but her chances for survival are better out there than back on Earth. Meanwhile, Taylor and Maia find themselves living off the generosity of rebel leader Sorra, an ikthian living a double life for the sake of the rebellion. With Maia's research in hand, Sorra believes they can deliver a fatal blow against the Dominion.

Desert Palm Press

All The Pretty Things
ISBN: 9781311061393
With the launch of her political campaign, the last thing Tess needed was a distraction. She had enough to deal with running as a Republican and a closeted lesbian. But when Special Agent Robin Hart from the FBI arrives in Cincinnati to investigate a corruption case, Tess finds herself spending more time than she should with the attractive woman. Things get a little more complicated when Robin begins to display signs of affection, and Tess fears her own outing might erupt in political scandal and sink all chances of pursuing her dreams.

Cover Design By : Rachel George
www.rachelgeorgeillustration.com

Note to Readers:

Thank you for reading a book from Desert Palm Press. We have made every effort to edit this book. However, typos do slip in. If you find an error in the text, please email lee@desertpalmpress.com so the issue can be corrected.

We appreciate you as a reader and want to ensure you enjoy the reading process. We would like you to consider posting a review on your preferred media sites such as Amazon, Smashwords, Bella Books, Goodreads, Tumblr, Twitter, Facebook, and/or your blog or website.

For more information on upcoming releases, author interviews, contest, giveaways and more, please sign up for our newsletter and visit us as at Desert Palm Press: www.desertpalmpress.com and "Like" us on Facebook: https://www.facebook.com/DesertPalmPress/?fref=ts.

Bright blessing.

Desert Palm Press

Made in the USA
San Bernardino, CA
26 August 2016